Summergreen

Summergreen

Janet Cox

Deseret Book Company
Salt Lake City, Utah
1981

First printing in paperbound edition, September 1987

Library of Congress Cataloging-in-Publication Data

Cox, Janet, 1947–
    Summergreen.

    I. Title.
PS3553.09194S9   813'.54   81-66051
ISBN 0-87747-864-3 (hardbound ed.)   AACR2
ISBN 0-87579-119-0 (paperbound ed.)

To Doug

ONE

"Hey, you'll be great." Phyliss reassured me and nodded toward Rebecca Niven, who was presently auditioning in a loud, brittle voice. "She's no better than the others, Anne. With your tone quality—and *looks*," she fluttered round blue eyes, "you've got it for sure!"

Her faith in me grated. After listening and watching for more than an hour, I wasn't feeling at all confident. This suave, dark-eyed Mark Staaton was a *professional*. His remarks so far had been painfully to the point, and I dreaded the moment when I'd have to take my turn to stand before him. At the thought my stomach lurched and my whole body got warm.

"I think—oh, Phyliss." I moaned softly and leaned forward to rest my forehead on the back of the pew in front of me, my trembling voice betraying my longing to be accepted in this renowned all-girl choir. "I haven't a chance, and you know it. These girls have had training." I lifted my head in emphasis, and then let it fall back on the bench. "*Training*! He'll see that. He will!"

The music stopped, and Phyliss, unable to answer in the silence, shrugged, unwilling to consider defeat—unshakeable as ever in her determination to make me a part of the Ashley Valley Singers. She was a member herself—had been for two years, and ever since she'd been accepted two years ago, I'd *dreamed* of becoming a member too, but despite months and months of practice, I couldn't summon courage to try out—not until that frightful Rachael Ashley, the choir's wealthy sponsor, had stepped down as director and imported this elegant Easterner to take her place. It was laughable that I'd hoped to have more of a chance with him. Mr. Staaton was every bit as formidable as Sister Ashley. In a different way perhaps, but every bit!

I closed my eyes and rocked my head back and forth against the bench. The wood felt hard and cool and good, making thumping vibrations inside my forehead that soothed me. *Thrr—ump, thrr—ump.* Smells of polish and wax lingered in the air and I wished it were Sunday—Monday—Tuesday. It didn't matter, any day but today. No, I wished it were years from now—years and years—some distant lovely summergreen day when I was old and married with children and all my problems solved forever.

Mr. Staaton's voice rumbled like thunder in the near emptiness of the chapel, bringing me bolt upright. ''Anna Jeanette Carrow.''

It hurt to breathe. My chest felt so tight it actually hurt to breathe.

Phyliss smiled and murmured, ''Good luck.''

I wanted to shout at her. *What was I doing here? I had made a terrible, dumb mistake.* I hunched down in my seat and froze, not daring to move a muscle despite the recurring jabs of Phyl's elbow into my ribs.

''Miss Carrow?'' Again he called my name, this time impatiently. ''Anna Jeanette Carrow, *next*!''

I slumped lower, and at Phyliss's outraged look, I pressed a finger to my lips, my eyes squinting a warning for her to keep quiet.

His brows rose as he surveyed the scattered few still waiting to sing. If I kept still he would go on to someone else, and then later, with his attention diverted—

He traced his hand down the side of his head and, with a sigh and rattling of papers, turned in his seat. He was about to select another application when Phyliss's harsh whisper rang out.

"*Oh, go on, Anne.*"

"Be quiet," I tried to shush her. "I've changed my mind."

"My name's on that application, too." Her voice rose. "I'm your sponsor!"

"Shhhh." The commotion brought his eyes to us, and I felt others turning to stare. I glared at my best friend turned traitor, but her fingers fastened to my arm as she pulled me up.

"You're not going to make me look bad," she insisted.

I forced a shaky smile for Mr. Staaton's benefit, muttering a low, "Let go," through my smiling teeth.

"Oh, Mr. Staaton," Phyliss sang out, "this is Anne Carrow."

My eyes widened in fury but she ignored me. With a bounce of her curls she gave me a shove. Mr. Staaton was growing impatient. He was standing now too, his eyes hard on me.

I straightened my shoulders and took a deep breath before stumbling to the front. There was no worry. I'd simply tell him that "something awful" had come up at home and I had to leave. I brightened and actually felt myself smiling at the doubtful looks I received from the other girls. But when I stood before him, I found myself blurting out the miserable truth.

"I just don't want to sing—I mean—it's not that I don't like this choir, honest." I pushed back a drooping strand of hair and swallowed. "It is a *good choir,* I know, but—" I half-smiled and bobbed my head. "Thanks anyway, really." I started past him, a hot stain surging upward in my face.

His hand on my shoulder halted my ungainly retreat. "Just a moment, Miss Carrow." *Miss Carrow, Miss Carrow.* His voice seemed to echo about my ears, and I bit my lower lip in confusion. Everything about the man threatened me, and the gossip with which Phyliss had filled my head in the past days didn't help; it clamored now in my brain, blocking all other thought.

"He's so beautifully tall and well-muscled," she had said. It was true! The bluntly carved features and squared jawline made me want to stare and stare, and the thick blackness of his curly hair was just as Phyliss had described, "gorgeously unruly." Feathery strands brushed the collar of his shirt and long sideburns lay against the tanned smoothness of his skin.

Phyliss, a great reader of romantic novels, had recited a passage about a dashing riverboat gambler and said the description fit Mark Staaton to a T. I had laughed it off, knowing her tendency to exaggerate, and had instead preferred to believe Peter Tate's rather dismissing report. After all, Peter—Papa's trusted hired hand—was reliable, and he'd said Mr. Staaton seemed dapper and bookish. "You know the sort, Anne."

But at first glimpse of Mr. Staaton striding into the chapel, I knew Peter had missed the mark by a wide mile. Dapper? I'd nearly choked remembering. It had been no scrappy derby Mark Staaton held, but a black velvet-banded slouch hat that matched the richness of his vested coat and ribbon tie. It did no good trying to will back the vision of that other man Peter's words had created. This was the *real* Mark Staaton, and he was no staccato-speaking educator with a bald spot and spectacles! In appearance, at least, he *was* Phyliss's gallant rogue.

I looked at the floor, then back to his tie. It was loose, as if the stuffy little chapel had been too uncomfortable.

"Come now, I'd like to hear you sing." His voice, gruffly mellow, was full of a practiced charm. "I assure you there's no need to be afraid."

"Oh, I'm not," I half-laughed. "I just, well—I ch—changed my mind."

His eyes swept over me and I winced, wishing I'd taken Mama's advice and worn anything but my gray dress. I'd always liked the way it fit, but the color, though it did match my eyes, now seemed drab and plain, and the fact that I'd made the dress myself made it all the more lacking.

The cleft Phyliss had told me about deepened in his chin. "I had gathered that, but why?"

Unable to even think longer, I threw up my hands. "Never mind! All right!" I thrust my music toward him and, without further explanation, began to sing.

"That wasn't so hard, now, was it?" With a brief nod he returned my music and asked me to join the others in the foyer.

I told myself I didn't care. What did it matter if he picked one of the others to fill Vinnie Bacon's vacancy? But as I found my seat at the foyer window I felt heartsick. I'd made a complete fool of myself.

I blinked back tears and, sniffing, turned from the curious glances of the other girls to stare through the glass to where Phyliss sat relaxed on the dandelion-covered grass, her nose raised to the sunshine.

"Oh, Phyl," I sighed inwardly, "I've ruined my chances, haven't I."

We had a long while to wait. The foyer was warmer than the chapel had been, and with the suspense eating at all of us it was unbearable just sitting. Someone sighed, and Meg Carter whispered to no one in particular, "He's certainly taking his time."

"But a man like that," Rebecca Niven teased loudly, "is well worth waiting for! There's something about Mr. Staaton's eyes and the way he looks at you that—" She stopped, suddenly face to face with the eyes under discussion. He'd come silently through the chapel doors and caught her mid-sentence. When he raised his brow she giggled, her face breaking out in blotches. He smiled at that and moved to the front of the group.

"Before I tell you who I've picked to fill the vacancy," he said, his gaze falling on the folded paper in his hand, "I'd like to thank you all for coming. You have talent— some of you very promising talent." He cocked back his head and his eyes met mine.

I quickly looked away and glanced at the girls around me, all sitting stiff as boards, each praying to hear her own name. Jeanie Parry, who was sitting closest to me, had tied her delicate lace handkerchief into an ugly lump. It was disgusting that it meant so much to all of us—disgusting!

Someone was asking if it were true that Sister Ashley was expanding the number of members in the choir, and I fought down my impatience. My dress seemed suddenly unbearably warm; the high, stiff collar and tight cuffs were stifling, and my skirt clung heavily to my nervous legs. I was baking, slowly cooking. *Which one of us? Just tell us and let us go.*

"Mrs. Ashley has said that will happen, Miss Carter, but as for details, I'm not sure. After the July concert we'll know better."

Didn't *any* of them notice the heat? How could they sit and wait so calmly? Mama would say I should think cooling thoughts. *I was wading in High Creek. The icy water swirled about me and stung my legs, took my breath. The canyon breeze blew the pins from my hair and the damp curls from my forehead.*

"No, Mrs. Ashley will only attend the practices prior to the concert, and, as she puts it, 'advise where needed.' "

I heaved a sigh and leaned toward the window, pretending to be absorbed with something outside. Those dark eyes were on me again, and I drummed my fingers against the glass. "Rude," Mama would have said, shaking her head at me. But I simply wanted the terrible waiting to be over and to get outside with Phyliss. There was no need to fret longer. The chosen application Mr. Staaton held would be Meg's or Jeanie's or someone else's. Not mine.

"Miss Carrow?"

Had someone spoken my name or had I only thought it? Mark Staaton was watching me.

I tipped my head and smiled as though I'd been listening all along. The room had grown awkwardly quiet. *What had I missed?* I turned my mind backwards but got nothing. Jeanie leaned over to me, the lump of handkerchief in her hand, and squeezed my fingers against it. The heat in the room swam about my neck, and my face felt scarlet.

"I expected *some* reaction." Mr. Staaton moved until he stood before me.

I wiped damp hands on my skirt. "Reaction? I— uh . . ." My voice dropped. "I didn't catch what you said."

The girls laughed, and the tight silence drained from the air.

"Miss Carrow," he took one of my hands into his, "I said, 'Congratulations on your entrance into the choir.' " Into my open palm he put my application. A large scrawling hand had written across the top "Accepted by Mr. Staaton, filling the vacancy of Vinnie Bacon, first soprano," and the date.

Stunned, I murmured a thank-you. I smiled up at him, suddenly humble, contrite, and, as the truth of it dawned, gloriously, unspeakably thankful.

"See you tonight, eight-thirty sharp?" He smiled at me, took back the application, and, after dismissing the group, strode back into the chapel.

It had happened. I was in—*an Ashley Valley Singer*—at last!

The late May sun, full-blown as a summer dandelion, poured out its warmth in a river, filling up the valley with a sleepy, hazy kind of heat that made Charlie Brinton nod and yawn next to me on the high wagon seat. The rhythmic plodding of the horses hooves lulled and soothed my bursting excitement, and I sighed with contentment and lay back. The valley had never looked more beautiful—*my* fields —*my* mountains.

It was a pity the black headlines of the *Ashley Trumpeter* would not read, "Lifelong Dream Realized, Anne Carrow Returns Victorious." But the grand celebration at home would more than compensate. Hadn't I done the impossible? And at the mere age of seventeen?

The jostling buckboard, spinning dust clouds behind us,

jerked to a sudden halt, and Brother Brinton pushed his tattered hat back and mopped his forehead with his sleeve.

"This is it, Annie. I'd drive you in, but I've got to get on to the Blavens'. Dell's away and Margo's needing supplies, though I hear she's sick again."

"Yes, Mama's been over."

"It's good they have you as neighbors. Poor Dell." He frowned. I knew what he meant by that. The Blavens were always having troubles, sickness mainly. Papa said Dell would never see his way clear until he could stop running down to Ogden for medicines every other week. But their problems, shack, and run-down farm were far away as I climbed from the rig, my new happiness rising.

"Thanks for the ride, Brother Brinton. If that blue silk comes in before next week—"

"I'll send word with Raymond. He's in a lot after school."

"But school's out next Friday."

He laughed and shook the reins, turning the horses down the Blavens' road. "Don't worry. You'll have that cloth soon enough. Say hello to your ma and pa for me."

Across the fields our house glistened white in the shimmering sun, and behind it the barn loomed like a sleeping giant cuckoo clock, the gaping mouth of the loft doors flung open. Orchards sprawled beyond, leafing full and green at last, and as I gazed over our portion of the wide valley, two skinny figures in short pants emerged from the back door of the house on the run—Gerald and Tommy Blaven, hightailing it through Papa's new alfalfa toward their place. I called a hello and returned their waves as they disappeared into the cottonwoods and willows that fell out of the mouth of High Creek Canyon and followed the wobbling stream through Ashley.

I laughed and whirled in the dusty road, the colors about me never more brilliant than at that moment. The sky was a robin's-egg blue, fleeced with snowy clouds miles higher than the cottonwoods. Impatient with the long lane stretching ahead of me, I raised my skirts, pulled off my shoes and stockings, climbed over the log fence, and cut barefoot through the fields. The barnyard was empty when I came into it.

"Papa! Peter! Hey, I'm home!" But there was no one about. I ran in the back door, through the empty kitchen, and let the screen door bang behind me. "Mama, mama!" There wasn't a sound. Only the marble clock on the fireplace mantel broke the stillness. The long oval mirror in the hall caught my reflection. I stared at the slim girl in the worn but attractive gray dress that matched her flashing eyes. Her cheeks were flushed, and despite the tousled hair, I had to admit she didn't look bad.

"Hello," I curtsied to the mirror.

"I see you're smiling, Anne. You must have made it."

I nodded at myself.

"You know, very frankly I *knew* you would. I'm right pleased for you."

"Well," I gave the mirror my best smile, "*thank you,* I'm awfully happy myself."

"You look older somehow."

I yanked my hair back from my face and surveyed myself carefully. "Do I? It's the *experience,* I think. Experience does that." I walked about holding my hair on top of my head. Yes, I was older now. I could feel it. Coming back to the glass, I put my face very close and, opening my mouth to an *ah*, sang up the scale and down again, just as I'd done so often in practicing for the audition, but of course with a new confidence behind it. Then in my lowest voice, "Why, Miss Carrow, you look lovely with your mouth open."

"Do I truly, Mr. Staaton? What a gallant thing to say."

Upstairs a door closed softly. Forgetting the mirror, I skipped up the stairs, and Mama met me at the top.

"What a racket! Shhh." She wagged her finger and cast a quick look back at the children's room. "Margaret's asleep and I've just now got Tyler settled."

"Guess what? Go ahead, Mama, guess!"

Her face creased into her most serious frown.

"Then I'll tell you. I've made it! They accepted me, Mama. I'm in that choir—Rachael's aristocratic chorus! Can you believe it? Me!"

She smiled, but with effort, and nodded absently. "Oh, that's so nice, dear. You must tell me about it, but later. Sister Blaven is so ill, Anne, and with Dell gone—he won't be home until late tonight—I was just going out to find your father."

"Nice? *Nice*! Is that all you can say when after all these years your own daughter—"

"She's worse, much worse. She needs a blessing and right this minute. Gerald and Thomas B. were just here after the elders. You run and fetch your Pa and Peter and tell them to *hurry*."

I turned and started back down the stairs.

"Oh, Anne, you're *not* barefoot, are you? Where are your shoes?"

"I took them off."

"Well, you'd better get them on again quick. Bill and Peter are fixing fences by the canal. Now hurry!"

I closed the screen door more quietly this time, Mama's scolding ringing in my ears, and pulled on my shoes without looking for my stockings. There was still someone to tell. Papa and Peter didn't know yet. With that renewing thought I ran past the swing and into the orchard. I could see Papa's brown hat and Peter's blond head above the grassy ridge of the canal, working near the headgate where, on a fall evening two years before, Phyliss and I had done our worst for Peter. He had been working for Papa only a few months then. Had he thought of it too, working so near the place? But why should he? It lay years buried, and today was a day for rejoicing!

While still in the cover of the orchard I began some nonsense tune, letting the notes come as my brain wove them. They searched briefly with their eyes, then Papa leaned to Peter and the two had a good laugh and went back to work.

"Ignore her and she'll go away," Papa had probably

said, for sing and carry on as I would, the orchards and I got not another glance.

Deflated, I sat down under a tree. It had happened—my wildest hope had been realized. Fireworks should be going off, cannons should be exploding. Leaves rustled in the warm air, and scents of new grass and living ground filled my head. Bumblebees as big as bullets droned in the lazy heat, and blossom-like butterflies flitted aimlessly. *It wasn't fair.* I shot to my feet and ran to a rise about a dozen yards from where they continued working, pounding, stringing wire. I'd make them fire those cannons.

"Don't you care how the audition went?"

Peter lifted his eyes and, propping his weight on his shovel, tossed back his head and laughed, his handsome bronzed face full of delight. "It worked. Flushed her right out." He dropped the shovel and ran toward me. "By the look of things, you made it!" His big hands spanned my waist, and he swept me off the rise into the blue, blue sky. My body reached that place where its spirit had soared all morning.

"Yes! Yes!" I cried. "I made it!" And hollering it repeatedly, we fled toward Papa. He gave me a somewhat patronizing smile from where he knelt, then went back to his fence. I knew that look.

"Congratulations, Anne." Peter's hands detained me. "I know how much this means to you."

"Thank you. A score of girls tried out, you know."

"And they picked the prettiest one."

I laughed, grateful that at least Peter was pleased, then I turned to Papa. "Didn't you hear, Papa? Out of all the applicants Mr. Staaton chose me. I'm in the choir. Aren't you glad for me?"

"Sure am, darlin'," he said fondly, smiling.

"Well, then, *do something*, Papa. What's wrong with you and Mama today? She was the same way—wouldn't listen, just sent me out on the run to find you."

"Find me? For what?" His brow creased into a deep furrow. "Nothing's wrong?"

I had forgotten, and Mama had told me to hurry. I glanced from Papa to Peter. "No, nothing at home. It's Margo Blaven. She's worse. She's requested that you and Peter administer to—"

"Anne!"

They were gone before I'd even finished. I should have told them right off instead of fooling around like that. I felt a pang of guilt as I watched them running back. Maybe Sister Blaven would die this time. Maybe she'd die before they even got to her—all because of me forgetting to tell.

I watched Peter and Papa until they disappeared into the orchard trees. Well, it was out, my precious surprise. And who even cared? I picked up the shovel Peter had dropped and pushed it into the soft earth.

"You look might ordinary to me, shovel—you stupid thing." I kicked at the blade a time or two and then ran over to the edge of the canal and flung myself down on the bank. I lay on my back, my head next to the water, and looked up into the sky again. Admitting the day was less beautiful than before, I cried a little. I knew why Mama and Papa weren't happy. Sure, I knew. Society things like that weren't important to them. Hadn't Papa said the rehearsals would pose a problem?

"And how will you be getting in to their two dozen practices a month?" he had asked the day I told him of my decision to try out. We were driving the cows home.

"Well, I can drive the buggy, Pa. Since when has that been a problem? And the practices will only be twice a week."

He frowned. He was a powerful man—large and tall with reddish blond hair as thick as mine. His face was weathered, rough, and tanned regardless of the season, and though I was old enough to look elsewhere, Papa was the most handsome man I knew. He stopped and bent for a slender green stem. "Don't you get your dander up, Annie! I don't want you going into town and coming home late alone."

"Oh, Papa, I haven't even made it yet. Can't I at least

try? Please? If I don't—'' I set my face stubbornly (Papa admired a strong will). "If I don't I'll always be wondering whether or not I could have done it. I'll wonder whether or not I could have soloed beside an Ashley—till my dying day I'll wonder. Till they put me under.''

Papa shook his head, trying to hide a smile. "I suppose you're set on it.''

"I am.''

"And your mother?''

"She said to talk to you.''

He sighed with exasperation. "All right then, Anne, since you're so determined to try.''

"Thank you, Papa.'' I reached up and kissed his cheek.

"The only thing is—,'' he turned away and squinted after his cows, "you try out and you're as good as in.''

"Oh, Papa.''

"And when you are, don't be forgettin' that this silly choir has caused some hard feelings in the valley.'' He looked down at me. "I don't like to step into something that walls another man out, saying 'yes' to me and 'no' to him.''

I agree, Papa, I thought. *But I want to sing. Is it so hard for you and Mama to see? I want to sing.*

The canal gurgled beside me. More water rushed down from the headgate. Someone above us had finished their turn. After a while I felt a bug at my ear, and I sat up and brushed it into the water. Raymond's and Katy's voices came to me from the direction of the swing. They were home from school. It was late. Mama would be wondering.

"Well, there's our lady of leisure,'' Raymond said as I walked past the swing. He was standing on the wooden plank, his fists around the rope.

"Where'd you get that, Raymond?''

"Mama said it before she left.'' He leaned back in the swing and began pumping higher and higher.

"And where is she?''

"Over to the Blavens'.''

"And Papa—is he back yet?''

"He and Peter are out in the shed getting their boots on.

It's—our—water—turn!" Raymond sang out each word as he soared in the swing.

Katy, Margaret, and Tyler were on the step by the house cracking apricot nuts with a large rock. Margaret had just smashed one and, with Tyler's eager help, was picking the white meat from the tiny shell pieces and putting them into his mouth.

"What about some nuts?" I reached down for the jar but Katy pulled it away. "Come on. Just a couple?"

She shook her head. "You'll have to wait until we mash another. Mama said we could eat the mashed ones. They're for divinity. Raymond's deacons quorum is having a candy sale this afternoon in town."

"This afternoon?" Panic seized me. "Raymond, what time are you going?"

"Five."

"Are you taking your horse?"

"No, the buggy. Why?"

"I've got to have it, Raymond."

He jumped out of the swing. "Sorry!"

"Raymond, this morning they accepted me into the choir. Tonight's my first practice. I couldn't go to a choir practice on a horse. I need the buggy. You see that, don't you?"

His face was noncommittal. "What time do ya gotta be there?"

"Eight-thirty sharp."

"Impossible. I couldn't get done that fast."

"Raymond—"

"Well heck, Anne." He kicked at a clump of grass. "We gotta get enough money to fix our tents for the August outing, and *I* gotta stay till all the candy's sold."

"Couldn't someone else?"

"I'm chairman."

"Oh, Raymond!" If I hadn't been so caught up in my own desire to get to the practice, I would have seen how much this candy sale meant to Raymond. But I rushed on. "If I'm late my first time—can you see how that would look? Just the thought of it makes me sick. Everyone will be wondering who filled the vacancy—they'll be announcing me. Oh, Raymond, I just can't go late. I just can't! Take your horse this time.''

"We'll all have boxes of candy and stuff. You can't haul that on a horse. I asked for the buggy weeks ago.''

I blinked back tears as I realized how hopeless things were beginning to look.

"Aw, Annie. Maybe things can work out. I'll get back as soon as I can.''

"Couldn't you leave early?''

"If you'll get my candy made.''

"I'll do it now. You go get ready," I cried as I ran to the door, "and you kids stop smashing so many nuts! *Hurry*!''

I was just finishing when Mama came into the kitchen.

"What a nice surprise! I thought you'd be worthless the rest of the day.''

"Thank goodness you're home. I've got so much to do to get ready myself. I thought if I could get Raymond off sooner—''

"Get ready? Where are you going?''

"To practice. It's at eight-thirty.''

"Tonight? But it's Friday." Mother laid her gloves and wrap on a chair. "You didn't say anything about it earlier.''

"I hardly had the chance. No one seemed to care much anyhow.''

"Anne!" She gave a deep sigh and shook her head. "Of course we're happy for you! I just wish I'd known about the practice. You said you practiced Saturdays.''

"Well, in the summer they switch to Fridays. You haven't made other plans for me have you, Mama? I *have* to go to my practice." She said nothing, but walked to the window. The afternoon sun coming through the glass caught her dark hair, graying it slightly. She looked tired standing there; she seldom let her shoulders slump as now.

"Mama?" The silence answered for me. She simply stood looking out toward the Blavens' place. I knew she'd promised Margo that I would sit with her and the kids until Dell returned from Ogden this evening. "Is that it?"

"What, Anne?" Her back was still to me.

"Did you promise Margo that I'd sit with her tonight?"

"Yes."

"Mother!"

She turned. "There is *no one else.* Your father and Peter have the water until late. I'll have to do the chores myself tonight because Raymond is going, and then even when he gets back I've got supper and the children."

She was right, I knew—she and Papa had been right all along. The practice was a problem, before it had even begun.

"Oh, Mama." Tears that had been inevitable all day began to fall. "What am I going to do?"

TWO

Raymond came down the stairs a little after four, wearing his good clothes and carrying a pail of paint under his arm.

"Well, I'm ready. Where's the candy?"

I was sitting on the back porch brooding, but I could hear him and Mama in the kitchen through the screen.

"Here," Mama said. "Better put it on the seat next to you. Whatever are you taking paint for?"

"To make signs. We need them all over town. How does this sound: 'Quality candy. Bargain prices.' What do you think?" Mama laughed and kissed him. A moment later Raymond came out to me, still smiling, pleased with his sign idea.

"You be ready and I'll hurry back," he said, peering over his boxes. "And thanks for making the candy." He bobbed his head and started for the buggy.

"No need for you to hurry, Raymond. You might as well take your time. I can't go anyhow."

"Can't go?" He whirled around, spilling the top box. "I thought you said you had to!" He stopped and gathered the candy. "I thought you said if you didn't go you'd be in for it. I've been rushing around this place—"

"I can't go." My voice trembled. "Mama's promised me as a sitter for the Blavens." Raymond set his paint and boxes on the grass, then sat down on the step beside me.

"Been crying?" He surveyed my eyes.

"Raymond, I can do without remarks from you."

"Well, you said you had to go."

"Yes, I said I had to, but I can't now. Who's going to take care of those kids if it isn't me? Katy maybe?"

He pulled a clump of grass, roots and all, and began shaking the dirt between his shoes, making a mess on the porch. "I suppose *I* could do it," he said casually.

His suggestion took a second to hit. Of course Raymond could do it! I'd get the kids and Margo fed. I'd have them all asleep, and Raymond could just sit and read a book or something. Then I could go to the rehearsal—maybe late, but being late seemed no longer to matter.

"Raymond, would you?" I was about to kiss him, but he looked so benevolent that I stopped myself. "I'll be all ready and make it easy for you, all right? You just come down in the buggy as soon as you get back."

He smiled, picked up his paint and the boxes, and disappeared around the side of the house.

"Thanks!" I called after him. "Thanks a lot, Raymond."

Thanks, I echoed silently, looking up at the afternoon sky. Clouds were beginning to darken the far arm of the mountains, but above me, the sky ran high and very blue—blue as a robin's egg.

I rode Raymond's horse over to the Blavens'. Peter left Papa watering and rode with me on his horse, carrying my new dress, lavender shawl, and shoes. We moved slowly so I wouldn't muss my hair. I really had wanted to be alone to think about it all—it imagine how it would be, the shocked expression on everyone's faces when my name was announced, how Mr. Staaton would look at me again with those wonderful eyes of his. Yes, I wanted to think it all over, but though I'd argued with him, Peter insisted on coming.

Lately it seemed easier to let Peter do what he wanted. I alternated between admiring and resenting his pushiness—but at this moment I resented it.

"Your hair's different. I like it."

I gave him a clipped thank-you and touched one of the pins at the nape of my neck.

"It means so much—this practice?"

I pretended confusion although I knew what he was about to say.

"The new dress, your Mom's shawl, your hair." He gave me one of his paternal smiles. "That's kind of going all out for a practice, isn't it, Anne?"

"Obviously *I* don't think so."

"Do the other girls do all this?" He gestured at the clothes he held over his arm.

"Well, how do I know, Peter?" I snapped the reins, and my horse loped ahead. I could see his point, of course. I'd walk in dressed for a grand affair while all the others would be casual. They'd see at a glance how important it was to me. But did it matter? Not tonight! I determined that nothing would spoil my first practice—nothing.

Peter hurried his horse. "I'm teasing you, Anne. You'll look great."

We rode along silently with the sun ahead of us and the late afternoon shadows stretching behind. As we turned down the Blavens' lane, Peter began to whistle and I thought back to his first summer with us, two years ago . . .

Peter had become a member of the family immediately on his arrival that June. We all flocked about him, easing the strangeness the best we could and trying to make him feel at home. But while he chummed with Papa and Raymond, hauled Katy about, cooed over Margaret's cradle, and propelled himself into action at Mama's slightest need, he gave no heed to me. Amid this sweltering of brotherly love and compassion, I watched woodenly, wondering often if I'd become invisible. Peter was cool and distant to me deliberately—at least, that's the decision Phyliss and I came to. We had lots of time to spend together those days, and we spent much of it trying to figure Peter and plotting ways to shake him from his strange, egotistical world. Most of the plans fizzled, but unfortunately, we did carry out one such plot—our very last.

Phyliss and I, in an undignified moment, climbed one of the big cottonwoods behind our barn. It was early fall, and the leaves were still green and thick enough to hide us. We sat looking across the fields when we saw Papa and Peter coming from the orchard. Papa, with one hand on Peter's shoulder and the other outstretched over his land, was boasting about what a team the two of them made. They stopped nearly under us and talked about the fence along the lower field that needed mending.

"I suppose we could do it tomorrow, Peter, but something else has me worried."

"The canal above the potato patch?"

Papa nodded. "I've got a meeting tonight, and I don't think we'd better let that bank go another day. The lower corner of the patch is rotting out."

"I'll fix it, Bill. This evening early."

"Would you, Peter? You know, son, I can always depend on you. You've been great this summer, really great. Let's get the cows in."

They disappeared around the barn, Papa's hand on Peter's shoulder again.

"*I'll* fix it Bill—early!" Phyllis mocked. "Ugh! I think I might retch." She held her stomach and groaned, her head hanging out over a limb and her jaw sagging open. "He makes me sick—sick—sick."

It hurt somehow to have Papa like Peter so much.

Besides, I reasoned, outsiders should be humble awhile—at least at first.

"Let's get him, Phyl. We can fix him good. Papa thinks Peter is perfect, right?"

"Oh, he *is,* my dear." She pursed her lips. "He is Mr. Percy Perfect." We laughed, trying the new name.

"He wouldn't be so perfect if he forgot to fix the canal."

"Forgot? Our Percy? "No chance—that is, unless—unless we *lure* him away with our beauty."

I grabbed a fistful of leaves, and we watched them whirling to the ground.

"Listen, I've got an idea! You stay all night. After everyone's asleep, we'll go out and break the bank open again. We could make it look like he never even fixed it in the first place!" Glorious visions of Papa disappointed in Peter's work filled my mind. I lay back against a limb and tossed another bunch of leaves into the air. "What do you think?"

Phyliss said nothing for a long moment. She sat looking up into the highest branches of the tree, turning the idea somewhere above her. Finally she asked if I were serious.

"Well, sure, Phyl. Can't you see it? We'd bring Peter down a notch or two!"

"Yes—we'd be doing Percy a favor, wouldn't we! We'd be giving him that endearing human trait—error, for," she put a finger to the air, "to err is human."

Even then I knew that I would regret it later, but I didn't care. Let the consequences come. We would do it.

That evening Peter came in late for supper. Mama, Phyliss, and I had already begun clearing up.

He looked lonely and tired standing by the door making his excuses to Mama. He had been fixing the canal, he said, and it had taken longer than he'd expected, but it would hold this time.

Phyliss winked at me over a dish she was drying. It struck me then that I knew nothing about Peter—not really. Perhaps he was an orphan and had no family of his own. Perhaps he worked himself so hard because he wanted to forget—to wipe a possibly horrid childhood from his mind.

Phyliss nudged me. "Going soft?" she whispered.

"I think—maybe we shouldn't—"

"Don't get dramatic. We're not going to hurt him." She gave Peter a big smile over her shoulder. "We're going to help him."

It was after twelve when Phyliss and I climbed out of bed. The house was still and dark except for a soft trail of moonlight streaming in the window. We pulled on coats over our nightclothes and crept softly down the stairs. Sometime before supper, we had hidden a pair of galoshes and an old pair of Papa's shoes along with a small trowel and shovel in the lilac bush outside the back door. Now I put on Papa's shoes (my feet nearly came out of them as I walked) and Phyliss took the galoshes.

The moonlight fell in soft patterns of shadow and light as we walked through the orchard. The air was still and cool. Crickets chirped softly, stopping as we approached and singing again after we had passed. We talked and giggled in low tones, our excitement growing as we approached the canal.

We found easily enough the spot Peter had mended. He had done a characteristically good job, and had even packed out gravel and lined the canal sides with it.

"There's a lot of water in the canal tonight." I stared down into the black liquid moving silently but swiftly westward. "I'd kind of hoped that someone above us would be taking his turn. Then we could get right inside to break the bank."

"We'll do all right."

We stood a moment looking at each other. "I guess we should get started."

"I guess so."

The work was less fun than we had imagined, and before long we realized our tools were useless—we didn't even have the strength to get the shovel blade into the ground. Peter had packed it solid. We put down the tools and began using our hands.

"It *is* too bad the canal isn't empty," Phyl said, taking off her coat and laying it a short distance down the bank next to mine. "That would simplify things. Then we could get inside and push it out with our feet."

I looked up at her. "Maybe we should come back another time when it is."

"Now or never, I always say."

We pushed and pulled at the bank until the moon that had hung over the eastern foothills stood above us and glimmered ghostlike in the inky water of the canal. But all attempts were useless. The bank held. I sat down on the ridge and gathered my nightgown about my legs. A canyon breeze had come up and the air was cooling considerably.

"Oh, Phyl, let's get out of here. What an awful idea."

"Of yours," she reminded me.

"All right, of mine. But I'm cold, and besides, he's done it too well. We'll be here all night."

"Leverage!" Phyliss cried, a bit wild-eyed.

"You're not making any sense, Phyl. What has leverage got to do with this?"

"Listen! We'll make the hole real deep, see, and then put the shovel handle down it and rock it back and forth. We'll use leverage to bust the bank open. It'll work, Anne. Jump!"

After we had broken through with the shovel, the rest went easily. When we had made our hole deep enough, we put the shovel handle down it and began swinging on it. It was working. Our spirits were renewed. The hole got larger and larger, and at last the bank began to give.

"He'll die," Phyliss laughed. "He'll really die. I can see him now when your pa lights into him." We laughed until we thought we'd fall down weakly into the water.

I flung a fistful of mud at Phyliss. She ducked and slipped backward toward the water, grabbing the handle to save her. It held only for an instant and then gave way, following her back into the canal. With that, the bank broke. The black water came over me in one long, loud gushing spout like a tidal wave, blowing the mud and gravel

23

of the bank with it. I tried to run, but Papa's shoes held me. When I had at last crawled up on a dry section of bank, I found my hair full of grit, I was soaked clean through, and worse, I had lost a shoe.

"Help me, Phyliss. I've lost a shoe."

She stood on the dry bank several yards away shivering and laughing between breaths. "I think that did it."

"Did it? Look at this mess. Papa's patch! Do you think we've ruined it?" Phyliss shrugged her wet shoulders. "Well," I said, "better find that shoe."

Though we searched in mud up to our knees and elbows for a half hour or more, we found nothing. It was gone, swallowed completely. We walked along the bank upstream to get our coats, washed as well as we could in the canal, and started back home—leaving Papa's shoe behind and the potato patch filling with water.

Phyliss left for home early the next morning after making me swear an oath to tell her everything. I suspected she used all the drama to obscure the fact that she was deserting me. We both knew we had gone overboard with our little joke.

I was making up my room when I heard Papa and Peter outside my window. Papa's voice came through in angry spurts. I had to lean out to catch it all.

"Well, if you did, you made a fine job of it. The entire patch is buried in water."

Peter stood quietly, taking his undeserved punishment. "I'm sorry, Bill, I'll—"

"Taylor Parry was up here this morning," Papa cut in. "He was fuming, and I can't say I blame him. We ruined his water turn. It took him the entire night to trace the leak."

"But I did fix it, Bill, and good too. I swear I did."

Papa sighed and walked back to the house, mopping his brow. Peter followed him with his eyes; then, as if he'd known all along that I'd been watching, he raised his gaze to meet mine—direct, penetrating. My cheeks grew hot and red. After a long, uncomfortable moment, Peter turned on his heels and left. I was ashamed—to the core!

I spent the entire day indoors. Mama was overwhelmed. I polished the front room until it shone, cleaned my room again and again, and helped prepare and clear up breakfast and dinner. Peter was absent from both. Late in the afternoon, when I'd run dry of chores, I gratefully remembered the needlepoint Mama had given me two summers ago, now tucked away in my bottom drawer.

"Are you ill, Anne?" Mama asked as I sat in the corner of my room sewing (something she knew I despised).

"No, Mama. I just thought it about time I got this done." Tomorrow it would go back in the drawer unfinished.

Peter was there at supper. Papa scarcely said a word, mumbling only now and then for something to be passed. Peter was quiet as well, but not so obviously as Papa. So Mama, with the help of Raymond and the girls, kept up the conversation and quite pleasantly. I too launched off bravely on several subjects, but my voice sounded loud and high-pitched.

Mother looked at me several times during the meal, puzzled. She seemed to know something was up. But it wasn't until after everyone was up from the table, and the kids and Papa had left for the parlor, that the boom fell.

I was starting to gather dishes when Peter asked if he might speak to me a minute.

"I'm sorry," I said, "but it's my turn to wash."

Mama waved a hand. "Nonsense, you've done well over your share today. Go out with Peter and get some air." She gave me a knowing, almost conspiratorial smile as we left the room.

We stood on the front porch. It was nearly dark. The full moon was out again, but a slight breeze was up brushing through the cottonwoods, reminding us that winter was near.

"Why?"

I was concerned, of course. Peter knew. Had he found the shoe? But it was Papa's, not mine. He did seem to know though—somehow.

"Why what, Peter?"

"Why did you do that to me, Anne?"

That was the first time Peter had called me anything except Miss Carrow. I put both hands firmly on the wooden porch railing. I wasn't going to confess. He couldn't make me.

"I don't know what you mean. Ask whatever you're wondering outright, or don't be bothering me, Peter Tate."

"But you *do* know what I mean."

"I don't understand why, Anne, but you and your friend did this thing deliberately." He came up behind me so close I could feel his angry breath on my neck. "Now why don't you tell me about it?"

I still said nothing. He'd have to prove it. I wasn't telling. We stood there like that for some time. I was beginning to feel terribly uncomfortable when Peter ripped me around and, with a heavy grip on my arm, pulled me off the porch. He began angrily striding toward the shed, pulling me after him.

"What are you doing? Let me go or I'll call Papa! I mean it, Peter. I will!"

"If anyone calls your father it will be *me*."

He shoved me through the shed door. It was black and close inside. What was he doing? I *would* call Papa. I'd scream my lungs out.

"Peter? Peter, I can't see. Let me out of here."

Behind me a lantern came on. My shadow loomed against the shed wall and rippled over the tools that hung there, over the shovel and trowel.

"If you won't talk, listen."

I turned to face him, but he held the lantern high between us. I couldn't see his face except as a vague shadow beyond the brilliance of the light.

I had no choice. "All right."

"As you well know," he began, his voice dry and controlled, "last night I fixed the canal. When I returned my tools, I noticed the other shovel missing, and with it the trowel. Well, I thought it pretty odd, since your Pa had gone, but I was late getting in for supper, so I decided to look around a bit after. When I did, they were still missing. Then this morning early, before I'd seen your Pa, I was walking in from the barn and noticed the shed door open. The trowel and shovel had been returned—both crusted with dry mud.'' He stopped, still holding the light high. Obviously he was waiting for some response.

Mud! We'd forgotten to wash it off. Weren't all farm tools dirty? Evidently not with Peter around.

"But why do you suspect me?"

"Suspect? I *know*." His voice was hard and flat. If he would just put the light down and let me see his face.

"You can't know. Why not Raymond?"

"Why would he do a thing like that?"

"Well, why would I?"

"That's just what I'm asking. Why, Anne?"

I turned away from the light—from Peter. He'd worn me down. He had won. Peter would always win.

"All right, Peter, all right. But I won't be talking to that light anymore." I felt a rush of self-pity. "It makes me dizzy. As you well know, I didn't get much sleep last night, and this day has been exhausting. Could we go back to the house and talk by the swing? Please, Peter?"

At last he lowered the lamp, but his face didn't look at all as though he had won.

THREE

The next day I told Papa.

"*You* broke the bank open?"

"Phyliss helped!"

"And you've just now come to me?" He creased his forehead and studied me a long moment."Anna Jeanette,do you know what I've done?"

He turned and looked out to the orchards, over the rows of beets and sprawling tomatoes, beyond that to his new corral, newly painted barn, and tool shed. I knew what he was thinking. Peter had worked for him like a son, and then at what seemed his first real error . . .

"Oh, Papa, I'm so sorry. I've talked with Peter and told him so. We didn't mean to go so far with it. It was just going to be a little—" The word *joke* stuck in my throat. Whatever we'd done, it was no joke.

Papa waited for me to go on, to give some explanation. Surely I had reason. Did I want Peter fired? Was that it? No, I liked him. I did—even more now. Then what did I want? I didn't know.

Papa continued to wait. "Well, Anne?"

"Oh, Papa, I don't know what to say. We—we just did it, Papa."

He shook his head and turned to leave. Wasn't he going to cuss me out as he had Peter? Wouldn't he call me what I was—dishonest, a cheat, a schemer? Hadn't I ruined his crop—cost him a great deal of hard work and money, and worse, eternally so, caused another to take my punishment—*while I looked on?* No. Though I would have welcomed a bawling out, even a thrashing, I would get neither. Papa was leaving me there with my mouth open and tears filling my eyes, unable to say anything in my own defense, because there was nothing to say.

Early September soon dissolved into late fall, warm still, though the days were rapidly growing shorter. The mountains had slipped from their velvety greens into burning reds and yellows and purples. Only the aspens stood holding their limey green against the darker evergreen of the firs and spruce, until at last they too had turned weak yellow and their thin, scale-like leaves began to fall.

The entire valley became frantically engaged in winding up the harvesting before cold weather set in. Papa and Peter worked round the clock, coming in only for short infrequent snoozes now and then, and in spite of Mama's pleading with them both to come in for meals, we usually ended up taking baskets of food out to them in the fields and they ate on their feet or in the shade of the wagon or a nearby tree.

Needless to say, that year there were few potatoes that needed picking up from the washed-out potato patch, but no one, not even Raymond, said much about the smaller number of burlap sacks that were filled and placed in the corner of the cellar.

And also needless to say, since my little episode with the canal bank, Papa's admiration and respect for Peter had grown considerably. He had proven himself a worker and a man.

"We're made from the same stuff," Papa said one afternoon as we walked in from the fields. "Reminds me of myself when I was his age. You mark my words, Annie, he said, smiling, "Peter'll make something out of his life. He's got what it takes to get what he wants, and more than that— he knows darn well what he's after. It's simply a matter of time."

Mama and Papa were away for the evening, and so there would be just Peter, the younger children, and I around the table at supper. It had been weeks since our little talk by the swing, and I had done my best since then to avoid any situation with Peter where I'd have to make conversation. Whenever I remembered back to our last talk, I broke into a cold sweat, more determined than ever to prevent it from happening again. Peter knew me now at my utter worst, while I knew him no better than before my nightmarish prank.

As the supper hour approached, a tight knot began to grow inside my ribs. There would be no way out tonight, no easy excuse to make. In a few minutes I'd have to face him without Mama and Papa as buffers. My major concern was the casual chit-chat I knew I'd have to make. What could I say to him? "Mended any canal banks lately?"

My mind kept going back to what Papa had said earlier about him and Peter being made from the same stuff. *No, Papa, I couldn't agree.* Oh, the two of them liked a lot of the same things: they both shared the same general view about religion and politics, and they got along well with one another. But that was a far cry from the same stuff. Papa was a man you could easily read. His feelings were there on the surface. But Peter seemed to have something hidden beneath the casual, confident manner he displayed with my family. He never ceased evaluating, analyzing, measuring one thing against another, and there was an uneasiness about him, as if there were something bothering him— something he couldn't or wouldn't quite let go.

The meal went smoothly enough. Raymond and Peter did most of the talking, with the children chiming in occasionally. I busied myself with helping Tyler and keeping the serving bowls filled and passed about.

"It'll be a real wingding," Raymond was saying. "Foot races, prizes, cakes and lemonade, and the big dance at the end of the day. I can go now that I'm twelve, Mama says."

"We're all going to it, aren't we, Anne," Margaret said

confidently, puddling her gravy onto her potatoes. "Well, aren't we?"

"I'm sure Mama and Papa are planning on us all going to the celebration. That's the most important part."

"But the dance, Annie?"

"Margaret, you're dripping on the tablecloth. Katy, help her get the ladle back in the bowl, will you?"

"Answer, Annie!" Margaret pressed.

"Yes, Anne," Katy said, "you're changing the subject. Are we or aren't we allowed to go to the dance?"

I felt Peter's eyes on me. "I'm afraid not all of us will be going." Peter raised an eyebrow that seemed to ask, *And you, will you be going?* "But of course, the dance is for older people, and we'd rather spend our energy on the cake walk and the races, now wouldn't we?"

"But I'm *ten*, Katy insisted. "That's nearly Raymond's age."

"My age? Hah! You're both too young to go for years and years and years."

"Now, Raymond." I gave him a warning glance.

"Well, I'm not so young as Tyler," Margaret pouted. "He's the one who'll have to wait for years and years and years." She began to chant and Katy joined her, "Tyler is the baby, Tyler is the baby."

I looked across the table at Peter. He seemed delighted at the sudden commotion. I wondered if he were now analyzing my ability to control children.

"All right, you two, that's enough."

Tyler grinned back at them both and calmly finished his milk, holding his little silver cup in both hands. Then he picked up the chant himself and began to shout it gleefully, a white milk mustache over his little mouth. They all giggled back at him, forgetting, for the time being, the dance.

Following the meal, Peter seemed to be in especially high spirits. He shooed the children upstairs to get ready for bed with promises of a scary story when they had their pajamas on.

"Do you promise to really scare us?" Katy asked wide-eyed.

Peter rolled his eyes wildly and began swinging his arms apelike with his back hunched over his head. Katy ran squealing into her bedroom.

I was lifting hot water from the top of the stove when Peter came back into the kitchen.

"Let me do that." He crossed the room in three easy strides and took the kettle from me. But instead of pouring it into the sink where I wanted it, he placed it back on the stove.

"But, Peter, I need it over here."

"I know, but while the kids are upstairs, I'd like to talk a minute."

I turned to the sink and began stacking the dishes. "I really can't. I have studies tonight."

"What is this, Anne? And why don't you look at me? You know you never do."

"Of course I do." I turned and forced my eyes to meet his. They were a deep blue against the tan of his face.

"You've made it awfully hard to talk, ducking about like you've been doing."

"Peter—" He always seemed to put me on the defensive, and I didn't like it—not one bit.

"Don't deny it. I just hope it isn't too late."

"For what, Peter Tate?"

"For the harvest dance. You haven't been asked, have you?"

It suddenly occurred to me that Peter was asking *me* to the dance. But that was incredible. I was certain this little talk would be some sort of progress check. That is, Peter measuring my advancement along a new road to honesty.

"You *are* going then. You have been asked?"

"No, I haven't. No one . . ."

"Will you go with me, Anne?" He crossed from the stove and stood before me, smiling again.

I remember thinking then that Phyliss would never

32

believe this, not in a million years. "I don't understand. You're asking *me*—after what I did to you?"

"You're talking about the canal thing, are you?"

"Oh, Peter, you haven't forgotten it either."

He threw back his head and laughed. "No, Anne, I haven't. But that's irrelevant, isn't it? I want to take you to the dance. Now will you go?"

"Well, I—" What could I say when he was charitable enough to ask me? "Yes, I'll go."

"Good!" Peter took the water from the stove and poured it into the sink. "I've hired a buggy. They'll have it here by eight. Oh, and Anne," he turned in the doorway, "I want you to wear that yellow dress—you know, the one with the big sash."

We turned our horses down the last bend of Blavens' lane. Peter was still whistling. We *had* come a long way in the past summer. There were times when we'd really had fun together, Peter and I. I glanced at his profile. He was very nice to look at—in a comfortable way. He wasn't at all like that mysterious Mark Staaton. There wasn't anything comfortable about Mark Staaton. I felt my spirits soar. I was happy again—happy it was spring, happy to be one of the lucky sixteen girls who made up the Ashley Valley Singers, and happiest now that I was going to my first practice after all.

Nathan and Connie, the youngest of the Blaven children, waited barefoot on the porch, whispering to one another. I waved a hello and they scurried back into the house, letting the door slam behind them. I thought of Margo Blaven, ill and trying to rest. Gerald and Thomas B. ran out to greet us.

"Is *he* tending us, too?" Gerald pointed a grimy finger at Peter.

I caught Peter's aggravated expression as the children jumped up on the gate and rode it.

"Your Pa and I fixed that gate this spring. That hasn't been a month ago." He looked back at the gate, where the two boys had begun giving each other rides. "Look at it now! And no wonder!"

"They're just children," I said. "Didn't *you* do things like that?"

I felt Peter's arms tighten as he helped me off my horse. "No, Anne," he said in an even voice. "Never."

"But Peter, surely—"

"*No*, and I wouldn't say it's normal to be destructive either. The boys should be helping out instead of tearing the place apart."

He seemed so angry that I thought it best to drop the matter right there. I followed him into the house and we cleared a place for my things.

"Well, Anne, I guess you're all set for tonight?"

"Yes, Peter, thanks."

"Will you be all right coming home alone?"

"Of course. I've done it before."

"All right then. I'd better get back. I'll be out watering until late, but I'll check to be sure the buggy is back before going to bed."

"Thank you, Peter. I'll be fine."

He smiled. "I'll see you, then. If those kids give you any trouble—"

"They will, that's for sure. If they didn't, I'd worry."

"You're too soft on them," he hollered over his shoulder as he rode out of the yard. I watched as he stopped at the gate and gave Thomas B. and Gerald the word.

I got supper over early. The boys played outside while two-year-old Connie trailed about as I cleared the dishes and set to work cleaning the house. Their mother slept soundly, waking only once when Thomas B. jumped onto the roof from the hut he and Gerald had made in the apple tree behind the house, and she stayed awake only long enough for me to give the boys a good scolding and feed her a little broth.

It was seven-thirty before I had everyone in pajamas. Connie went to sleep immediately, but the boys romped across their big iron bed, socking one another and turning somersaults. The show, I gathered, was for my benefit, but my time was running out.

"All right, boys," I decided to start right off with bribery, "get into bed and I'll tell you a story."

I told them two—"Beauty and the Beast" and "The Three Little Pigs"—both of which I thought would appeal to boys.

"They're silly," Gerald said as I finished the line about the pigs never seeing the wolf again.

"Yes, I guess they are, but they're fun too, aren't they?"

"Yeah, more." Nathan clapped his hands.

Thomas rolled over next to Nathan and propped his head against his brother's arm. "More."

"No!" Gerald set his jaw in a stubborn line. "Pigs don't talk."

"All right. I'll tell one especially for Gerald. But this time about three little boys who wouldn't go to sleep. They were very much like you three—in fact, nearly the same ages. But they were young princes, and they hadn't gone to sleep for weeks and weeks. Oh, their mother made them go to bed all right, but they never closed their eyes. Not once.

"Why don't you lay on your backs and pretend to be them—but whatever you do, don't close your eyes!"

Nathan and Thomas lay on their backs blinking at the ceiling.

"Anyhow, throughout the entire kingdom the best doctors and wisest men came to counsel with the king. 'I will give half my kingdom and the hand of my beautiful daughter in marriage to anyone who can save my sons,' he said. 'If they don't go to sleep soon, their eyes will be useless and they will go blind.'

"The wise men and doctors thought and thought and counseled and counseled, but to no avail. There was nothing they could do. The king became angry and sent them away. In great despair he at last called his three sons to his chamber. They stood before him yawning like this." I yawned several times and rubbed my eyes. " 'My sons,' said the king, 'why will you not sleep?'

" 'Father, we dare not,' said the oldest.

" 'Father, we dare not,' said the youngest.

" 'Father, we dare not,' said the one in-between.

" 'And why do you dare not?' demanded the king."

Gerald, still sitting up, listened with great interest. Nathan and Thomas B. were busily staring at the ceiling, concentrating more on their eyes than on my story.

"Why do you think they dared not?" I asked Gerald. I was quickly trying to think of why myself.

"I don't know," he said, bewildered. "Maybe someone's trying to steal the king's gold."

"Exactly," I said. "Brilliant! Someone *was* trying to steal the king's gold, and the king's three faithful sons dared not close their eyes lest the thief should strike while they slept."

"But who?" Gerald's eyes were wide.

"The king's closest servant. He had helped the king so long that now he thought he should have a kingdom for himself. But as soon as the plot was discovered, the king had him exiled to a distant land. At last his sons were able to sleep, and they slept happily ever after."

Gerald sat a moment, letting the story settle in his mind. I was certain he'd enjoyed it, but he said simply: "You can tell us another, but we'll still be awake. It's still light outside. Who goes to bed when it's light?"

"But it's not early, Gerald." I looked at my watch again, and noticed with a jolt that it was straight up eight o'clock. My stomach did a turn. I wasn't ready, and there was so much to do. "You see, in the summer the sun is up longer than it is in the winter. The days are longer and the nights are shorter. But we still need the same amount of rest, so we have to *try* to sleep even though it isn't dark."

"Can we talk?"

"Try to sleep first." I closed the door behind me and said a little prayer that they would go to sleep quickly.

The lane was empty. Raymond wasn't in sight. I hurriedly slipped into my nice dress. Mama had made it for me from a light spring print Charlie had gotten in from the East. It was bright pink with small splashes of blue and green, ruffles at the throat and cuffs, a wide flounce around the hem, and a wide tie in back. I did up as many of the tiny buttons as I could reach. Raymond would have to do the others.

The Blavens had only one mirror. It hung on the wall in the kitchen and was so smoky and narrow I could scarcely make out my reflection, but what I could see would do. The brilliant pink of the dress made my cheeks glow. I would look like a different girl from the one who had sung trembling before Mr. Staaton in a gray cotton that morning. And the curls high on my head made me appear quite sophisticated. I would be proud tonight—even sitting next to an Ashley, next to Delores.

I began talking out loud to myself by eight-thirty. The fastest anyone had made it into town from our place was twenty-five minutes. Unless Raymond came soon— *Raymond, come, please!*

I took the rocker out on the small porch and began watching the bend in the road. I looked at my watch again. Mr. Staaton would be walking into the chapel right now. He would survey his group; all of the girls would be in their seats except Phyliss—she would be waiting by the door, pacing.

"Shall we begin, Miss Langley?" He would turn to Phyliss and invite her to take her place.

"But, Mr. Staaton, Anne Carrow hasn't come in yet."

Everyone would turn to look at my empty seat. "Anne Carrow? *She* took Vinnie's place? Well, where is she? Not late her first time surely?"

Raymond . . .

It was nine o'clock before I realized he wouldn't be coming. The sun had set and it was growing dark rapidly. I had watched the bend till my eyes ached. I got up from the chair, stretched my legs, and went into the house.

I put on my dark cotton again and hung my pink dress behind the door where I wouldn't see it, then went through the hall and into the children's room. Connie slept in a little bed next to the door. Nathan was on the floor under the window asleep, and in the bed, Thomas B. also slept. Gerald sat up as I came in.

"They're asleep." He said it as if they had betrayed a code.

"Why aren't you asleep, Gerald?"

"I told you. I don't sleep when it's light."

"But it isn't light any longer. I'll be lighting the lamp soon. Help me get Nathan back into bed, will you?"

Ten-thirty—the practice would be over.

"Anne Carrow," they would shake their heads. "He's new or he would have known better."

I had moved the rocker back inside and placed it next to the open window. It was a warm evening, and the canyon breeze coming from High Creek fluttered the faded curtains at the window. I found a book inscribed "to Margo" in a delicate leaning hand. It was poetry—Wordsworth's. I opened it and stared at the pages for some time before realizing I wasn't reading. I leaned my head back in the old rocker. The book slipped from my hand to the floor. I felt very tired.

"Annie." A little shadow was standing in the hallway just beyond the lamplight. It was Connie.

"What's wrong, dear?" I picked her up and held her close in my lap.

"I want to sleep with Mommy."

"But your Mommy's sick." I felt the little head nod against me. "Why not sit with me for a while?"

It was soothing holding her there. We seemed so isolated, the two of us in that tiny pool of light surrounded on all sides by empty darkness. I began singing quietly to myself as much as to her, and to stop myself from asking any longer, *Why, Raymond? Why didn't you come—why—why?*

My voice came to my ears sounding far off—distant—as if I weren't singing at all, but someone else deep in the blackness.

Tiny Princess, sweet the night,
Close your eyes in slumber tight,
Soon enough these stars will fade
And the sun will light the dew
But for now your swing hangs silent,
And waits for dawn, and you.

The warm night air washed over us, bringing with it the gentle sound of the blowing cottonwoods—hush, hush.

FOUR

I woke, cold in my chair. The soft blue light of morning filtered through the one smudged window in front of me. Barely dawn. Brother Blaven had not returned.

The front room and kitchen lay in that cold blue shadow. Brown walls. Brown floor. Brown chairs and table. Brown and cold. Brown and still.

An uneasy sensation played about my throat. Morning at home was never like this. Our house was not quite so near the hills, and it caught the sun earlier as it crept into the warm kitchen, brushing the yellow curtains. Mama's cherry-colored apron would be at the stove, and the blue rose china on the table. Smells of freshly sliced bacon, creamed eggs, and griddle cakes would shake us from our beds to the warm kitchen or the roaring fire Papa had built in the front room fireplace. "It's awful morning," he'd call cheerfully to those still in bed. "Awful morning" meaning simply that it was very much morning, and we needed to *get going*.

I stood up in the pale light and wrapped Mama's shawl about me and stepped out onto the porch. The lane was empty. Raymond's horse, tied to the gate, stood statuelike in the shadows. As I looked at the bleak yard, I shivered. The trees about the house were steeped in gray darkness, looming silently against a dreary sky, and the air, wet and cold, was heavy with the smell of rain. Except for the low, far-off thunder of High Creek, everything was still and intensely quiet.

Last night I hadn't shed a tear over missing the practice, but with this sudden feeling of desolation the tears came— slipping silently down my face. No one had come—not Raymond, nor Papa, nor anyone. They had let me miss the practice and stay here all night unprotected. Horrible visions of dangers that could have befallen me broke my silent weeping into painful sobs. I thought of Chester Bailey with new fear.

Chester was the twenty-four-year-old retarded son of Hec Bailey. He was a tall, blank-looking man with a swollen head and pale, almost colorless, protruding eyes. He had a way of walking with his large, irregular head slumped nearly to his chestbone, and then abruptly swiveling it to the side to catch a long, gawking stare at something that interested him. Chester was a good boy and had never given anyone cause for real alarm, but he was strong and broke things without meaning to. I'd always been kind to Chester. Papa said someday we'd meet him again in the celestial kingdom, and that Chester would look out of clear and intelligent eyes to judge those who had ridiculed him. I wanted Chester to smile at me then and remember that I had been his friend. But at this moment the many occasions I had talked with him, and our familiarity, frightened me. Because his father was often drunk and locked up, Chester roamed the countryside on his own, often sleeping as he was against a canal bank or in a pile of leaves or compost. Papa had, on more than one occasion, found him skulking about at night and invited him in—smelly clothes and all—to sleep on the couch. Of course, Chester didn't ever mean any harm, but I shuddered to think of the things he could do without meaning to.

Then there were the Indians. They hadn't been around much in the last ten years, but Wally Brinton, Charlie's son, said a small band was camped on the steep bluff above South River nearly all last summer. They were *real* Indians, he said, and were responsible for the stock pilfering many Ashley farmers experienced in August.

I couldn't remember even seeing what I considered a *real* Indian. There was on occasion the same group of old men and women wrapped in grubby blankets and begging food in Huntsville, but people called them *diggers* and said their own people were ashamed of them. In my mind real Indians (like the Utes or Snakes that once held the valley as their summer home) were giant, strong, red people like those described in the Book of Mormon, with savage and passionate appetites. A girl was better off dead than taken by *them*, I'd heard many times. My tears came even harder when I thought about that. I wouldn't even be able to kill myself to keep from being captured. Suicide wasn't moral.

Overhead the rain began in a silent drizzle sifting through the trees. I wiped my eyes. There was nothing to do but go back to the dark house and wait.

I sat at the rain-spotted window and watched the lane, my ears straining at the silence around me, half afraid I might see a hunched figure moving through the shadowy brush outside (there was no bolt or even proper latch on the door), and half-knowing such an idea was preposterous.

Outside the day gradually came, though still overcast, and at length, a buggy rounded the bend and hurried toward the house. Papa's buggy!

I flung myself out the door and ran under the drenched trees and swung the gate wide.

"Papa," I shouted, tripping over my wet skirts as I ran down the lane to meet him.

"Anne?" The buggy lurched to a stop and Peter jumped down at my side. "What on earth has happened?" His face had never seemed so compassionate and understanding as it did then.

"Oh, Peter," I sobbed, "nobody came for me. I missed the practice, and—" I looked back with horror at the ugly house squatting beneath dripping trees—"and I stayed here *all night*—alone!"

Peter held me against his warm shoulder and began patting my hair. "Kind'a scared, huh?" I nodded. "Raymond ought to be licked good for this. Poor Anne."

It was all of it unreal—the dim sky above, the man at my side, the bleak house, the falling rain—all a vague, unhappy dream.

Peter put me into the buggy under a cover. "I'm taking you home!" He disappeared into the house and emerged with my things.

"I don't think I should, Peter. Dell's not—"

"He's back, Anne. He's talking with your pa right now. He'll be here before anyone wakes up." He untied Raymond's horse and slapped his flank. Then he climbed in beside me, took off his jacket, and put it around my shoulders. The horse loped for home.

"Warmer?" Peter smiled, his face close to mine. "You'll never miss the practice again, I promise. From now on I'll take you in myself." He brushed at a tear drying on my cheek and, lifting my chin, leaned and kissed my mouth. "Now, don't you feel better?"

I closed my eyes against the bleak morning and nodded numbly, not knowing if I felt better or not. A new uneasiness had begun inside me.

Peter shook the reins and, smiling at the road in front of him, took me home.

"All right, Raymond. Where were you?" I stood at the foot of his bed, keeping my voice as low as I could manage. The entire house was still sleeping except for Papa, who, along with Peter, hadn't gone to bed during the water turn.

By the time I got home, my self-pity had left me. I only knew that I had missed my practice and that Raymond, who now slept peacefully without a care in his young mind, had caused it all. His sunburned face looked babyish and innocent. He didn't stir in the least at my voice.

"Raymond, wake up!" I shook the bed hard. The serene expression clouded slightly as the bed rocked, but settled again. I put my mouth next to his ear. "Raymond, answer me! Where were you last night? I waited and waited. You *promised* to come!" The eyes fluttered open.

"What are you doing? Leave me alone."

"You stayed and played with the guys! I knew it!"

"I said I'd try to get there, Anne, *try*. Now let me sleep, and I'll explain later." He rolled over and covered his head in the blankets.

"Oh no you don't! I want to hear it now," I demanded, pulling at his head. "You tell me why you didn't come!"

"Let go. Let go." His voice was muffled under the knotted bedclothes.

"I'm not letting you sleep until I know." I bounced the bed up and down again with my weight as I pulled at the blankets.

"Anne, stop that!" Mother frowned from the doorway. "You'll wake everybody. We've already been through all that with Raymond. Now let him sleep and I'll tell you about it." She motioned for me to follow. Raymond's eyes appeared above the blankets as I left.

"Come and sit." Mama held out her hand and took mine in hers. She pulled me down beside her on her bed. "If it will make you feel any better, dear, your father and I got after Raymond quite thoroughly not an hour ago."

"Raymond—" I began bitterly.

"No, listen. That was before we knew his side of it. He wasn't to blame after all. Circumstances beyond—"

"Circumstances! What circumstances?"

"If you'll listen, I'll try and tell you."

I tried to fight my anger down. There was no sense in getting Mama upset. But I was certain that nothing Mama could tell me could justify Raymond's actions—*nothing*.

Mama smoothed the lap of her dressing gown. "Raymond says he was ready to come home by seven-thirty —the candy sale was over. He was just about to leave when Sister Lacey came with her goods, a basket packed to the

44

brim with cookies and candy. Raymond said it looked like she'd been working for days. He tried to tell her the whole thing was over but she didn't understand. She's getting so old, you know.''

I thought of the little white-haired woman who whispered so loudly in church while everyone pretended not to hear.

''What was he to do, dear?'' Mama gave me her bright proud-of-her-wonderful-son smile, which told me just what he did do.

''He stayed and sold her stuff.'' I couldn't help but say it belligerently.

''Just what *you* would have done under those circumstances. He thanked Sister Lacey, and when she asked where all the other boys had gone, he told her not to worry, he'd go door-to-door himself until it was sold.''

''And when was that?''

''He finished just before nine. Your practice had started. If Raymond had come straight to the Blavens', then you still wouldn't have made it. It was just one of those things. But because he knew how important it was to you, Anne, he waited until after the practice was over and spoke with Mark Staaton about it.''

''He didn't!''

''Oh, I thought that was a wonderful thing to do.''

''Mama, I can imagine—''

''I'm sure he handled it fine. You needn't worry about what the girls thought. He waited until they had left the chapel and then he slipped in and told Mr. Staaton in private.''

The thought nudged me that Raymond had tried. ''Do you know what he said?''

''I suppose that you were tending to a sick neighbor and her family. Mr. Staaton's a fine man. I'm sure he found that a legitimate excuse. In any case, it couldn't be helped, and you mustn't be angry with Raymond.'' Mother pushed herself to her feet and began straightening the room.

''So that's that,'' I mumbled. I understood and yet I felt

no less frustrated and angry, if not at Raymond, then at the disappointing turn of things. I had missed my longed-for, dreamed-of practice because a confused old lady had brought her candy to a bake sale hours too late.

"You're *still* angry?"

"I can't help it! Surely Raymond could have done something. *Someone* could have done *something*!"

"What? Anne, just tell me what?"

"Well, he could have come out there and told me instead of sneaking off to bed and leaving me there alone, wondering and half-scared all night."

"He said it was late and he assumed everybody was home. He just went straight to bed."

"Did everyone just assume I was home?"

"I suppose you mean I forgot you too."

"Well, you never go to bed and assume *any* of us are home. When I'm with a boy the whole darned house waits up."

"Your father came in about eleven for a rest. He saw the buggy was back and so naturally we thought you were here and in bed. It wasn't until Dell came by this morning and mentioned that he hadn't been home yet that your father realized someone hadn't come home. He checked your bed. Then he woke Raymond, and you know the rest. We sent Peter right over after you. And honestly, Anna Jeanette, it didn't hurt you to spend the night—someone would have had to anyway. I'm sorry, but—"

"Things happen."

"Yes, they do. Now don't mope. After all, the important thing is that you're in the choir now and there's always next Saturday."

"Friday!"

"Next Friday then. Oh, Anne, let's be happy, shall we? Why not get another hour of sleep? You look as though you could stand it." Mother sighed and patted my hair in much the same way as Peter had done earlier.

I jerked away from her hand.

"Anne?"

"Can't you understand? I don't want the whole business forgotten!"

"Stop it, Anne. You're tired."

"Yes, I'm tired. I'm sick and tired of doing for everyone else—*everyone else*. And when I need *one little favor*, no one—*no one* can manage it. I'm supposed to smile and forget it just like that!"

"A lot's expected of you, that's true." Mama's voice wavered slightly and her eyes reddened. "But it isn't an easy life. There's always those that need special help. We've needed it from others in the past. And when the Blavens need *us*—choir or no choir—we're going to help. And that means *all* of us. Now go to bed. I don't want to hear another word about it." Mama stood shaking before me for a brief moment and then turned and walked out of the room, crying. I had made my mother cry.

I went straight to my room and, after changing into some dry old clothes, slipped out the front door into the drizzling rain. It would be best to be absent at breakfast. Papa would ask Mama about the tears, and there would be the children and Peter wondering too. And where would they place the blame? On me, of course.

The skies were still lead gray—the worst of the storm yet to come. I saddled Dandy and turned toward the lane. Sleep? I doubted if I would ever sleep again. I had to talk to Phyliss.

"Well, here she is. Ashley Valley's newest member of the upper crust. Doesn't look like the nervy type, but then again I don't look mysterious."

"Don't, Phyliss." I walked past her and sat in a rocker that faced away from the door.

"How could you do it to me?"

"To *you*?"

"Yes, *me*!" She pushed the door shut and padded across

the room, still in her wrapper and slippers, to stand in front of me. "Who do you think got snubbed from Delores's group when you didn't show up? They couldn't snub an empty seat, could they? Who do you think got asked a dozen times, Where is she? Why isn't she here? Who does she think she is?"

"Phyliss—"

"And who—who do you suppose got cross-examined by an angry Mr. Staaton afterwards?"

"Angry? He was angry?"

"Was he ever! And why shouldn't he be? You're the first vacancy he's filled in the choir. How do you suppose that looks for him when you just don't show? I can't say he was raging—his type doesn't rage. But he was, well—put out. That's the word for it. He was downright put out. He was grinding his teeth under that closed jaw—I watched the muscles work under his cheekbone." Phyliss rocked her teeth in a closed mouth to illustrate. She was really having a good time. She was obviously teasing, but I couldn't take any more. I lay back and closed my eyes, and there was a silent moment.

"I'm sorry for making fun." Her tone had altered. "So what happened? You wouldn't have missed it except for a good reason, and that's what I told everyone. I said, 'I don't know why she isn't here, but I'm sure she's got a good reason.' " Phyliss narrowed her eyes and sank into a chair. "Tell me about it."

I wasn't convinced, but I told her the whole thing—how I waited for Raymond, watching the lane until it was too dark to see; how Sister Lacey had wrecked it, unknowingly; and then how Raymond went to bed without even opening my door to say boo, and how Peter and Mama had patted my head, telling me to forget it—as if I had a bruised knee or something. Reciting the horrible events made me cry. Phyliss, seeing the tears, left her chair and began staring at something through the rain-flecked window.

"My, you've been through it all right!" She turned, biting the lower edge of her lip. "I shouldn't have given you such a rough time. I was exaggerating, as always. The girls didn't say anything much—except for 'Queen Delores,' " Phyliss gave me a little bow, "and Mr. Staaton was—well, I think he just wanted to know where you were. That's all. He asked me to have you go in and talk to him early in the week."

"Talk to him?"

She turned back to the window. "Oh, he probably wants you to pick up your music so you can start practicing. No big thing. Isn't it the gloomiest day? Want some hot chocolate?"

"No, thanks."

I left Phyliss and rode for a long time in the rain. It came now in long heavy sheets that slapped against my back and took my breath. No big thing. That seemed to sum up very well everything I cared about. I hit the reins hard against Dandy's neck and we lunged down the sloppy lane toward the hills, while all around us the world was coming apart.

The familiar poplars and cottonwoods were dark and strange and shook wildly against the charcoal sky. The alfalfa lay flat and floating in the fields. The road became a river, and the clouds dropped lower and lower till they fairly skimmed the treetops. With every clap of thunder, the valley groaned under us, and over us, in the blackening hills, the wind bellowed and lashed the long grasses till they danced like frantic waves upon some sea.

"No big thing," I cried in the wind. "No big thing!"

I don't know how long I drove Dandy like that, but I didn't head him homeward until we had long since crossed the South River bridge, a good hour and a half's ride in dry weather. But when I finally turned down our lane, Dandy and I were both a part of the soaking wet world around us. I slipped past the house, tied him up in the barn, and looked for the clean, dry rags Peter kept in the shed. I knew that if

Pa saw me like this, he'd lick me good—not only for being so drenched myself, but for endangering Dandy as well. I knew better. He was an old horse.

I got out the entire lot of rags and dried him off as best I could. He seemed none the worse for our ride. In fact, his big black eyes were full of excitement and youth. I think somewhere in his horse's mind he was thinking about old times with Pa when they and the valley were young.

I did the job hurriedly lest I be caught, and before I knew it, all the dry rags were gone. My own wet clothes were now painful to move in and my hair clung heavily to my head and still sent small rivulets of chilling water down my back. I was finishing Dandy's legs when I heard someone come into the barn behind me. I didn't turn but stopped drying the horse and began stuffing wet rags back into the box. *Don't act guilty,* I thought, *just don't act guilty.*

"You're drenched." It was Peter. I breathed a sigh of relief. He stood for a long moment at the door surveying the horse, the rags, and me; then he came forward and sank down on the straw beside me, a hand clamping my shoulder. "You know, you get into more stupid jams than any girl I've ever met."

"Who says I'm in a jam now?"

"I do."

"It's none of your business just the same, Peter."

He stood up abruptly, his temper flaring. "I'd say it was very much my business, Anne. Your folks—"

"Well, it isn't," I snapped. "Stay out of it. Leave me alone. You seem to have a talent for catching people in the wrong. Don't you ever do anything but toe the mark, Peter? In your saintly life have you done even one original and new wrong thing?"

"Anne—" His voice was on edge now, warning me.

"Or an ordinary run-of-the-mill sin? Have you Peter? *Ever?*"

He reached down and jerked me to my feet. "You'd better cool off, and right now. You're overwrought. It may have been a bad day, but—"

50

"It has. Now *please*, Peter."

"It's time you grew up. The choir's just not that important!"

"I know, I know." I pushed past him out of the barn. The cold wind swirled about my wet head and drowned my cries. "No big thing," I called into the storm, but only the whistling air fell on my ears.

"Annie?" It was mother's voice. "Annie, are you ill? You've been coughing all night."

I opened my eyes to see her sitting in the dim light at the edge of my bed. I heard myself moan. My entire body seemed to ache with cold.

"I'm so cold, Mama, and my head—"

She put a cool hand to my forehead. "You're burning up. Oh, Annie, you shouldn't have gone off like that." She kissed my cheek and sighed. "I'll get some more blankets. You say your head hurts?"

As soon as it was light I heard Mama send Raymond for Dr. Lawrence Sloan. He arrived soon enough, though the roads were still muddy and made traveling by buggy slow. He came up to my room alone and talked over my bed, turning his white head to one side and then the other.

"So you took a ride in the rain, young lady?"

"Yes."

"A long ride?"

"Up to South River bridge."

"In that rainstorm? Why would you do that?"

I shifted under the covers.

"You were unhappy about something." It was a statement, not a question.

"Why is this important, doctor?"

"It's very important to know how my patient feels." He smiled and opened his black bag.

"My head hurts. My throat hurts. Yes, I'm unhappy."

He took my temperature. Then, while checking my ears and throat, he told me about a time when, as a young man, he had run away from home.

"She's a sick young lady all right," he told Mama. "A little done in to boot," he added—wisely, I thought. "But I think three or so days of rest should do it fine—that," and he turned to me with something good in his eyes—understanding, "that, and some extra loving care."

It seemed somehow fitting that I should be sick. Though terribly miserable with my raw throat and aching head, I was really quite content to be so. The family at last was penitent for their late mistreatment of me. I didn't go to church at all that Sunday. The rest of the family went, except Mama, who stayed home to nurse me. Raymond and the children passed by my bedroom before leaving for Sunday School. They promised to hurry back and said they'd help me have a "real good time" that afternoon.

After church, Katy brought me up her button-on-a-string but I was too sick to work it. Later Raymond got out the checkers, and he and Margaret played for two hours at the foot of my bed where I could watch.

Mama fussed about me a great deal, coming in with broth and juices or a fresh towel for my head, and Papa—Papa kissed me and gave me a quarter.

By Tuesday I was able to get up. The fever had gone and I felt completely well, with only one hitch. I could barely talk. "Laryngitis," Raymond explained to the girls. "Lare-run-gy-tis."

Of course, I didn't go talk to Mr. Staaton as he had requested. In fact, I was glad to have an excuse to put it off until Friday.

I sent Raymond in for the music with a note to the effect that I was a little run-down. I didn't actually say it, but I implied that this was caused by my unselfish stay with our sick neighbor Friday night. This solidified the excuse Raymond had given him then, and it gave Mr. Staaton a little insight into my fine character. I signed the note using my full name, "respectfully, Anna Jeanette Carrow."

"Remember, Raymond—not a word about my laryngitis," I squeaked. "Tell him I'm nearly well and will be quite fit by Friday."

By Friday I was fit to be tied. Phyliss came out to hear me sing. "Oh, oh, here we go again."

"It's that bad?"

"You sound awful." She put her head in her hands and studied my face. "You'll have to fake it tonight. When you sing just move your lips and try not to talk at all."

"I'm getting an ulcer. My stomach's been aching all week. This stupid choir's giving me an ulcer!"

"Well, don't lose your head. I'm with you." I smiled at that. Phyliss was a strong person—independent and willful. She had a way of making life toe the mark. But if ever it didn't, if things got too rough or uncomfortable, she lit out and stayed away until things settled again. Though I knew she wouldn't always be, I was comforted by the thought that she was here now. My troubles couldn't be too bad.

"You know, you don't sound so hoarse on your first few words. It's only after that that your voice goes haywire. The secret is in saying short sentences. Never any more than four or five words."

"Like?"

"Like, 'Good evening, Mr. Staaton.' Try it."

"Good evening, Mr. Staaton."

"Good. Very good. Now relax your vocal cords completely a minute. Don't talk. You see, tonight you won't have to do much talking anyway. And for your first practice you can mouth the words when we sing. You don't sit right next to Delores, so you'll be fine."

"Phyliss, if you're just trying to—"

She put up a hand. "Don't talk. Save your voice. You've got to relax the rest of this day and be completely calm tonight so you don't ruin everything. Now say, 'Hello, girls.' Just that and no more."

"Hello, girls."

"Fine. You sound fine."

FIVE

The little churchhouse stood on a low hill, just off the main street of Ashley. It was made of red sandstone and sometimes—not often—when the sun sank behind it and slid down the western range of mountains, the sky became pink and blue all at once, and the golden-white rays of the dying sun jutted out from the dark peaks like celestial fingers that danced about the hill, turning the red rock of the churchhouse fiery orange, while the slender tower and steeple glittered in the sunset.

Friday evening the valley was blessed with just such a sunset. As I walked up the street toward the dancing flames on the hill, a tall, square-shouldered figure swung out from another street a block in front of me. He too walked toward the church, taking long, easy strides that increased the distance between us with every step.

"Mark Staaton," I half-whispered, feeling at once breathless, and hurrying my own pace.

Phyliss was waiting for me on the lawn.

"Where's Peter?"

"Where should he be?"

"Anne, you've become cynical! He told me he would be bringing you in."

"Not tonight. Papa had to see a friend at Brinton's store. But I don't think he'll wait—Peter will be here for me after."

She got to her feet. "Better not talk anymore. You need to save your voice."

We walked into the small foyer, and seeing it empty, I asked if we were too early.

"No, about right." Phyliss put up a warning finger. "Now, don't say *anything* tonight unless you absolutely have to. Remember—" Mr. Staaton appeared suddenly before us from a small anteroom off the foyer. He smiled at us, waiting for her to finish her sentence before speaking. "Remember," she fumbled, "uh, remember, we're in the churchhouse." She smiled weakly, looking from me to Mr. Staaton. He burst into a hearty laugh at that, knowing that Phyliss was obviously about to say something quite different.

"Good evening, girls."

"Good evening, sir."

"And how are you tonight, Miss Carrow?"

"I'm fine."

"And your neighbor?"

"Better, we think."

"Glad to hear it. It was kind of you to stay with her."

"Yes, but I was sorry to miss the practice. You see, my mother—"

His hand came up. "Please, don't worry about it. Your brother explained completely." He began to smile. "Raymond's a very loyal fellow. We had quite a talk."

What *had* Raymond told him? The report he had given me was in his usual garbled style.

"Well," Mr. Staaton said, glancing toward the chapel, "it's nearing time to start. If you'll excuse me?" The strange smile I was beginning to find most enchanting brushed his lips again as he disappeared into the anteroom off the foyer.

"So you think it, too!" Phyliss nudged me away from the door.

"Think what?"

"That he's handsome and charming."

"I suppose he is, for an older man."

"Older? Not much older than Peter. He's twenty-six. I have it on good information."

"If he's twenty-six, he's the smoothest—"

"Your voice, remember? You don't have to worry anyhow. He's taken."

"By whom? And I'm *not* worried."

"The 'Queen,' of course. I'd say Delores was the number one reason Rachael brought Mr. Staaton to this valley." Phyliss leaned closer and her voice lowered confidentially. "You can't tell *me* it was to give her precious choir over to a stranger with different ideas. And he's got them—I can tell you that! Sister Ashley can't keep away from these practices. She's so worried he'll change something, and I think it's beginning to get his goat."

"Do you think Sister Ashley would sooner hand her *granddaughter* over to a stranger with different ideas?"

"Of course not. But granddaughters have to be given to *someone,* don't they? Delores isn't getting any younger, and it's easy to see she's bored stiff with the fellows around here." Phyliss glanced back at Mr. Staaton's door and dropped her voice even lower. "Mark Staaton may be a stranger to the choir and its policies, but he certainly isn't one to Delores or her family."

"You're talking riddles." I swallowed with effort, my voice tiring. "Come on, Phyliss, he'll be coming."

"My source says Delores and Mr. Staaton are old acquaintances."

"But Delores has lived *here* all her life."

Phyliss gave me a smug little smile. "You're forgetting the summer in the East while she was in that finishing school."

"You mean in Denver."

"That's the 'East' when you hear Delores tell of it. Anyway, they saw each other in Denver, but they didn't meet there—at least not according to the information I've received. Get this—Mr. Staaton was born here himself!"

"Here?"

"According to my source." Phyliss cocked an eyebrow

and narrowed her eyes. "And he's a baptized Mormon—one of us. Very, very eligible, wouldn't you say?"

"Who told you all this?"

"I've only been waiting for you to ask." Her face split into a wide grin. "Delores—*the queen.*"

"Delores?" Then it had to be true. Delores and Mark Staaton. I felt acutely disappointed.

She sighed. "It really isn't a secret at all. She's been telling everyone who'll listen, and I think it's just like her."

It was, I thought. Mark Staaton was the most impressive man this valley had seen, and if he were an old acquaintance of Delores's . . .

A group of chorus members came up the stairs and into the foyer. It was eight-thirty. Time to go in.

Laurie Lewis sat immediately to my right. She was older than I and prettily plump. I'm ashamed to admit that on seeing the choir perform throughout the years, I had often wondered why she had been accepted into such a sophisticated group. But now I discovered she had a delicately beautiful voice, and I was angry that she had never been allowed to solo—but then, an Ashley usually took the solo parts.

Delores sat on Laurie's right. Delores was a daughter of Rachael's third son, Daniel, and his now deceased wife, Delight. She was one of five daughters, the "darling Ds" as Phyliss put it: Dorothy, Darla, Denise, Delores, and Debra. While all of the Ashley women were attractive, Delores's flaming auburn hair and wide-set green eyes placed her apart from her sisters and cousins. Her skin was smooth and white—she didn't have a freckle on her face. (I doubted if she had ever chased cows, or spent a day in the fields, or picked even one apple with her white dimpled hand.) If she had a flaw, it was her mouth—so tiny it seemed always in a pout, yet when she smiled she outshone anyone near her.

Delores's grandfather, Johnathan Ashley, was among the first settlers in the valley. He was an outstanding leader and church member. The people who came to Ashley loved and respected him. Though Rachael, his wife, was hardly the pioneering type, she was strong willed and determined to make life in the valley bearable and even cultured. Everyone knew that Rachael had given up a singing career in the East to come west with Johnathan. Sometimes in testimony meeting she would stand and, with tears streaming down her face, tell how she could have been an opera star with real wealth and fame, but because she loved her husband and the Church she left it all behind. To hear her talk, that had been her biggest hardship in life, and though I never dared say it aloud, I thought she got off pretty lucky. Many in the congregation, Papa's family included, had left loved ones along the way in unmarked graves they never saw again.

But Rachael never forgot her dream. Shortly after the founding of Ashley, she became director and soloist with a group of singers that she established. At first they practiced in her home—the largest in Ashley even today, built by her husband, who tried to make up for her earlier hard years in the valley. Papa said Rachael made it clear from the start that *her* choir was not church affiliated, but civic, and culturally minded.

She kept the chorus membership down to a select few, and auditions were few and far between. Many people in the valley, especially the leaders of the church, were unhappy with it. However, Rachael made it a good choir with excellent musical standards; and though many, like Papa, shook their heads in disapproval, it was respected, as was Rachael herself.

I tried hard to like Delores, but her loveliness and complete self-assurance were painful to me. She was never flustered or unsure of herself. She never laughed too heartily or enjoyed herself too much (as I was so often apt to do). Her hair was always perfection—each strand in place—and her grand clothes were impeccably made to accent her very best features. Worst of all, Delores had a *maid*—a woman servant who took care of the two girls left at home, Delores and Debra. Phyliss said the maid even hung up Delores's clothes and brushed her hair out at night. I don't know how Phyliss knew that, but I took it for truth just the same.

When Phyliss told me I was to sit next to Laurie rather than Delores, I was plenty grateful. Mouthing the words made me uncomfortable enough, but though Delores sat a person away, several times throughout the practice she leaned over to tell me not to be afraid to sing out.

"I can't hear you at all, dear. You mustn't hesitate to use a little volume. That's better. Yes, I do believe I hear you now. You really have a lovely voice. We've always been proud of our section. If the sopranos aren't loud enough, the altos go flat."

Mr. Staaton, too, gave me doubtful looks throughout the practice, and finally, later in the evening, he said he wanted to hear the sopranos sing "Cast Thy Burden" alone. But as he did so, three rowdy boys tumbled into the chapel, socking and chasing about and causing such a disturbance that Mr. Staaton forgot us, and I was spared the agony of being found out.

"I suppose you know we're singing on the Fourth of July," Laurie whispered to me near the end of the practice. "One of us will have to sing the solo for the *Elijah,* and Mr. Staaton hasn't picked her yet. If *you* want a crack at it, you'd better sing louder next time."

"But aren't all solos reserved for—" I gestured toward Delores.

"I don't think *he'll* do it that way." She smiled with satisfaction. "Things are changing."

Following the practice Delores caught me at the door and asked if I would wait for a few minutes. She and the choir president had a "few points of policy" to discuss with me.

"I'll see you later," Phyliss said as Delores went for Shirley Green, the newly elected choir president.

"What do they want?"

"Oh, something Delores mentioned to me last week. I meant to tell you, but I guess they can do it now. It's just one of Rachael's silly by-laws."

"By-laws? Have I done something wrong?"

"They're coming back. See you tomorrow. Oh yes, I've got some great news. Superintendent Anderson has a teaching job for me this fall. I'll tell you about it later." She gave me a cheery wave and disappeared out the door.

When I saw Shirley I relaxed a little. She put a hand into mine and welcomed me to the choir. "We're really very happy to have you with us, Anne. I meant to come out during the week, but . . ." Her pale eyes shifted nervously to Delores.

"Yes, welcome," Delores added, waiting impatiently for Shirley to continue.

"I, well, we . . ." Shirley stopped again.

"Shirley means to say that there is just one small matter that we need to clear up." Delores looked at me levelly, her voice low.

"What is it?"

"Your absence last week."

"But my brother explained to Mr. Staaton. He said I didn't have to worry."

"Yes, well," she shrugged, "you must realize that Mark is still rather new. I'm certain he's acquainted with our policy on absences." She paused, then went on. "If a member misses *two* rehearsals without giving *prior notice,* she is let out. I'm afraid we'll have to count last Friday as your first miss."

"It doesn't make any difference that it was impossible to give notice?"

"*If* it was impossible, perhaps we could make an allowance this once. Maybe if you gave us the details?" She arched her brows.

My fingers plucked at a button on my sleeve as I struggled with where to begin. "I—Mama—well, you know the Blavens? There's Margo and—I mean, they've been sick, real sick—at least Margo has . . ." My fingers closed about the button again and it dropped loose into my hand. Had Delores seen? I stiffened. "Never mind. Count it. I don't want any special privileges."

Shirley shifted uneasily and looked somewhere past me out into the darkness. But if Delores was at all unnerved, her smile didn't alter in the least, and her eyes still rested coolly on mine.

"Is there anything else?" I glanced toward the door.

"Yes, your dress." But I wore my best dress tonight— my very best dress! "Have you ordered the fabric?" She meant, then, my costume for the choir.

I nodded. "Last week after my audition."

"You should have checked with us first. We've had a color problem with different dyes. I hope you sent along a slip of material with the order."

"No, not unless Charlie Brinton knew and sent it for me. I'll check." I touched the ruffles at my neckline and noticed that Delores's dress had lace—pleated lace.

"Fine," she said, her slender hands entwined beneath her chin, "you can understand why we want everyone in the same shade of blue."

"If that's all, someone's waiting for me."

Delores nodded a dismissal in much the same way as would Mark Staaton or a schoolteacher—and Delores was only two years older than I.

As I left the chapel and climbed into the buggy beside Peter, I felt that penetrating gaze still on me.

"How'd it go?" Peter was settled back in the seat, his head against the upholstery. He was obviously in no hurry to leave.

"Fine—can we go?" I flashed a look back at the church. Delores was gone.

"You don't sound like it went fine. Trouble with your voice?"

I shook my head. "They just thought I was bashful— afraid to sing out my first time."

"Well, that's great, Anne." He smiled. "You must be very happy. You've wanted to be in this choir a long time."

"Peter?" I leaned close to him. "You like my new dress, don't you?"

"Of course, you're spectacular in it!"

I smoothed the skirt about me. "Am I really? You're not just saying that?"

"Not at all." He put a hand over mine, his smile gleaming in the darkness.

"Well, I think it's plain—plain and terribly homemade!" I yanked my hand from under his. "And I hate it!"

He stared some moments and then, muttering to himself, whipped the reins over the horse, and we lurched away from town. The light from the church was gone and we rode in silence. I turned back for one last glance. The diminishing hill was a tiny cake of darkness.

SIX

Because school was out, the choir went on a two-prac-tices-a-week schedule, Wednesdays and Fridays. In the days following my first practice, I memorized every piece in my folder; and because I was finally able to use my voice again, I sang them over and over all day long until my family began to complain about my singing as often as they did about Katy's piano practicing.

"If you're going to sing all the time, you might as well sing something that makes some sense," Papa said one morning.

"Oh, you're just not used to *good* music, Papa."

"I'm just *too* used to good music. That's the trouble."

By Wednesday I felt confident in every piece, especially the solo from the *Elijah*.

"My goodness, you can sing," Laurie said to me after we had gone through the first number. "What was wrong last time?" She felt so free about talking between numbers that it made me a little nervous.

"Laryngitis." I looked up at Mr. Staaton, but he was busy with the second altos.

"Really? I just figured you were scared or something."

"Well, I was that, too."

Delores leaned over Laurie and tapped my knee. "Shh."

"I'm sorry," I whispered back to her. "I just had to answer a question." She nodded as if to say, "Yes, but we mustn't talk all the same. You understand, of course."

In spite of Delores I enjoyed the practice. Because I knew the songs so well I was able to really sing out, and I noticed girls from the other sections turning to look at me and smile. *They like my voice*, I thought. *They accept me now.*

"What're you trying to do?" Phyliss asked me during the break.

Across the chapel, Delores and Mr. Staaton stood talking to each other—she leaning her head back against the wall, and he, with his boot hitched up on a bench and his hand just above her head, smiling down at her.

"What did you say, Phyl?" Delores laughed then at something he had said and playfully brushed back the lock that had lain on his forehead all evening.

"I said, *what are you trying to do, singing so loud.* You stand out like a sore thumb. Didn't Delores tell you to quiet down?"

"You were right," I said, still watching them. "He *is* taken. Wouldn't you think he'd have better sense?"

"What? What are you talking about?"

I nodded toward Delores and Mark. Phyliss sat down on one of the wooden benches and propped her head in both hands. "Oh, well, I told you, didn't I?"

"I know, but I just didn't figure him for her type. He's so nice and everything. I think he's being taken in unawares."

"You've got a lot to learn," Phyliss said, shaking her head. "No man in this world gets taken in—unless he wants to be. It looks pretty clear to me that *he* wants to be."

The tinkle of Delores's laughter drifted over to us, and then, seconds later, he threw back his head and laughed with her. He was enjoying himself so much I had to turn away.

"Come on, Phyl. Let's get some air."

At ten, following the closing prayer, Mr. Staaton asked the first sopranos and any others who wanted to try out for the solo part to stay after.

"It should take just a few minutes. I won't ask you to stay for the decision," he added. "I'll give myself some time to think and then drop by tomorrow to inform whomever I pick. I guess that's it. Goodnight to the rest of you."

Shirley Green raised a hand. "Mr. Staaton, you forgot—"

"Oh, yes. We need to move our Friday night practice to Saturday this week. Any objections? There's a ward outing on Friday."

"You going?" Laurie asked as we waited for the chapel to clear.

"Yes. Wally Brinton and I are in charge of the games until noon. What about you?"

"Wouldn't miss it. I love North Fork!"

I loved the area, too. It was full of aspens, firs, and spruce and sat against the major range of mountains. Ben Lomond Peak, the tallest and loveliest mountain in the Ogden area, looked right down on the North Fork River.

"Raymond's given me the best idea for a new kind of sack race . . ."

"All right, let's have it quiet now. Miss Green, you sing first." Mr. Staaton closed the large oak doors against the last few girls to leave. Shirley took her place by the piano and began.

"He watching over Israel,
Slumbers not nor sleeps . . ."

"Fine. Now Miss Lewis."

"I'll mess it up," Laurie whispered as she left my side. "I don't solo anywhere but in the tub." But she sang it perfectly. Mr. Staaton nodded.

"Delores?"

She gave him an intimate smile. "I'd rather be last, Mark."

He shrugged his shoulders. "All right then, Miss Carrow."

I stood by the piano and faced the large hall, my back to the other girls. Before beginning I closed my eyes and thought of home and how I'd sung it there. I took a deep breath; then, opening my eyes, I gazed into the eyes of Mr. Staaton—dark and reassuring.

"Ready?"

"Yes, please." I sang then as I had in the fields with Papa. The hall seemed to ring with overtones. I'd never sung with such ease; and all the while, Mr. Staaton watched me, smiling as if he knew something no one else did. When I had finished I waited for the sound to die in the hall before returning to my seat. Though he didn't say so, I felt that he'd liked it too. His eyes had never left mine.

"Delores?" He called her name from where he sat below the podium. She went forward—but down in front to him rather than up by the piano.

"I feel ridiculous, Mark. You've heard me so often."

"You'd rather not try?"

"Don't be difficult. You know I want the solo, but it's senseless to sing for you."

"It's not senseless if that's what I require."

Her voice fell to a whisper. "Mark, please." She looked up at Shirley, Laurie, and me, and her gaze caught mine and held for a long moment.

Mr. Staaton shook his head impatiently. "Delores, just go ahead and sing."

"No," she said, still looking at me. "I won't give you the pleasure. I'm declining the audition." She swept out the side door without looking back.

"Oooh," Laurie breathed next to me. "She's furious."

Mr. Staaton stood up, the smile wiped from his lips. "That does it. It's between the three of you. I'll let one of you know before the next practice." With a clipped thanks to the pianist, he began gathering his music from the podium. As he did so something Phyliss said rang in my ears: *Oh, he wasn't raging—his type doesn't rage. But he was grinding his teeth under that handsome cheekbone.*

And now, just faintly above the curve of his jaw, I watched the muscle tighten and relax and tighten again. *Yes, Phyliss, I see what you mean.* He looked terribly grim—dangerous, even.

Shirley, Laurie, the organist, and I hurried out into the foyer. Then, turning back, we caught a glimpse of Mr. Staaton disappearing out the door Delores had taken.

Late the next afternoon, I was walking in from the Blavens' house when Raymond's piercing whistle sounded across the fields. He was playing with the Blaven boys, and they chased down the lane toward me. Though there was a larger gap between me and Raymond than between any of the other children (Mama had lost a little baby boy three years after I was born), he and I were close. When chores were done, like today, and even sometimes when they weren't, we'd race down to the road and walk back balancing on top of the log fence that ran the length of the lane. The real skill of it wasn't just in keeping our balance, but also whistling at the same time—not breaking rhythm even when nearly teetering off the fence.

We thought it a great feat because we could do it very well, both having had years of extensive practice. Lately, to increase the challenge, we had quickened the pace to a near run, the one coming second pushing faster and faster, hoping to fluster the other into falling off.

"Let's have another race," Gerald Blaven called. "You and Raymond on the fence, us on the road!"

Raymond bounded to his place on the log. "Come on up, Annie. Let's show these two we can beat 'em."

I laughed, loving the challenge. Hitching up my skirts, I climbed up beside him. "Ready!"

We were off, with Gerald and Thomas B. shooting ahead of us.

"We're beating! We're beating!" Thomas B. called over his shoulder. The two of them whirled through the gate and stood panting on the lawn under the trees. Gerald dropped to his knees.

"Hit the dirt!" he screamed. "Get down, Thomas B.! Them dirty rebels are comin'."

Raymond and I, nearly to the gate now, saw two yanks in the grass aim a Gatling gun at us.

"Ratatatatatatat, ratatatatatat."

I hollered and threw my hands above my head wildly. Raymond grabbed his stomach. "They got me, Joe. I'm a goner," he wailed, falling off the fence into the alfalfa.

"Ratatatatatat, ratatatatat."

"Uh, oh, ugh," I moaned, twisting my body in mock pain. I grabbed at my side to whirl around on the fence top. Only yards away I caught sight of Mark Staaton on horseback coming up the lane toward me. It was too late. I was already keeling over into the alfalfa beside Raymond's motionless body.

The sweet smell of blossoms filled my nostrils and the buzzing sound of insects surrounded me as I lay still. Perhaps he'd think I was someone else. I had only to lie there with my eyes closed until he passed by.

The thud of horses hooves slowed and stopped. I guessed him to be very near and opened my eyes for a tiny peek. The sight was so painful that I snapped them shut again. He was leaning over the fence, his head tilted to one side, studying me as I lay in the deep green. I kept still.

"I think we got her, Jed," Gerald cried, "dead!"

"Yup, dead!" Thomas B. replied.

"Dead!" Mr. Staaton echoed, and moved off toward the house. He was laughing softly.

Raymond leaped to his feet and jumped the fence. "Hey, that's Mr. Staaton, Anne!"

"Is he gone?" I whispered.

"He's knocking on the door."

"Tell me when he goes in."

"Get up! I bet he's here to see you."

"*Tell me when he goes in, Raymond.*"

"He's going now. What's the matter with you?"

I pushed to my feet, not bothering to adjust my skirts or petticoats. Then, flying over the fence, I ran into the orchard until I was deep enough into the trees that the house was no longer in sight. There I dropped exhausted to the grass and pulled the skirt of my dress over my head. I'd never live this down, never!

Listening to the pounding in my throat and my hard, anguished breathing, I sat there for some time. From the direction of the house came Mama's voice. "Anne, you've got company!"

A few minutes later I felt the thud of bare feet on the orchard floor. "There she is," Gerald and Thomas B. chimed together. "We see Annie's bloomers. We see Annie's bloomers."

"Anne," Raymond said, yanking my skirt off my head, "he wants you. You'd better come."

"Tell him I'm not home."

"But he knows you are. He saw us running the fence, remember?"

"Raymond," I pleaded, "get rid of him for me."

"I can't. I just went in and he and Mama are talkin' in the front room and she asked where you were."

"You *didn't tell?*"

"Well, sure I did." Raymond jammed a fist into his pocket. "I said you had hightailed it for the orchard."

"Oh, Raymond!" I pushed my dress back over my head.

"You don't have to be embarrassed about playing with us kids. Mr. Staaton's my friend. I can fix it up for you."

"No, just leave me alone, please."

"Look, Annie, they know you're out here. You're gonna be in dutch if you don't get in there." He pulled at my skirt.

I looked at the three pairs of eyes watching me. "All right. I'm going, but you kids stay here." Smoothing my hair and dress, I couldn't remember when I had felt worse. At the back door I glanced hurriedly in the mirror and searched for a brush.

"Anne? Is that you?" Mama's voice came to me from the other room. My face was dusty and streaked. "Anne!"

"Yes, Mama, I'm coming." I took a dish towel from the hook above the sink and wiped my face hurriedly. I tried to smile back into the mirror, but it was no use. I looked a mess. I wouldn't even let Peter see me like this.

"Anne—," Mother was irritated now, "Mr. Staaton's waiting!"

I dropped the dish towel on the sideboard and went through the hall, past the stairs, and into the front room, mumbling a hello. Mr. Staaton, who was sitting in Papa's big chair with his back to the door, stood as I entered.

"Hello, Miss Carrow. Nice to see you." His handsome face broadened into a smile, almost a laugh.

"Goodness! What *have* you been doing?" Mama jumped to her feet and, with a worried scowl, crossed to brush my hair away from my face. "You're so flushed," she exclaimed, clicking her tongue. "It's because she's been out in the sun," she explained to Mr. Staaton. "And your dress, Anne." Her fingers fidgeted with my blouse, tucking it about my waist.

"Just leave it, Mama, please."

She whispered, "You should have taken a moment to clean up." Then she smiled at Mark. "If you'll excuse me, then, I'll leave you to your business." After another doubtful look at me, she left.

"Please sit down." I motioned to Papa's chair and crossed to the couch.

"Thank you." Slashes deepened along his jawline. "I'm sorry if I interrupted something out there."

I straightened and looked into eyes dancing with laughter. *He knows how horrible this is and yet he laughs!*

"You're pretty good at that—incredible balance."

I rubbed at my nose. "I guess that's because I've had so much practice at it."

He burst into laughter then. "I'll *bet* you have! No, stay, please. It was just so funny! My new soprano up on a fence, her skirts flying." He continued to laugh. "And you are good—I've never seen anything like it—and when they shot you, it was just so—"

"Funny!"

"I'm sorry," he laughed, full throated, "but it was . . ." He closed his eyes and shook his head, but still the laughter came.

He looked pretty funny himself laughing that hard, I mused. And then, suddenly I saw it as he did, and I began to laugh despite myself. It was delightful—like having the giggles with Phyliss, only better. "Please stop," I cried at last, "I'm hurting." But I didn't want those wonderful minutes to end—not ever. We had become friends, and from that moment on Mark Staaton would call me Anne.

He had come to tell me I was to be his soloist for the *Elijah*. I was elated, but had he come to tell me I would never sing in the choir again, I would have been as thrilled.

"What was that all about?" Mama asked after he had gone.

"I'll be right back," I hollered as I rushed by her out the back door, around the barn, and through the cottonwoods that lined the south field. Over the fence and up the hill I flew until, nearing the top, I threw myself down into the growth, peering over the steep incline to where the hill met the lane below. I lay close to the soil I loved and waited for him to pass. And come he did, riding high on his horse, the late sun full on his face, the wind lifting his black hair beneath the brim of his hat. I lay until the sound of hooves had died, and then rising and brushing myself off I headed home again with the song of *Elijah* on my lips:

"He watching over Israel,
Slumbers not nor sleeps . . ."

SEVEN

"Jump, Chester. Hurry. We can win. We're ahead!"

It was a perfect day for the outing. The sun was warm, and the canyon breeze was up, rustling the new grasses and millions of tiny aspen leaves surrounding the small meadow Wally and I had selected for the games.

We had divided the children into two large groups for the races, the red team and the blue team. So far the red team had won everything but the egg relay. Now, on the final race of the morning—Raymond's sack race—the blue team looked as though they might make a showing at last.

Chester, the retarded son of Hec Bailey, had only thirty more feet to jump before he would cross the finish line to his teammates, and the licorice sticks Wally held in the small brown bag would go to them.

"*Come on*, Chester. Jump faster!" Raymond hollered from where he half knelt in the grass. "*Move, Chester*. They're gaining on you!"

Chester, nearly at the finish line, stumbled, his large body twisting, and fell backward to the ground. He sat numbly, his head on his chest, looking at the sack tangled around his big shoes.

"I, ah . . . fell."

"Well, get up, Chester. Hurry!"

"I, ah . . . fell . . . down." He shook his head slowly.

Wally's voice sounded across the open meadow. "The red team's done it again!"

A victorious whoop rang out as Mary Bacon jumped across the finish line. Raymond's teammates moaned as they watched Wally pass out the long dark sticks to the winners.

"Heck, Chester, you let a *girl* beat you. Why didn't you just get up?" Raymond began untangling the sack from Chester's feet.

"We . . . lost?" He looked up slowly. "We lost . . . again?"

"Sure we lost. You just sat here and let them take it from us."

Chester's childlike eyes blinked against the sun, and a slow expression of the vague failure he so often felt came across his wide face. "I . . . ah . . . fell."

"I know," Raymond said, patting Chester's shoulder. "You couldn't help it. You did real good anyhow."

Already most of the adults had arrived—girls and women in colorful dresses and starched bonnets, carrying baskets filled to the brim with their specialties; men in clean work pants and freshly ironed shirts, watering their horses in the cool creek and tying them near the road away from the crowds. The children, finished now with the games, sought their parents for a spot of shade and something cool to drink. Blankets were spread under the white aspens, and after a general blessing on the food by Bishop Holt, everyone began eating.

Raymond and I had gone to the outing in the wagon with Peter. Mama, Papa, and the younger children were among the last to arrive, and because most of the better spots were taken, we spread blankets a little distance from the group. Raymond had found the spot and wouldn't hear of us moving closer.

"This is the best place in the canyon, Pa," he cried. "Look at it—shade, grass. It's perfect."

It *was* a nice cool area, and the cascading river sounded especially pleasant. But I had hoped to sit closer in to the Ashley group.

"But shouldn't we be closer to our friends?" I asked Papa. "We don't want to be unsociable."

Raymond grabbed the blanket and began spreading it beneath the trees. "Anne just wants to be by her choir teacher. She doesn't care if *we* get sunstroke."

"Don't be silly, Raymond." I looked about our little group, but no one seemed to take much notice of Raymond's remark except, maybe, Peter.

"Well," Papa said, grinning, "we're not getting any fatter standing around. Emily, pass out the food. Let's eat."

Following the meal, Peter hauled our things back to the wagon, and Mama took her needlepoint and went to chat with some of the ladies while Papa stretched out for a snooze. Katy went off with Margaret, Tyler, and the Blaven children to take a "nature walk," and Raymond, on top of Chester's shoulders, disappeared into the trees.

Papa's heavy breathing told me he was already asleep. *Who was I to visit with*? Phyliss wasn't here—she had left town for an interview in connection with her teaching job and wouldn't be back until Saturday. I surveyed as much of the crowd as I could from where I sat and couldn't find anyone with whom I felt really comfortable. I would have liked to stroll past the Ashley blanket and smile at Mark Staaton, but I couldn't very well do that alone.

"Would you like to walk down to the river?" Peter asked, coming back from the wagon.

"Yes, I would. I think we're fairly close, by the sound of it." He helped me to my feet, and as we moved away from Papa he took my hand. "And then after we see the river, maybe we could stroll through the camp and talk to our friends."

"We ought to ride up here often. I like to get away."

"It is nice, isn't it."

"You look very nice today, Anne. I like you in green."

"Thank you, Peter."

He smiled, and his face seemed especially good looking and confident just then. His clear blue eyes surveyed my dress as we walked.

"It isn't new. It's last year's."

"I know, but it fits the occasion. I'm glad you know how to dress for a picnic—watch that branch. So many girls have no sense at all. They don't know how to let their hair down."

I thought then of Delores. She and Mark Staaton had paraded past the meadow during the last minutes of the final race. She was wearing an all-white, eyelet-trimmed dress with a very tightly fitting bodice and full skirt that had made me acutely aware of my light green cotton. But I was sure her skirt would be streaked with dirt and grass stains before the party was half over, even if she did nothing but walk about showing it off.

"Anne, there's a place I've been meaning to show you." We reached the river and sat down on a large, dry boulder. "I've been thinking about buying it."

"Really, Peter? Buying it to *live* on?"

He scowled. "Of course. Why else would I buy land?"

"I don't know. I guess I never thought you'd want to live here in the valley."

He gave a quick, impatient sigh. "From the first summer I spent with your family, I've wanted to stay. They've made me feel that *this* is my home."

"Well, you don't have to get angry, Peter. I'm *glad* my folks have made you feel welcome."

"*Welcome* is something you say to an outsider. I said they make me feel *at home*."

I took my hand from Peter's and grabbed a branch of boxwood leaves, threw it into the water, and watched it spin for a moment, trapped in a tiny whirlpool and then whisked downstream. "Do you know how to make paper boats, Peter?"

He ignored my question. "This piece of land, well, it isn't a lot, Anne. I mean, it isn't as big as your father's place, but it's green and there's water available, and I think it's all we need to start with. We could always buy up more later."

"We?" I stared at him. But he was more upset than

ever. I seemed to have the knack for making him angry lately. I decided it best to ignore his mood. "Papa can make the best paper boats I've ever seen. He's shown me a lot of times, but I can't seem to get it. Mine just break apart as soon as they touch the water." I shrugged and looked uneasily at Peter. "I must not fold them nearly tight enough, or maybe I make the sides too low and the water gets in. In any case, I think Papa has a secret that he hasn't told."

Peter stood up abruptly and, without so much as a word, left me talking to myself.

"Peter? Peter!" But he didn't answer or even look back. I sat down on the rock and watched the racing water. I could get angry too!

I should have *made* him tell me just what he meant by that "we" he was tossing about so loosely. I didn't understand him at all. Why couldn't he be frank and open like Papa, and come right out with it rather than talking in riddles?

Behind me somewhere in the trees I heard a twig snap. I heard it again, and then again—one, two, three, four, five times.

"Who's there? Peter?" I searched the heavy growth with my eyes. The trees moved easily in the warm breeze, and above my head in an overhanging limb a large gray bird shrieked and flapped its wings for flight. Otherwise there was nothing.

I slid down the boulder closer to the water and propped my head on my knees. The river, swift and high this time of year, looked inviting. Phyliss and I could have had the greatest fun if only she were here.

The snapping sound had begun again—one, two, three, four, five—almost in rhythm.

"Peter?" I called over my shoulder. "Peter, stop being sore and come out!" I heard someone then, coming through the brush, and I fully expected Peter to emerge. But he didn't. When no one appeared, I moved off my rock and peered into the growth with straining eyes.

"Look, I know someone's there." The roar of the racing river filled my ears. I was alone and yet—I wasn't alone. Someone was watching. I knew it. The mere thought of someone crouching in the trees made me shiver. The group seemed suddenly very far away, and I could reach them only by going back through the trees. But I could always holler. That thought reassured me. They weren't that far away. *But they'd never hear you*, a voice said within me. *You're too close to the river.*

I was being silly and I was scaring myself. What could happen to me here? The snapping had long since stopped, and I turned back to the water, but though I wanted to ignore it, my heart had begun to race. I could *feel* eyes watching.

I cleared my throat and tried to sound calm, but my voice came as a hoarse, trembling whisper. "Whoever you are, you'd better come out. And now."

A low chuckle came from just beyond the rock. *Run, run and don't stop.* But this is North Fork. I love North Fork and I'm safe here, safe! *But you aren't, you know. You heard someone laugh.*

I thought of Papa sleeping calmly under this same sky. "Papa," I cried aloud, and as I did, it began again, *snap, snap, snap.*

"*Papa!*" I ran then, along the bank as far and as fast as I could. At one point, after nearly falling into the water, I changed direction and cut away from the river, hoping to come out fairly close to the crowd. The ugly laugh came again, just behind me. I had come the wrong way. I turned frantically about. "Oh, Papa!" Where was I? Which way should I go? The bushes moved behind me as I ran. It was following—following just beyond my sight. A large dry branch suddenly caught at my hair and dress. Trying to free myself, I pulled my hair loose and tore my sleeve. I ran, unaware then that I was sobbing with terror, until at last I stumbled into the clearing below the camp where we had played the games just a short time before.

I was on the far side of the group now, and had come farther than I had realized, but I was in sight of people, and safe. The dense growth behind me was suddenly very still. I stood at the edge of the clearing and tried to collect myself. There was nothing in those trees, nothing even remotely sinister. But that couldn't be. *I had been chased.* No, no one could have known we were so close to the meadow. He would have stumbled out too—that is, if there had been someone.

I laughed at myself. How silly I was! I pushed the pins back in my hair and brushed off my skirt. The reassuring voices of the crowd floated over to me. How foolish to be frightened here in North Fork. I should stay alone more and get used to the feeling.

Walking back, I decided to go around on the far side of the meadow to avoid passing anyone—my disheveled hair and dress would cause questions.

I was nearly to our blanket when I heard a familiar voice in the aspens ahead of me. Then I caught sight of a white dress and auburn hair.

"Oh, let's! But first I must get something for my head. My skin won't tolerate sun. I'll just be a minute."

It was too late to duck her. Delores was suddenly in front of me.

"My, my! What have *you* been doing?"

"Walking—I ran into a br—"

"Oh, I'm sure you have." And as she left me to fetch her bonnet, I heard her laugh. "Walking indeed!"

I felt the heat rise in my face. It was just like her to assume the worst!

I stalked off in the direction of our blanket. Papa was still snoozing, and Peter and Raymond were sitting on a nearby rock, whittling. I had gone only a few steps when I heard Mark Staaton's voice behind me.

"Anne? Is something wrong?"

I turned. "Hello."

"Hello." He gave me a friendly smile. I felt my pulse quicken as he came toward me. I knew I looked a sight, just as I had yesterday. Perhaps he'd think this is how I always went around. "What's happened?" His dark eyes took in my disheveled hair and dress, and then, as they stopped on my sleeve, he frowned. There was a triangular tear across the shoulder seam. I had forgotten that. I touched the torn corner and tried to push it up and make it stay in place.

"I—it really isn't what you think." I stopped and tried to calm my voice. "I was just running through the growth along the river and, well, a branch—" I looked from his face to my sleeve again. My cheeks were burning.

He took my hand from my dress and studied my shoulder. "You're hurt, aren't you!" His hand came away and he rubbed a spot of blood between his fingers, staring at me—obviously recalling what Delores had implied—*walking indeed*.

I fought the tears that suddenly swam behind my eyes. Surely he didn't believe her! I had just had the scare of my life, and now I had the misfortune of running straight into Delores Ashley and *him*—looking like this! How unfair life was!

"It's nothing but a scratch."

"It looks like more than that to me. You ought to—"

"Please, let's just forget it. I've done a great deal more than this, racing the fence, I assure you."

"All right, if that's how you want it." He looked in the direction Delores had gone. "We're going to walk. Delores says she knows this area very well. I rather doubt that she does."

"Walk? Around here?" Peter was suddenly at my side. "Unless you stick to the immediate area, I'm afraid you'll have to hike."

"Well, I suppose we can make it a hike then."

"Sounds fun." Peter's hand tightened on my shoulder. "Let's get a group together and hike up the falls."

"The falls?" I nudged him with my elbow. What was he doing now? What had come over him today? "Sure, Anne. You've hiked them before."

Mark glanced again toward the Ashley blanket. "I don't know . . ."

Peter chuckled. "I guess a musician isn't the type to go in for hiking."

"I was thinking about Miss Ashley."

"Oh?" Peter ran his eyes over Mark's black ribbon tie, white shirt, and dark pants.

"So here you are!" Delores came into the trees tying a white bonnet beneath her chin. "I'm ready. Let's be off, shall we?"

"There's been a slight change of plans. We're going up the falls."

Delores gave a little laugh, indicating that she thought the idea as ridiculous as I did. "Really, Mark—the falls?"

"Yes." He took her hand. "Mr. Tate has suggested it for us, and I think it's a fine idea. I've never been there."

"We'll need a group," Peter said. He turned and hollered to Raymond. "We're going up the falls. Get some fellows together—five or six should do it." Raymond was off in a flash.

"I don't know, Mark—we might get lost, and it's rather rough for ladies." Delores's voice was suddenly small and timid.

"Nonsense." He put an arm about her. "Mr. Tate knows this area very well, I'm sure. And it must not be too rough, or he wouldn't have suggested it for *us*. Right, Mr. Tate?"

"Well, it shouldn't be difficult if we have enough capable men along to help."

"You see, Delores, we're in good hands." He looked at Peter's strong hand on my shoulder, a curious expression in his eyes. Was he amused, I wondered—amused that Peter liked me?

"Peter." We had left Mark and Delores and had gone after Raymond. "Why did you do that?"

"Do what?"

"Move in on their little walk. They had no intention of hiking, and you know it. You just had to make it into a big affair and invite us and half the ward along."

"You don't think it will be fun?"

"That's not the point."

"It *is* the point. It's our party. Staaton doesn't have to come. He's the intruder."

"He's no more an intruder than you are." I turned on my heels. It was my turn to leave in a huff.

"All right, everyone. We're heading out," Peter called across the group that had assembled for the hike. "Pair off and keep track of your partners."

We crossed the river along a large fallen tree and started up the first gentle slopes toward the springs. There were thirty-one in the group, and everyone talked as though we had embarked on some great and dangerous trek.

The young men were making the most of it. Ahead of me one of them whispered to his girl, "Stick close, Amelia, I'd hate to lose you." She giggled softly and moved closer to him.

"Watch your step, ladies," someone called from the rear. "These hills are infested with snakes." Several girls shrieked and had to be calmed by their companions. I laughed to myself. There were certain to be a few snakes around, but we were hiking on the eastern slopes. Rattlers found a warmer and cozier home on the western, sunbaked hills—and the men all knew it.

Though I was still upset with Peter, I had to admit the hike was already very exciting. I walked up front with Wally Brinton, and looking back through the happy faces of the group, I noted the men walking taller than usual, their young women deliberately dependent.

Delores and Mark near the end of the party were engrossed with one another. She picked her way carefully, chatting as she did so, and he walked protectively at her side.

An hour and a half later we reached the bottom of the falls. The white, foaming water dashed over the first twenty-foot-high drop. Most of the group were now a little tired, and some of the earlier glamour had worn off.

"It's too early in the season to hike the falls," Wally said. "Look at that water come down. Half these girls will never make it."

But as it turned out, half would never try.

"I'm not taking my girl up there," someone called from the rear. "Me either," another voice agreed, adding, "and I wouldn't go up on a bet."

"We'd better vote on it," Billy Parry suggested. He and his younger brother, Jason, had come with Raymond.

"You're all getting alarmed over nothing," Peter said, stepping back to the center of the group. "The first fall looks frightening, but we can station men all along the ledges in zigzag fashion and hand the girls up. It's really very simple."

"What do you say, men?" Raymond hollered from a rock high above the group. "Do we quit before we've even started or do we go on?"

"Well, I'm not going on!" One of the girls left the young man at her side and walked to the rear. Several others joined her and were followed shortly by their companions.

"Are you coming back, Anne?" one of them called.

"No, she isn't," Peter answered for me.

"Let her speak for herself, Peter."

"I know the water is high, but I really think we'll be all right," I answered. "It's gorgeous up there."

Laurie Lewis emerged from the rear of the crowd and said, "If Anne's going on, I am too."

"All right then." Peter joined Raymond on his rock. "Everyone who's going on step up here by Anne. The others stay back."

We waved good-bye to eleven persons. And to my surprise, Mark and Delores weren't among them.

"I'm going on, certainly," Delores said, her chin high. She suddenly lowered her eyes and looked at Mark, clearly inviting him to disagree and insist on her going back with the others. He, however, took her hand and walked up by us.

"Perhaps I was wrong, Staaton," Peter said. "The water is high. It will be rougher going than I had thought, and you'll get plenty wet. Maybe you and Miss Ashley should reconsider. Once we start up, we've got to stick together. There'll be no turning back."

"We don't mind a little water, do we, Delores?" She shook her head, but I saw her turn and watch the other group leave with regret in her wide eyes—and that was something I hadn't seen there before.

"All right! Let's go."

The mist from the falls was cooling, and the beauty of the white pools, garnished with brightly colored mosses, was breathtaking against the lush green of the trees and ferns. Enormous amounts of crystal water rushed off the smooth, bleached rocks into large, hollowed-out basins below. It was hard to believe that they had been formed from years and years of running water. It seemed somehow more plausible that intelligent hands had fashioned them. I said so to Wally and he smiled.

"Intelligent hands did fashion them."

"If you think this is fun," Raymond said, "you ought to see the slippery slide farther up. You won't believe it! It's got to be twenty-five or more feet long, and at the bottom, a narrow pool stops you just before you crash into a solid rock wall. Everyone's gotta try it on the way back. You can't say you've been up the falls unless you come down that thing!"

We did very well all the way up. By the time we reached the top we were all tired, wet, and elated. I felt a near kinship with everyone there—even Delores.

She was having an especially rough time and was complaining a little. But she had come. The front of her dress was smeared with green moss, and her skirt now hung limply. She'd lost her bonnet, and her hair hung loosely about her shoulders. But despite it all she was beautiful.

As for the rest of us, we were in a similar condition. But no one seemed to mind. It was an adventure. In the past several hours we had defied real danger together and had won. It was a glorious feeling to have conquered the falls.

"We'll rest a while before turning back," Peter called from the front of the group. "There's a beautiful lookout if you want to rest there. I'll show you." He crossed to the brink of the hill but no one followed. They scattered instead, staying relatively close but pairing off for the few minutes' rest we would take.

Peter stood and surveyed the valley below. He had done a good job of conducting the party safely up the falls, and as yet no one had said a word of thanks for his excellent skills. I crossed the springs and stood at his side.

"Well, you did it, Peter. We're all here safe and sound. You certainly do know these hills."

I suddenly felt a rush of warmth for him. He was a fine person—always doing for others, my family and me especially, rarely thinking of himself. I knew practically nothing about the life he lived in the seven months he went home each year. He never talked about his past or his family unless we brought it up.

"It is beautiful here." Peter broke his silence. "It's spiritual almost."

I sat on the soft green facing the valley. "You know, you've never told me about your family."

"What do you want to know?" He knelt beside me and took my hand into his.

"Everything."

"Well, I did tell you that I'm the youngest in my family. There's a big gap between me and my closest sister—ten years. It was like being an only child at home, but with none of the benefits." He told me then of his young life—how he had gone to work when he was very young because his father had suffered a stroke and was so ill he could no longer hang on to his farm. "My parents are good people—more like my grandparents in some ways, but good." He never wasted time, he told me. "Not a minute. But I don't regret anything," he said, fingering my hand gently in his. "And here in this valley I have plenty of friends and time enough to enjoy them when I want to." His eyes scanned the expansive view below us almost caressingly. "I'm happy here, Anne."

He *was* happy—happier than I had ever seen him.

"You're a fine person, Peter Tate. Papa says you know what you want and where you're going. I believe him." He put my fingers to his lips.

A breeze danced across my arms and face and through my damp clothing, tingling my entire body. *I care for Peter*, I thought incredulously. *I care for him—very much.*

EIGHT

"If you've rested enough, ladies, I think you should be heading back." Raymond swaggered as he and his two friends left the shade of their tree.

"I think you mean *we*," Wally Brinton said.

"My men and I are going on to the top."

"Of the *mountain*? Three of you?" Wally laughed and called to me. "Hear that, Anne?"

Peter and I joined those who had begun to assemble.

"He's teasing," I laughed.

"I'm dead serious," Raymond replied. "We're nearly there." We all turned to face the highest visible point of the mountain. "I might never get a chance like this again."

Peter shook his head. "The top's not any closer than two or more hours of steady hiking, and most everyone's about had it."

"We're not talking about the others—just us."

"We've been the lead the last hour," Billy Parry chimed in. "We aren't tired."

"Well, has anyone here been to the top?" Wally asked. Everyone shook his head. I stepped forward.

"I don't want you to go, Raymond!"

"Our grandparents walked across the plains, and we can't even hike one little measly mountain in our own dooryard."

"Ben Lomond isn't measly," Peter cut in. "It's the highest mountain in the Ogden area. From the valley floor to the peak—"

"We're not talking about the peak. We just want to look over and see the lake from any place on top."

This was getting entirely out of hand. Raymond *was* serious about it, and I knew I couldn't go back down the falls without him. He might be tough and smart, but he was reckless too, especially when he was feeling cocky and too sure of himself, as he was now.

"Papa would be furious," I insisted. "Let's drop it!"

"We want to go," Billy scowled.

"Last chance for anyone to join?" Raymond was paying no heed to me. "No one? All right then, see you back in camp after a while. Let's go, boys." They were going. There was nothing to be done.

"Raymond, come back here!" But he just smiled back at me and gave the silly comic salute that he used with the Blaven boys. A vision of him lying dead in one of the pools or crushed at the bottom of some ravine flashed through my mind.

"Peter, do something. He'll get hurt. You know how he is."

Peter gave me a fleeting smile. "Anne, I know that he won't listen to me. He never has. All right, everyone, I guess we might as well be on our way too." The rest nodded in agreement.

They were all letting Raymond and the Parry boys go! I looked for Mark, but he was busy with his own problems. He and Delores stood apart from the group. He was standing above her, his hands palms up as though he were trying to make something clear, and she turned from him. I supposed she was angry about the hike and blamed him. In a way he had maneuvered her into coming.

"Raymond'll be fine, Anne." Laurie Lewis touched my hand as we started back toward the falls.

"But he won't, Laurie. He has no—no judgment." And that was true. Raymond was a showoff. I turned to watch the three boys now some distance above us, scampering through the deep grass and up the sloping hills. I should be with them. I knew it. But I was tired, suddenly very tired. How I wished I were off the mountain, that all of us were back in camp playing ball or tossing horseshoes, or just sitting in the shade and chatting. I could imagine how Delores was feeling, and I couldn't blame her one bit.

"Anne, why not come up front?" Peter called from where he stood surveying the terrain below.

We were leaving. In another few minutes it would be too late to do anything.

"Laurie, how do you feel?" I asked in a rush.

"What do you mean? Am I tired?" She pushed back a sleeve. "I'm just getting warmed up."

"Then go with me—up the mountain. I can't go down and leave them."

"Well, it's fine with me, but your Peter won't like it." *My Peter.*

"Anne," Peter called again, and he held out a hand to me. But when I told him Laurie and I were going after Raymond, he became angry.

"Now just a minute. Your pa thinks you and Raymond are with me. What will he say when I walk back into camp without either of you?"

The group closed in about us, expecting a showdown, the men smiling and obviously delighted with the difference of opinion, and the girls visibly impatient with me—and my brother—for detaining them.

"I'm serious." I spun around to glare at him. "I can't leave. I'll worry all the way down. Don't any of you understand?"

"Everyone rest another minute or so." Peter took me by the elbow. "This won't take long." He led me some distance from the group.

"No, it won't take long!" I swung around and faced him. "You let my little brother go up this—this *huge* mountain alone, and I'm not going back without him!"

"I didn't let him, Anne. What could I do? I have no say over Raymond's actions."

"You could have at least *tried*." I shook a fist. "Now I'm going!"

"The falls are your limit. You're tired and you're not built for this. Raymond is. He's tough. He's always going off on his own. You know perfectly well he'll be fine."

I tried to sidestep past him, but he caught my arm and pulled me back.

"You're *not* going."

"I am. Now let go of me."

Peter's jaw stiffened and his face deepened into crimson. His hand tightened on my arm until it made me wince. "For once you're going to listen to *me*!"

"How dare you try and stop me!"

"I *will* stop you, Anne." His eyes held a dangerous glint. "You're making a fool of us both. They're laughing at us."

"Let them laugh. It's my brother!"

"Anne, I mean this. You're not taking another step up the mountain. *I won't—*"

"Excuse me." Mark Staaton was standing just behind Peter.

"What is it?" Peter nearly shouted at him.

"I think I can help."

"You can help by staying out of it," he exploded.

"Obviously," Mark's tone was low, "that's not what I had in mind, Tate."

"I'm going up the mountain," I insisted. "*No one's* going to change my mind."

"I'd feel the same in your place, Anne," Mark said, "but you must agree that you and Miss Lewis can't go alone. I'll go with you, and Tate here can take the others down."

Peter swore. "How much assistance can you give when you don't know anything about this area? If anyone goes with her, it will be me—but of course I won't. She's tired.

She shouldn't go on, and,'' Peter's fingers clenched on me again, "she isn't going to. That's final!"

"Peter, stop trying to run me." I tried to pull my arm free. "Let go!"

"I think you'd better," Mark said gently.

Peter's angry expression faded. "All right, you can go. But you can rest assured that I'll come too. I wouldn't miss it for the world—the blind leading the blind." He laughed disagreeably and released my arm, nearly throwing it at me. I was furious with him. How dared he act that way!

We split the group again. Everyone turned back but six of us—Laurie, Wally, Peter, Mark, myself—and Delores. I dreaded her coming. She would only slow us down, and I was impatient to catch Raymond.

Mark and Peter tried to talk Delores out of coming, but for some reason nothing could dissuade her.

"Mark, I came up these stupid falls with you and that's how I'm going down them. If you don't want me to keep on, that's fine. Come back with me. But if you go, I go. I won't be abandoned!"

There was a long pause.

"She's going," Mark finally said. And as he said it, Delores flashed me a triumphant smile.

Two hours later, we had stopped for our umpteenth rest. So far we hadn't seen any sign of the boys. They had vanished. Each conquered rise only led to another, and another still more steep than the last. The grassy, meadowlike hills above the falls had given way to rocky cliffs, and now the ragged terrain stretched endlessly above us. We had come to a towering, gray cliff. There seemed to be only two ways up, and these were runoff gullies on each side of the cliff. After close inspection, Mark decided we should take the left one.

"The right is wider and reaches the top sooner," Peter interjected from the back of the group. It was the first real sentence he had uttered since we'd left the falls.

"That's true," Mark said. "But the right is full of shale and loose rock. We couldn't climb it without bringing several tons of it down on our heads."

The men went ahead to find a way up the cliff, which appeared even more impassable than anything we had come to. After what seemed hours, though it could have been only five minutes or so, they reappeared and waved for us to come ahead.

"I guess we'd better get going." I pushed to my feet, though I wasn't at all sure I could go on myself. My legs felt numb and my shoulder, which I'd hurt earlier in the day, was giving me trouble.

"I won't go another step," Delores said. "You're quite a little heroine, risking all our lives for three foolish boys— the leader of which is *your* brother."

"Help me up, Anne." Laurie extended her hand to me, and as she rose she said, "You didn't have to come, Delores."

"Oh, no? I suppose I could have gone back alone."

"You'd have hardly been alone. Most of the group turned back," I said.

"You'd like to show me up, wouldn't you. You were clearly after my solo when you joined the choir, and now I can see you're foolish enough to go after my beau."

"I can't imagine where you get that. I assure you I'm only after three foolish boys, as you call them, who could be in great danger at this very moment. Now please, let's go."

"You deny it then?" Her nostrils flared.

"Deny what?"

"*Deny what?*" she mimicked me. "That you're after Mark—as if *you* could turn his head."

"Come on, you two. This is no time to quarrel." Laurie pulled on my arm. "The fellows are waving for us to come. They've found a way."

"I said I'm not going another step, and I'm not." Delores settled herself firmly on the rocky ground.

"Fine." I shot a look at Laurie as I passed her. She understood. *Leave them alone and they'll come home.*

Delores waited until we were nearly out of sight before getting to her feet and stumbling after us.

"Raymond!" We called over and over again as we climbed. "Raymond! Billy! Jason!" But there was never any answer. And still the mountain grew above us.

"I can't go any further, Mark. I can't really." Delores's eyes swam with tears. We had come through a narrow pass filled with thorny shrubs that left our bare arms and hands scratched and tingling with pain.

"I know," he said sympathetically, taking her hand in his. "But what can we do but go on?"

"Go back! Go back!" She screamed, suddenly hysterical. "Go back and let this little witch find her own brother!"

"Delores!" Mark looked from me to Delores. But I felt he agreed with her, that they all did. They blamed me.

We each found a place to rest, and an awkward silence fell over us. I felt close to tears. Blinking, I got to my feet. "I apologize for Raymond. I'd like to wring his neck. But Delores is right. It *is* my problem. All of you have given too much already. I want you to go back."

I don't know what I expected then—maybe for someone to disagree with me and to insist that they all keep on. But no one said a word—not one word.

Suddenly anger streamed through my veins. If they wanted to go back, let them! And let them try and live with themselves when they buried the boys and me!

I dashed the tears from my cheeks and ran, my hands in front of me, securing the way as I went up the loose rocks, climbing the face of the cliff in front of me. I was amazed at my own agility as I pulled myself up the steep wall. My feet found all the right crevices, and my frantic hands found the ledges above. I wasn't wasting an instant. I would find those lost boys myself. I would, so help me, or die trying.

"Anne! Anne! Come back. Stop at once!"

"Not that way—you'll kill yourself!"

The shouts came behind me. But I wouldn't wait or look back. I was through feeling guilty.

I had nearly gained the top of the cliff, and I marveled at

my daring. I was quite able to manage on my own. Pulling myself on to the top ledge, I looked back triumphantly. But as I did so, the ground swayed. I grabbed for anything, but my hands came away empty. I was falling toward the edge. I thought for a terrible instant that I was about to die—I couldn't fall that great distance and live. But as I began to tumble, a miracle happened. A long, strong arm caught me and firmly pulled me back from the rim. It was Mark.

"Fool!"

I gulped for breath. "How did you get up here?"

He ignored my question. "What a stupid, *stupid* stunt."

The faces of those below had disappeared. They were coming up too, using a path. I could see it now, sloping upward from the side. In my anger I hadn't even noticed it. Instead, I had come straight up, over the top. I *had* been stupid. I could have been killed. I laughed uneasily.

At my laugh Mark seemed to explode. He yanked me roughly to him. "Do you know you could have been *killed*?" He shook me. "Answer!"

"Yes, I suppose."

"You *suppose*? You gave me—us—the scare of our lives!"

It was strange, I thought. I had nearly lost my life, and yet I was much more composed than my rescuer.

"I'm sorry," I mumbled, though I hadn't the faintest idea why I should apologize for nearly killing *myself*.

He closed his eyes for a moment, and when he opened them again I was relieved to see that he had calmed considerably.

"Then why—why in the world did you take off like that?"

"I don't know. My mind's in such a blur." But the scene at the foot of the cliff came rushing back. "No. You had deserted me—all of you. You were sorry you came and you blamed me."

"I did no such thing."

"But you did! You *let* her say those things," I cried accusingly. "You agreed with her!"

"I *didn't* agree with Delores. But I couldn't very well scold her. She didn't mean it. This has been a strain—more than you know. Delores is really tired. And whose fault is it? I shouldn't have brought her up the falls to start with. It was an impulse. I wanted to come and," he smiled in self-derision, "would you believe I wanted to see Miss Delores Ashley in a situation other than the phony backgrounds she always finds for herself."

I'd had the same thoughts. Of course, mine went a lot further. I'd secretly hoped she would lose her poise. I should be happy, I mused. She *had* done that, though Mark apparently thought none the worse of her for it.

"She's hated it all the way," he continued, "but I guess she's got more spunk than I gave her credit for. She wouldn't go back."

"But you didn't say anything when I told you to go back without me. No one said a word."

"You didn't mean it any more than Delores meant what she said."

"Anne, Anne!" It was Peter. "Thank God you're safe!" He rushed to me and swept me into his arms. He held me for an awkwardly long moment, while Mark watched me with coolly interested eyes. "Thank you, Mark," Peter said. "Thank you."

He held me at arm's length, and his eyes looked deep into mine. The concern I saw there made tears spring into my own. "Anne, I really thought I'd lost you. When you started to fall . . ." He hugged me again. "You know, I lost my head. I tried to climb the cliff right behind you. You went so fast, I couldn't catch up. Thank heaven Mark had the sense to come up the other way."

I blinked. What was I to do? Peter loved me! I didn't have the courage to look at Mark again, so I closed my eyes while Peter held me.

The near disaster had given us all strength and, more remarkable, had eased feelings between Peter and Mark. The petty competition was off—for the time being at least. We were renewed.

96

The last portion of the climb was uneventful. The sun had long since slipped down the other side of the mountain and left us in its cool shadow. We found ourselves on the very back of the now nearly bald mountain. We climbed by clinging to the roots of straggly evergreens that grew crookedly out of narrow cracks and crevices in the rock. After several hundred feet of such scaling we reached a decision. The men would go on to the top, take a quick look for the boys, find them (we hoped), and return as rapidly as possible. Laurie, Delores, and I found a place to sit and began to count the terrible minutes they would be gone.

Peter and Wally started up immediately, but Mark held back to speak to Delores. He said something to her and she answered in a trembling voice, "I will, Mark." Then he edged his way up to me.

Raymond was fine, Mark assured me—no, promised me. And he kissed my forehead and was gone.

Delores watched as I touched the spot where his lips had been. Had she seen him kiss me? I doubted it. But even if she had, it was a parental sort of kiss, given purely to reassure me. She'd scarcely mind after what I was sure he had given her. That thought hurt. But wasn't it obvious? Mark lived in the Ashley home. Rachael undoubtedly gave them many opportunities to be alone. I could see it clearly. Supper over, they would go for a stroll.

"Take your time, youngsters," Rachael would call as they left arm in arm.

Yes, I was certain Mark had given Delores many a moonlight kiss.

It was Raymond who first scrambled down to us. My prayers had been answered. They were safe—all three of them.

"Where have you been? I've been half out of my mind with worry." I pulled him to me and gave him a hug.

"I've been doing exactly what I told you I'd be doing."

"You've been hiking all this time?"

"Well, no. We've been up there for a while. But it was fantastic. The Great Salt Lake was pure gold in the sunset. You should have kept coming. It was the most beautiful sight of my life, Anne. It was like looking down from heaven —honest, it was!"

"Raymond, I'm glad it was beautiful, but don't ever scare me like that again."

He pushed me away self-consciously and looked toward Laurie and Delores. "I'd do it tomorrow."

"You would!" Delores said sourly.

But though he wasn't repentant, I was thankful he was safe. And after everyone returned from the top, all nine of us gathered in a prayer of thanks.

NINE

For a while we made much better time going down the mountain than coming up. The air was cool and refreshing, and we didn't have to stop nearly as often. I knew that Mark and Peter were concerned about the time. I'd heard them discussing it, and both expressed a fear that we might be spending the night on the mountain.

After coming some distance down the mountain the men changed our course, explaining that by doing so we would miss the prickly shrubs we had passed through on the way up. The change seemed at first to be a good one. We descended rapidly and avoided many of the treacherous cliffs. But then, after what seemed like several hours, we came to very dense growth. It was gloomy and shadowy in the failing twilight, and picking our way down was a slow process.

Delores began to complain again, but now her complaints were directed against Raymond for causing the "whole mess," as she put it. "I'll never come up this mountain again."

"Yes, you will," Raymond said.

"If I ever do," she said, shaking her fist at him, "after such a terrifying experience, I won't deserve to descend it again. How callous of you to run off like that! You have absolutely no consideration for the comfort of others, and you've no idea the trouble you have caused us—nor the expense.''

''Expense?''

She touched what was left of the eyelet of her now ragged and dirty dress. ''It was new,'' she moaned, ''new.''

Mark was leading the party now. He and Peter had decided to change courses again.

''We're coming down the wrong ravine,'' Raymond protested. ''We should be further north.''

I had been thinking the same thing. Surely we hadn't passed through anything like this on the way up. Perhaps we were lost. I mentioned this to Peter and he told me to leave the worrying to him. ''But, Peter, suppose Raymond is right?''

''Anne,'' he said wearily, ''we are *purposely* further south than we were going up. We know what we're doing.''

We kept on. Wally stuck close to Laurie, helping her whenever he could, and I began to realize that they liked each other in a romantic way. Though I'd never before pictured them together, I liked the idea.

''Raymond,'' I whispered, ''is it true what you said about us coming down the wrong ravine?''

''I'm positive we're going to miss the camp. We could hike right on past it this way. We could hike till morning and longer.''

''But they have a reason, Peter says.''

''Of course, he'd say that to you. He doesn't want to worry you.''

Yes, that would be it. We were lost, and Peter wouldn't want to level with me because I would be frightened—or so he would think. Gradually I worked my way up the line until I was behind Mark, who was now leading. Delores had fallen back, so I could talk to him openly.

''Mark,'' I whispered as I made my way behind him. I certainly couldn't go on calling him mister, especially after he had kissed my forehead. ''Mark, it's me, Anne.'' He paused.

"I don't want you to think that I don't have faith in you or Peter," I went on, "but are we lost?"

"What makes you ask that?"

"Raymond and I have been discussing it. We both feel that we are too far to the south, and that we should change our direction. I spoke to Peter about it, and he put me off. I want to know. I can take it."

"I'm sure you can. Yes, I suppose I must tell you. The truth is," he paused as if to brace me, ". . . the truth is, we're not lost."

"We aren't?" I had the impression that he was stifling a laugh. "Mr. Staaton, surely you don't think me as gullible as that!"

"You're angry? Angry that we're not lost?"

"I thought you'd be straight with me, but you're putting me off just as Peter did. Worse—you were—"

"Yes?"

"I know very well you were laughing at me. You don't fool me a mite!"

But I had been fooled again, I thought, as I let him go ahead. I was foolish to think he would take me into his confidence. I was a pupil in his choir. He would always think of me as such. Let Delores have her precious beau. They deserved each other.

"Anne?" Peter caught me by my shoulder as I brushed past him. I must have cried out, for he asked if I'd hurt myself.

"My shoulder's still aching from this morning," I snapped.

"I haven't noticed."

"Of course you haven't. You've been playing the big shot all day—and anyway, it's been hurting me, not you." As soon as the words were out I was sorry. I had lashed out at Peter when I was angry with Mark. Peter loved me. He cared. "I'm sorry. Please forgive me."

"You know I do." He put his arms around me and held me against his chest. "You're tired. It's been a nightmare for you, hasn't it." He smoothed over my forehead—over the spot where Mark had kissed me.

Yes, I thought, wipe it off!

"We are purposely not heading down the ravine we climbed," Peter said gently, "because we aren't going to attempt the falls."

"*Why not?*" Raymond made his way to us.

"Because it would be much too dangerous in the dark."

"I disagree," Raymond said. "It will take hours going this way."

"It doesn't matter if you agree or not," Peter said stiffly, moving off.

I breathed easier knowing that our guides knew what they were doing. Mark had leveled with me after all! I was thankful then that we *had* gone after Raymond. I knew that if he, Jason, and Billy had been left alone, they would have come back by way of the falls and something would have happened—something awful. I shivered.

It was difficult to tell if we were making any progress at all in our descent. We had been going for what seemed hours.

"I don't understand it," Peter kept saying over and over. "We should have come out long before now."

Later we tried shouting for help. But our voices fell weakly on our own ears.

"Suppose we're lost!" Delores's voice was shaken. "Suppose we never get off this disgusting mountain!"

"We aren't lost," Mark said.

"Always so sure of everything, aren't you. You haven't set a *foot* in these hills before today—and you're sure!"

"I am."

"But could we be lost?" This from Jason Parry. It was a small voice, and I guessed he was about to burst into tears.

"No, silly," I said laughing.

"If we continue just going downhill we ought to come out somewhere," Billy, Jason's older brother, suggested.

"We could fall off the mountain, Billy," Raymond teased.

It was hardly the time for teasing, I pointed out to him.

"But we don't know the territory, Anne. The leader could disappear without warning, and then one by one . . ." He gave a long, tapering whistle to indicate someone falling a great distance.

"Raymond!" I wanted to fly at him. He had caused the situation, and yet he was doing *everything* to make things worse. But I didn't have the strength for anger. He was teasing and Jason knew it. But he'd gotten to Delores, for when we started off again, she moved to the back of the line. If anyone fell off the mountain, it wouldn't be her.

At last the dense growth cleared and we came to a point where we could view the valley below. To our dismay we were still very high. It was barely light in the valley, but here, close to the mountain, the darkness crawled down the trees and slunk along the damp ground.

"Surely they're looking for us by now," Laurie said.

"Certainly they are!" Peter agreed too heartily. "Half the ward is probably on this mountain this very minute. We should be keeping a sharp eye out for torches or fires."

Though I knew he was only trying to lift our spirits, his suggestion that they might have built fires to show us the way made me feel considerably better. Of course, they'd think of that. Of course they would.

At last we were out of the dense growth for good, and into meadowlike places where we could walk—no, run. *And we ran.* No one spoke. Only the heavy chorus of our breathing and the soft thudding of feet on spongy earth came to our ears. Occasionally someone would shout a caution, but that was all. We were all feverish to be down.

Suddenly in the distance we saw the fires, and we were encouraged. Mark and Peter had been very accurate—we would come out fine.

"We're not lost!" Jason Parry tugged on my skirt.

"No."

"You know what I'm worried about now?"

"No, what?"

"My mom! I'll get a spanking for this."

We had been walking through damp earth for some time. The hills were covered with springs and in some spots the ground sloshed sloppily around our ankles. Our final trial could have been spared us, had we only listened to Delores, but she had complained so much it sounded rather like "wolf, wolf."

"We're in that nasty stinging nettle again. My arm stings fiercely, Mark!"

"I don't feel a thing."

"Honestly, it does. It feels nearly like a bee sting." I had had it with her. We were nearly down the mountain and still she complained.

"*Beeeeees*!" Raymond screamed.

They were everywhere. I felt their fuzzy little bodies under my collar and clinging to my arms. In three seconds flat, the group had scattered, yelling and slapping at themselves. Finally we assembled again several hundred feet below and counted heads. "We're all here," Mark said. "Everyone all right?"

With, I was sure, half a dozen bee stings, I could smile—even laugh. It was ridiculous. Delores had warned us and we hadn't listened.

A voice cut across ours. "Hello! Peter? Is that you and the others?" Someone was waving a light. We were down!

"Well, well, well," Luther Jennings said behind the light, "if you're not a sight for sore eyes."

"We made it!" we shouted to one another, slapping backs and hugging. Even Delores joined in. "We're down!" We, all of us together, had done it.

The Parry boys let off war whoops, and Raymond's shrill whistle sliced the distant night's calm for what must have been miles around.

"I told you, didn't I?" Mark swung me about. "We weren't lost—not for a minute!"

"Of course not. It was all in your plan."

He inclined his head very close to mine, his hands spanning my waist. "Of course."

Luther fired his gun into the air three times to signal the others, then led us to a fire where we found blankets, biscuits, and enough horses to take us across the river and into the nearly empty camp. By then it was midnight.

"We prayed you'd have sense enough to bypass the falls." Papa's arm came around me. He and a large group of searchers had just returned from the base of the falls. "Thank heaven you did!"

"It was because of Peter and Mark."

"Thank you both," he said, shaking Mark's hand and embracing Peter. "Thank you for going after Raymond, though I'm sorry you had to. I know he can be a handful, and you can be sure he'll never do anything like this again!"

Peter's arm came down on Mark's shoulder in a brotherly clasp. "You know, now that we're down, well, we'd do it again. Wouldn't we, Mark?"

All around us men were leaving to join their families at home. With tired—but happy—faces they waved and hollered their good nights as they rode out.

Behind us, Daniel Ashley was hitching up his buggy. Delores had behaved admirably while she waited for her father and the other men to return to camp. But on Daniel's return, the hold she had on herself broke completely. "Papa, oh papa!" she cried, flinging herself through the crowd and into his arms. "It was dreadful!"

As he helped her into the buggy, he flashed the rest of us a hard look of disapproval. Then her face disappeared beneath a blanket as he quickly drove off.

Papa's wagon had become stuck in the mud, so while he and Peter and Raymond tried to pull it out, I wandered over to sit on a log by the fire, pulled off my wet, muddy shoes, and tried to warm my feet by the embers.

I was disappointed that Mark hadn't hollered a good-bye as the Ashley wagon passed, but it *was* late, and the Ashleys *were* angry. I touched my forehead and saw again his dark eyes smiling into mine. How exciting it had been! How things had changed! I wondered what my relationship with Delores would be now. It certainly would be altered, because I wasn't afraid of her any longer. Funny, I mused, I hadn't realized before that I had been afraid.

The fire had burned down to crumbling embers. The air was crisp and clean, full of the comforting sound of crickets and the low roar from the creek. A light wind brushed the ghostlike aspens around me, and perhaps somewhere, far up the dark mountain, that same wind skimmed a towering cliff and tossed a deserted white bonnet into a glistening black pool.

I put my hands flat against the familiar loam of the valley. It was so good to be back. Tears filled my eyes and I let them come. Alone, by the dying fire, I realized my many blessings and how I loved this valley, this soil.

"Unhappy?" A figure moved out of the shadows.

"Peter?"

"No."

"Mark!" I thought you went with the Ash—"

"They left me." He eased down beside me on the log. "Peter's offered to drive me in, in your father's buggy, but knowing the Ashleys, I'll probably be locked out too."

"They're that angry?"

"Oh, I don't know. Mr. Ashley didn't say anything to me—just took off."

"I'm sorry."

I felt him shrug next to me. "I expected it. They see things a little differently than we do."

Excitement tugged within me. I began to trace with a willow through the embers.

"You've been crying," he said.

I continued to play in the fire with my willow and destroyed what appeared to be a smouldering white snake.

"We're back," he said, taking the willow away and giving it a good toss. "It does feel good."

We sat for a while listening to the night sounds and enjoying the comfortable silence together. The soft wind shook the aspens and pines and cooled the air, and above us, towering magnificently powerful and indifferent, Ben Lomond slept in darkness as it had for ages.

Mark slipped his hand over my wrist and moved closer. The warmth of his fingers stirred my pulses, and I thought I'd never been happier, or more content in my life.

We watched the fire fade into complete blackness. At last we got to our feet, and turning from the dead fire I saw a silhouette hurrying from us—Peter.

The ride home was a silent one. Papa and Raymond went back in the wagon (Papa had sent Mama and the younger children home hours ago with a neighbor), and Peter and I took the buggy.

"You're more than welcome to stay with us tonight, Mr. Staaton," Papa had told Mark. "It's a long ride into town, and we have an extra bunk in a room off the barn. Not luxury, eh, Peter? But adequate."

"No, thank you."

"Son, the Ashleys just might not have those home fires burning tonight, and that's our fault. Why not stay and let things settle a little?"

Mark laughed. "You could be right, but I'd like to go in just the same. Look, I don't want to put Peter out. Could I borrow a horse? I'd ride out in the morning and return it."

"It's yours! Keep it as long as you need." Papa looked at Peter. "You'll see to it, Peter? But think about staying, will you?"

At that Papa shook the reins and the wagon moved off. Mark climbed up beside me in the buggy, and Peter tucked a blanket around me before we started off. Home and sleep were less than an hour away.

I sighed heavily. "It's been quite a day, hasn't it?" The pale road unwinding ahead of us rose and fell and rose again.

"That it has," Mark drawled absently, his eyes on the trees and brush moving past.

"It was an experience, wasn't it?" When I got no reply I added cheerfully, "The kind of thing we'll *never* forget." Mark held his silence, still watching the passing growth. Peter grunted and hurried the horses, staring at the dim road ahead of him.

I pushed back into my blanket and let the grim silence alone after that. I was too exhausted to affect an easiness that was no longer with us. I closed my eyes against the crisp air that fell over my face and dug deeper into the warmth of wool about me. At length I dozed.

I awoke with my head against Peter's shoulder. We had stopped at the barn door, and I had the very real impression that we'd been sitting there for some time. I sat up a bit dazedly and peered through my sleepiness at the place beside me where Mark had sat.

"He's gone." Peter's arm came around me.

"Already?"

He laughed, pressing my head against his. "Hardly already. He's probably fast asleep by now in one of Rachael's featherbeds."

"How late is it?" The stars still blinked dimly above us.

"Three o'clock at least."

"Three! Then he should have stayed, Peter. How could you let him go off?"

"I didn't let him go off," he snapped. "I took Turner's lane into town and dropped him at the corner. You seemed comfortable enough, so I didn't bother coming here first."

"He wanted you to drive him in?"

"He didn't object. Now come on. Let's get you to bed."

"But why didn't you just let him take a horse? He must have thought we wanted to get rid of him, and Papa said—"

"Give him a horse to be returned in the morning? It's nearly dawn now." He laughed, then took the blanket from around my shoulders and lifted me from the buggy. "You're very light." He set me on the ground but his hands held my waist. "Your head felt good against me."

"Peter, I'm so tired!" His face blurred and swam before me.

"I know you are." His voice was low—a whisper.

"Then let me go in—it's late."

But he held me still. "It is late." His eyes gleamed, and when he spoke, his words were silky. "I just want to say good night, Anne."

"Then *say it, please*!" I put an impatient hand to my forehead.

I should have felt it coming. A girl always does, they say. But as his mouth fastened over mine, half my brain seemed drugged. I tried to turn away—push away—but he kissed me for what seemed an eternity. When he finally released me, I staggered back against the rig and would have fallen, but he caught my elbow and steadied me.

My head cleared. I was furious. I put the back of my hand to my mouth and glared through the darkness at him.

"Anne," he was smiling, "I'm sorry if—"

"You should be!"

"I'm not apologizing for the kiss, my dear, but I am sorry if I scared you."

"Scared me?" But he had. "You—you have *insulted* me."

He laughed and moved close again. "I've waited an awfully long time then—to insult you. Two years for you to grow up."

"Stop talking like that, Peter. It isn't like you at all."

"It isn't like Papa's hired hand, you mean."

"No, it isn't." I pressed back against the rig. The horses swayed, impatient to be stabled.

"Look," he took my shoulders hard, "we've talked, your pa and I. He doesn't see me as hired help and neither does your family. *Son*, he calls me now, *son*! I've worked hard here—very hard."

It was clear he felt he'd earned something. What, I asked myself—me?

"Anne, we haven't talked much. Talking isn't always necessary. But we feel something special for each other." He turned to me again and gave a little laugh. "The canal incident, remember? You said you didn't know why you did such a thing. But if you'd think about it, you'd see it yourself." The anger had gone out of him and he spoke very gently. "Anne, you wanted my attention. You wanted me to notice you—as if I hadn't already."

"Oh, Peter, it was just a prank to bring you down in Papa's eyes. I was *jealous*."

"Stop trying to fight it. I told you before, I know you better than you do yourself."

"I object to your saying that. It's not true."

"Isn't it?" Peter's face was a shadow in the blackness. "Then tell me you don't like me, Anne."

"Of course I like you."

"Tell me we're wrong for each other."

"I—Peter, *please*, I'm tired. You're pushing me." I felt my hands knot into fists. "Peter, I may be a great deal younger than you, but I *won't* be pushed. You tried to run me today on the hike. You assume a position over me as though I haven't got a head to think with. I don't like it! I mean it! Don't do it again."

He gave an impatient sigh. "You were my responsibility, Anne."

"I'm not your responsibility! I'm not! Where do you get that? Stop pushing. Don't ruin a good thing."

"Sometimes we all need a little push in the right direction."

"You aren't even listening!" I moved out from against the buggy. "It's late."

"I've waited a long time, and I have no intention of letting anything or *anyone* ruin this."

"You're doing a pretty good job of it yourself!" I flung over my shoulder as I ran toward the house.

"Anne—"

"Good night."

"It's Staaton, isn't it?" That stopped me cold. I stood a moment trying to think of something to say, but because I could find nothing in my throat, I went on.

"Anne!" Peter called to me. "Answer that!" I didn't turn back, and as I closed the door behind me I heard him curse. "That's getting to be a habit," I said half aloud. "Papa ought to hear you now."

TEN

I went to the practice the following day two hours early. Papa was driving in to Charlie's store, and I decided to go along.

"No need, Anne," Papa said. "Stay and have your supper. Peter can drive you in later, and you won't get your pretty dress all dirty in the wagon."

"But my fabric—I want to see if it's in."

"I can check for you."

"Oh, Papa, I *want* to go with you." I kissed his face, which was still soft from his recent shave. "Besides, I'd like a hair ribbon."

"So that's it!" He laughed. "Your Pa's pretty easy, isn't he. All right. Get your things."

But the cloth hadn't arrived.

"It's the dye, I'm afraid," Charlie said, frowning at me over his counter. "I sent a slip along and said if it didn't match I didn't want it." He shrugged. "I guess it didn't match, Annie. I'd have it by now."

"But the Fourth is nearly two weeks away. They won't let me sing if I'm not in costume."

"Nonsense," Papa said. "Put some mosquito barre in too, Charlie, and let me see one of those buckets behind you."

"They won't, Papa. It's a rule."

"Then they'll break it. You're singing the *solo*—the featured event. They need you."

"Check with me next week. If it's not in then, you'll have to talk to Miss Delores. If you're singing a solo they'll figure something out. I'm sure she's as anxious about it as you. She's been askin' regular too."

Papa finished his purchases and loaded them in the wagon.

"Your ribbon. Nearly forgot." He fished in his front pocket. "Here's a dime. Enough?"

"Thank you, Papa."

He swung up onto the seat. "Peter'll be in for you after. Have a nice practice." He started the horses down the dusty street.

"Papa?" I called after him. "Raymond said he might come for me instead."

"You don't want Peter?" His eyes narrowed as if he were looking into the sun. "When a pretty gal turns down a handsome escort like Peter, she's not thinkin' clear."

"But twice a week, Papa? We take advantage of him. Let Raymond do it for a change."

Papa laughed at that. "You mustn't worry about it, Annie. I assure you Peter wants to do it." His blue eyes twinkled. He and Peter had talked, that was clear. "See you later."

He was gone. I returned to the coolness of Charlie's store and settled down to the business of selecting ribbon. I chose yellow to match the gingham dress I was wearing and took some pink for the new dress Mama had made me. I slipped the pink inside my music folder and asked to use the large mirror in the little room at the back of the store.

"Hold up a minute, Annie." Charlie came around and tapped on the door. "I got myself a part-time clerk this morning. He'll be sleeping in the back till Cora can find him a room somewhere.'' When no one answered, he glanced in. ''It's all right. Use the mirror. He's out.''

The little room looked neat. Cora had washed the blue curtains at the one window above the narrow cot, and the small panes of glass and mirror had been freshly wiped. My reflection came back to me unclouded as I combed my hair back and tied the ribbon around it in a large flat bow at my nape. How smart I had been to wear the gingham, I thought, staring at the image in the mirror. The large, flouncy sleeves hid all my scratches from the hike, and the yellow of my dress and ribbon made my complexion warmer. My dark hair and eyes looked almost black.

Charlie winked at me from the door. ''Nice. You're blossoming, all right. If I were a younger cuss—'' He laughed, his long face disappearing around the door. I heard him pulling shades and closing up.

I picked up my handbag and hollered up to him. ''Thanks! Keep an eye out for my cloth, will you? I'll just go out this way.''

''Fine.'' He waved, jerked the front door shut, and mounted the small ''closed'' sign in the window.

I bounced along the alley and down the street feeling pretty. As I passed the store front I caught my reflection in Charlie's windows and watched my bow bob with each step.

I crossed the street in front of the blacksmith's shop and started up the hill toward the churchhouse, calling hellos to the many faces I passed. But as I walked, I remembered that I still had a good hour's wait before the practice would start, and so I made my way toward Laurie's house.

As I approached her street, Wally came by in a buggy. ''Hello. Need a lift?''

''No, thanks. It's nice walking.'' I smiled up at him, waiting for the compliment I knew he'd give.

''You look lovely, Anne.''

''Oh?'' I laughed. ''Thank you. Are you going to see Laurie by any chance?''

''Yup,'' he said grinning. ''Thought I'd take her for a ride or something.'' He waved. ''Take care.''

114

I waited for him to reach her gate before turning back again.

As I passed the blacksmith's, Egan Stone, a former member of the ward, stepped onto the street.

"Well, Brother Stone! How nice to see you again."

"Miss Carrow," he sputtered, "this is a pleasure." He shook my hand vigorously.

"How's your family?"

His face clouded. "Lost my wife—two years ago last November. Typhoid."

"How awful for you and your children. I'm sorry."

"Yes, well . . ." He nodded, and I glimpsed a bald spot on the top of his head. "I thought I might ride out and call on you—and your family. But Jake here said I should ask first. He saw you pass earlier."

"Of course you should come out." His face broke into a smile. "Mama and Papa would love it, I'm sure."

"Well, it's you—uh . . ." He began to blink rapidly, and his mouth stiffened.

How very nervous he's become, I thought.

"Come out, do, please." I touched his shoulder and began up the street again. He certainly had grown strange. I turned back to smile at him, and as he stood watching after me his whole body seemed to twitch.

As a child I had thought of Egan Stone as attractive. He'd always had money and knew how to wear clothes, but the years had worn him down and taken his confidence. How tragic life was for some. How very tragic! I shuddered and, shaking my head, remembered my new bow. With the bounce back in my step I climbed the hill.

It wasn't until I'd reached the churchhouse that I remembered my music folder. I had left it in Charlie's store.

Delores wasn't at the practice.

"I wonder if *she* gave prior notice," Phyliss whispered as Shirley took the roll.

Mark didn't come in from his office off the foyer until eight-fifty. He strode through the oak doors briskly, took up the baton, and began the rehearsal without a word of explanation for his unusually late entry.

"He's never been late before," Laurie whispered. "I wonder if Delores's absence has something to do with it."

"I don't see how it could." I shrugged, and she looked at me with an expression I could only guess at. Sympathy? Pity? I wondered why.

The three of us, Laurie, Shirley Green, and I, carried the soprano part well that night, and I sat in my seat with an easiness I hadn't felt with Delores there.

Throughout the practice I smiled down at Mark, remembering the hike and the moments by the dying fire. Surely he thought of it too, and as the rehearsal progressed, I noticed with growing pleasure that his eyes kept finding our section. He was attracted to me. I knew it, and the knowledge bubbled and swelled inside me.

During the break Phyliss and I slipped outside and sat on the steps. Crickets chirped in the warm night, and below us, the windows of the little houses had begun to glow. I could hardly wait to tell her about the hike—about the kiss on the mountain and the moment by the fire. But she immediately began to tell me about her interview.

"I think I've got it. Superintendent Anderson is sure they'll place me in Mendon."

"You, a teacher!" I laughed. "You deserve it after all the misery you gave Miss Carroll."

Phyliss primped her mouth. "I saw that, young man. In the corner with you this instant! And I promise you'll not have a recess this week. Hah, hah, hah!" Her eyes narrowed to slits, and she made her head tremble violently. I thought uneasily how very like the spinster, Miss Carroll, Phyliss had looked just then.

She laughed. "Convincing, yes?"

"Very. Don't let it become real. I couldn't bear to think of you like that."

"Maybe that's me already. Who knows?"

116

"Don't be morbid. You *are* happy about this job, aren't you?"

She got to her feet. "Why shouldn't I be?"

Following the practice I took my time leaving the chapel. I hoped that Mark would want to talk with me, but as always, he was surrounded with girls and questions, and so, not wanting to feel conspicuous, I left. He'd be sorry to see me go, but, of course, I had no choice.

It was Peter in the buggy. As I approached he climbed down and came around to help me in.

"Yellow." He smiled at my dress. "My favorite."

Sunday was always the special day of the week at home. The Lord's day—the Sabbath, when Papa wore his white shirt all day long. It was a day when we could nap or read or visit at will. The baking was done on Saturday, and for the entire weekend the house was filled with delicious smells— roast beef or pork, baked chicken or ham, pies, cakes, puddings.

Each Sunday morning we took both the buggy and the rig into town. Because Papa, Peter, and Raymond had priesthood meeting before Sunday School, they'd go early in the buggy. Later the rest of us would take the wagon. Papa had built a little bench that fit into the wagonbed and converted it into a carriage of sorts.

"What we need is a proper spring carriage," Papa often said. "Next year maybe. When the potato crop comes in." But we never bought one. The wagon worked fine.

Each Sunday evening all the family rode into sacrament meeting together. And during the lovely summer months, this was my favorite part of Sunday—waving to other families as we rode and listening to Papa tell about his early days in the valley and how it had all looked then.

But this particular Sunday evening it was Peter who talked as we rode. He sat on the wagon bench with the children, and as he spoke, I marveled at how little any of us really knew of his past and his life outside our valley.

"When I was eighteen I got myself a job with the railroad," Peter began. "They didn't pay me much, but they did give me a free pass now and then, and on my days off, I'd ride the line as far as I could go and still get back for work the next day."

"You rode the trains?" Katy climbed over Raymond to sit at Peter's side.

"I rode the long ones." He smiled at her.

"Chooooo wooooo, choooooo wooooo," Margaret called to the passing view. "Let's pretend we're a train."

"Hey!" Raymond clapped a hand over her mouth. "Let him finish. Go on, Peter."

"Well, one time while riding the train north, I met a man. He was the kind of person I wouldn't normally have had anything to do with. But I had this impulse to try and talk to him, and so I did. I found that his name was Stephen Caine, and that he'd left his wife and children with the intention of never going back to them." Peter paused. "He's going to speak to us in meeting tonight."

"*This* Stephen Caine?" Mama asked over her shoulder.

"The same."

Stephen Caine leaned low over the pulpit. His shoulder and head swayed as he spoke. His story was so fascinating that every time his fist came down with a thud on his Bible, there was a resounding silence. Even the children kept still.

"It's not often you find a man of his years with such spiritual strength." He was talking about his conversion years ago through Peter. "Because this lad, then only eighteen, cared enough to stop—stop and share the gospel, he gave me—and my family—a new life. We'll be forever grateful. You see, brothers and sisters, I'd lost sight of everything." His heavy voice broke. "I was no longer any kind of a provider, and if you can believe it, I loved the bottle more than I loved my family or my sweet wife. I was a drunkard!'' His fist came down again. ''I lived to drink.''

Several people breathed soft exclamations behind me. Katy put one of her braids into her mouth.

Brother Caine's voice went on. ''You know, I tremble to think where I'd be today if Peter hadn't straightened me up.'' There was a long, uncomfortable moment when he pulled a handkerchief from his vest pocket and dabbed at his eyes. ''I . . . I hope—'' his eyes caught mine, ''you appreciate him.''

There was a marked hush as he closed and then moved from the pulpit to his chair by his wife. How moving it had been. Beside me, Mama wiped her eyes, while I found myself trying to swallow the emotion that had risen in my own throat. I glanced over at Peter, who sat at the end of the row holding Tyler in his lap. Though I couldn't see his eyes, I imagined they held the image of his friend with remembered sorrow and compassion.

Following the meeting, the family scattered and stood about the lawns talking to their friends. A large group had gathered around Peter and Brother Caine. I noticed, as I approached, how many of them were girls—attractive girls. Karen Sorenson hung at Peter's side. The Green twins pressed timidly forward to shake his hand, and behind them Delores and her younger sister, Debra, waited.

How tall he stood among them! How manly he was! I thought of the kiss he'd given me, and excitement surged through every vein. Forgetting that I'd ever disliked it, I edged my way to his elbow.

''Peter.'' I barely touched his arm, and his eyes left the faces of the crowd and found mine. ''Peter, we're ready to go home.'' I smiled up at him.

But he didn't smile back. Instead his brows arched curiously, and I felt my face growing warm. I grinned stupidly at the crowd around us, suddenly desperate. But then Peter smiled and took my hand in his. Envious eyes were watching.

''I've got a meeting with the elders quorum presidency.

Brother Thomas said he'd drive me home. Tell your pa to go without me."

"Fine." I dropped my eyes as I'd seen Delores do so many times with Mark. "See you at home?" He nodded, and I worked out of the circle of people and toward our wagon.

"Anne!" Phyliss crossed the lawn, dodging groups as she came. "Anne!" She stopped in front of me breathless. "Mr. Staaton's hunting you. I just heard him ask Laurie if she'd seen you."

"Oh?"

"I wonder what it's about!"

"I don't know." Another surge of excitement rushed through me. How nice it was to have *two* suitors.

"He's been acting strangely lately. I noticed he didn't sit with any of the Ashleys today." Phyliss gave me her most conspiratorial look. "I think they've had a spat, those two, and from what I hear he's moved out and things are—," she rocked her head from side to side, "a little shaky right now."

"He's left Rachael's house?"

"That's what I hear. Remember last night how his eyes kept shifting to Delores's seat?"

"I didn't—"

"Well, take my word for it, they did! He was looking over there all night long. Some of the others noticed it too."

But he was looking at me, I wanted to shout at her. *Me!* As I opened my mouth to speak, I saw him coming across the grass toward us.

"Shhhh, he's coming."

"Maybe you'd better brace yourself, Anne. He might have bad news for you. I'll see you later." She melted into the throngs of people. Bad news? How silly Phyliss was. But of course she knew nothing about the hike.

"There you are." He smiled down at me, and I was again taken back with his striking good looks—the strong squareness of his jaw, and his dark eyes, which swept over me with open approval.

"Hello." I put my hand out to him.

"Good evening, Anne." He took my hand between both of his, and had he put it to his lips I wouldn't have been a bit surprised.

"You seem to have needed no recovery from the hike."

"I feel lovely!"

He tipped his head to one side, surveying me. "You look it, too!" He winked and laughed as I blushed. "I have something for you." He pulled my music folder from under his arm. "I think this is yours."

"But where did you find it?"

A broad smile spread across his face. "I found it on my *bed* last night!"

"Well, *I* certainly didn't leave it there. The last time I had it was in Charlie's store. Perhaps Charlie found it and gave it to Sister Ashley and she put it there."

"More probably Charlie put it there himself."

I thought that was rather unlikely. Charlie's store was a good two miles from Rachael's home. "Well, I guess it doesn't really matter who put it there, does it?" I laughed again. "The important thing is I have it back." And as I spoke I remembered Phyliss's remark about his having moved out of the Ashley home.

"You're frowning. Something wrong?"

"They haven't made you move, have they? Just for taking Delores on that hike?"

"I wouldn't put it that way exactly."

"But you've left."

"Yes, it was a good opportunity. I sleep behind Brinton's store."

"You're not the clerk!"

He laughed and inclined his head. "What would you like today, madame? Needles? Thread?"

"And you sleep on that dreadful cot? Where do you eat?"

"Mrs. Brinton brings me my meals."

"Oh," I hugged the folder to me, "I'm so sorry, Mark."

"Don't be. She's a good cook."

"You know what I mean. It's my fault. If you hadn't gone with me to find Raymond, it wouldn't have happened, would it?"

"Things were awkward anyhow, but I guess the hike did bring everything to a head."

"Then it *is* my fault. I'll have to explain to Rachael."

He put up a hand. "Don't! I'd hate to wring your pretty neck. I *like* my independence, and believe me," he rubbed his jaw, "life's been a lot simpler since I moved out."

"Oh?"

But Mark had no intention of explaining further. He simply stood leaning over me, his hand propped against the tree at my back.

I realized that I had seen him stand just this way with Delores in the chapel. As he looked down at me with an enchanting expression on his face, I had the strongest urge to put my hand to his forehead and push back the tumble of locks that perpetually found their way there. But not being Delores, I smiled lamely instead. "Well, thank you for returning this."

"You're very welcome, Anne." His eyes danced as if a thought had just come into his mind that he enjoyed very much. And I was certain he was about to say something when he glanced up and his hand came abruptly off the tree. "I think," he coughed, "that your family's waiting for you. Your little brother's waving at us."

Raymond came running and hollering over the lawn. "Anne, why don't you come? The whole family's loaded and waitin'." He waved his arms furiously, a scowl on his face.

"In a minute, Raymond."

"All right, but we're leaving, Anne or no Anne."

"You'd better go." Mark took my arm.

If I hadn't been so happy—so thrilled, I would have bitten Raymond's head off for ruining that perfectly idyllic moment. But since I could scarcely breathe with the happiness I was feeling as Mark walked me to the wagon, I forgot my anger immediately. Life had never looked so beautiful!

Mark handed me up into the wagon, apologizing for keeping everyone waiting, and, with a polite nod to me, was gone. Phyliss would never believe it, and I doubted if I'd even want to tell her about it.

Raymond heaved himself into the rig next to the younger children. "That's everybody."

"Peter's got a meeting tonight. We can go without him," I sighed.

"Yes, dear, we've known that for sometime." Mama smiled. "All right, Bill, let's go."

"Wasn't it the most wonderful meeting tonight!" I threw my arms over my head and folded them there.

"It certainly was." Papa was thoughtful. "Every day I learn something good about that boy. I'm proud to have Peter with us."

As the horses hurried down the darkening road of the hill I began to sing a hymn and the family joined me.

"Our mountain home so dear,
Where crystal waters clear
Flow ever free,
Flow ever free . . . "

And as our voices rose to part the hush of the coming night, I turned to see a tall, square-shouldered figure move out from the shadows and stand in the street watching after us.

ELEVEN

"Look who just walked in." Laurie gave me a gentle nudge. "I don't know how she kept away this long."

Rachael. She'd come to hear us rehearse, now that the concert date was so near. And to hear me sing the solo her granddaughter should have had, I thought with a jolt. I took a deep breath and let it out in a steady slow stream. I was not going to worry. There was *nothing* to worry about. I'd sing as I always had.

And after I had sung my solo that night, Rachael smiled, seeming pleased. "You have a sweet voice, child."

She said nothing else to me, but I was thrilled with her comment and immensely relieved. I half laughed as I rode home with Peter. "You know, I actually thought she'd take the solo away from me." I laughed again, feeling prickly beads of moisture breaking along my forehead. "I really thought she would."

That Wednesday was the final practice before the dress rehearsal Friday. The concert was scheduled now for Tuesday evening, the third of July. Again Rachael came to hear us rehearse.

"Our concert will launch all the other festivities for the

Fourth," Rachael said from her chair just behind Mark's podium. "How flattered we should feel that we have been selected by the committee for that spot." Her high, sallow cheekbones had been dusted lightly with color, and I noticed that when she spoke of the choir, her eyes took on new luster.

One had to admire Rachael. She would never stop kicking—not till they buried her.

"The presidency will be pleased to hear that our flag is ready for us. We need only to pick it up. You other girls might be interested to know that it was especially made for us and is a good deal larger than the flag we've been using in past years. We've decided to hang it as a backdrop behind the soprano sections. I am told it is very elegant, befitting a choir such as ours." She paused for a long moment, then drew herself to her feet, her face breaking into smiles. "Girls," she said, taking a lace hankie from her belt as emotion rose in her throat, "*dear* girls, may I tell you that if Johnathan were with us today, he'd be proud. You do his name honor." She gave us a slight smile. "Shirley now has some points of business to discuss. Shirley?" With that she eased back into her chair.

I was certain Shirley would say something about my fabric not arriving, but after a tedious list of announcements she said nothing. Perhaps Rachael didn't mind after all.

The practice proceeded as usual. Mark took us from one number to the next without pause, and after each, Rachael nodded her satisfaction. When it came time for my solo, I sang easily, and after the strains had died out in the old hall I turned to make my way back to my seat. Mark smiled at me and I knew I had sung it well.

"No, don't go yet, Miss Carrow," Rachael said.

"Yes?"

"I want to hear it again."

"Again?" I looked from her to Mark. He sat back on the front row of benches almost as if he'd expected this and nodded for me to comply.

I took my place once more and began to sing it again,

but I'd barely started when Rachael cut in. "Miss Carrow," she shook her head at me, "do you *like* the song?"

The interruption so unnerved me that I found it impossible to look at her. "Yes," I said, running my hand along the wooden railing at my side, "very much."

"Well, then," she drew a slow breath, straining to keep her patience, "you must tell us so in your voice."

I nodded. But of course it was already in my voice. I felt this song as I never had before. Surely she knew that. I looked toward Mark, but his eyes had found the ceiling. He grimaced, annoyed at the delay.

"Are you saying I'm not putting feeling into the piece, Sister Ashley?"

"I'm not denying your efforts, my child, but I am compelled to tell you I'm not happy with your solo—as it is. This isn't a Sunday School song—it's a sophisticated piece. Try and sing it that way."

Her words cut. How did she think I was singing it—like some child? I looked over at the pianist. She gave me a quick smile, and I thought of the girls behind me. Surely they were all sorry too, except maybe one.

I sang it again. But though I tried to sing with feeling, there was none in me, and my voice came to my ears sounding cold and harsh.

Rachael left her chair and walked to the banister below me. "You're very nervous, aren't you." She made a quick appraisal of my trembling hands, the stiffness in my lips.

"Please." I despised the tremor in my voice. "I—I was nervous that time—but the other times were good."

"I assure you," she touched my hand, "if you are nervous with an audience of two, you shall be quite unable to manage yourself with one of two hundred or more. Now, do you think you can get ahold of yourself and sing it again?"

She crossed back to her chair, and as the piano began again she wagged a finger. "We're all friends here, Miss Carrow. It's only perfection we're after."

I closed my eyes as I sang. I tried to relax, to sing as I did in the fields at home, but there Papa smiled and the valley listened with love. Here an old woman with tight lips waited for failure, and my friend Mark was far away.

As I finished, Rachael's severe expression burned the phrase "pearls before swine" into my mind.

Rachael was speaking again but I no longer cared. I sank into my chair, tears aching in my throat. Laurie's hand found mine.

"Hang on, honey," she whispered.

"Your final lines were nearly inaudible," Rachael's voice at last penetrated. "One more time and I think—"

"That's quite enough, Mrs. Ashley." Mark spoke at last. But his voice was unfamiliar. *I didn't know him anymore. I've never known him.* I held my lips together and fought the tears that seemed so bent on coming. *Show him you don't care. Show him it doesn't hurt.* But I hurt so much I wanted to die.

Someone gave the closing prayer and then there were several more announcements. But I didn't hear any of it.

"Well, it's clear she wants Delores in the solo spot," Phyliss whispered as we moved to the door. "To tell you the truth, I thought Mark was going to tell you that Sunday. You see, I've heard that—"

"Please, Phyl, I'll see you later, okay?" I hurried through the group of girls standing at the door, and as my hot face met the cool night I heard Mark's voice behind me.

"Anne, wait! I want to talk to you, Anne," his tone brooked no argument, "over here!"

I moved on through the darkness and climbed into the buggy beside Peter. It wasn't until we had left the hill a good distance behind us, and Peter asked if I might like to look at the land he'd selected, that I started to cry.

TWELVE

"I'm quitting the choir," I told Mama the next morning. I had said the same thing on going to bed the night before and she had told me to sleep on it.

"Say your prayers and tomorrow you'll feel differently, dear."

But I didn't, and I told her so as we finished the breakfast dishes.

"You're taking it all too personal. It's likely that Rachael would behave the same to anyone in your place."

"I don't care about her. It has nothing to do with that."

Mama gave me a squeeze. "Of course it has, Anne. You felt very different yesterday before going to practice."

"Last night only opened my eyes. I don't fit in. You and Papa were right all along. I shouldn't have joined."

"It's your decision. But I do think it would be better to resign when you felt better about it. You'll remember your time in the choir now as a bad experience."

"That's just how I want to remember it," I said. "I'm going up to my room."

Later she came up with a bowl of fresh strawberries. "Thought you might like some." I took the bowl not because I especially wanted to, but because Mama would be hurt if I didn't. "Anne," she began as I ate, "don't you think you're being a little hard on them? Delores and

Rachael have been especially close since Delight died . . .''

"Mama—please. I'm not being hard on anyone. They both behaved exactly as they always have." (It had been Mark's behavior that surprised me. I pushed that thought away.) "You know, I knew it was coming. I couldn't figure it out the other night when Rachael was so nice. 'A sweet voice,' she said. It wasn't meant as a compliment at all."

Mama shook her head. "I hate you to feel like this." She sat on the edge of my bed and watched me finish the strawberries. "Why don't you ride down to the baby's grave with me? We haven't done it for such a long time."

And again, because she was trying to make me feel better, I gave in and went.

The early morning sun made soft lights in the quivering cottonwoods and poplars along the road and cast long, stretching shadows behind them, over the white lane and green fields. We passed the Miller houses and waved at Maud and Leela, first and second wives to Jared Miller, each carrying water from the one pump that stood between the two houses. And turning there, we began winding our way up the steep rise toward the graveyard.

"Anne, you don't remember Delores's mother, Delight Ashley, do you?"

"Mama, please, let's not talk about them anymore."

"Just let me say this. Delores means a great deal to Rachael, and not just because she's her granddaughter or because Rachael has taken care of the younger Ashley girls for so many years. There is something special between those two. Delores looks so much like Rachael did when she was younger. The resemblance is still there even though Rachael's an old woman now. Her beauty and her voice have slipped from her; the romance and prestige she knew in the early days have gone. But through Delores, she can see herself, Anne, and she can—in a way—live it all again."

It was true, but even so, I couldn't bring myself to feel

sorry for Rachael. She'd had a full life and should be content to grow old with dignity as Grandmother Carrow had done.

We gained the top of the hill, and our buggy swung onto somewhat level ground and lurched to a stop at the gate.

The long grasses blew over the wild, unkept cemetery. The spring flowers had blossomed and died on their stalks, and weedy morning glory had spread over a good many of the headstones so thick the names were no longer visible.

"I hate to see it like this," I said as we crossed to the Carrow plot where Papa's parents and the baby were buried.

"I'd rather have it overly wild than overly manicured," Mama said. "I like it natural."

I thought about that and finally decided I agreed with her. Here, these graves were still a part of the living hills, the surroundings like those these people had known and loved in life.

"Richard John," Mother said aloud as she placed a small bouquet of snapdragons on the mound. "He'd be fourteen." She stood looking down at the little headstone for some time. At last she straightened herself and we walked back to the buggy.

By the time Mama pulled Dandy to a stop in front of the barn I'd reached a decision.

"Mama, may I take the buggy into town?"

Her eyes smiled into mine. "You're a good girl, Anne."

I changed into the pink dress with the ruffles at the neck and, after brushing my hair until it shone, began to tie the new pink ribbon in what I thought was a very stylish bow. But even as I finished, I was tugging it from my hair again. A bow wouldn't do for today. I had to look all of my nearly eighteen years.

As I headed Dandy back down the lane, the heaviness I'd carried since the practice retreated, and in its place I began to feel a curious kind of peace.

130

Thirty minutes later, I drew the horse to a stop in front of Charlie's store.

"Charlie," I called as I entered. "Hello, Charlie?" It seemed especially dark inside, a sharp contrast to the brightness of the street.

"Anne." I stiffened at the voice. His tall frame came into focus as my eyes adjusted to the dimness. Though he was wearing work clothes, he hardly looked the part of a store clerk.

"Is Charlie here?" I looked hard at the candy jars, amazed at the steadiness of my voice.

He came from behind the counter. "No, no, he isn't." After a long pause he added with a smile, "But *I* could help you, Anne."

"No," I heard myself saying. "Thank you, but I need to talk with Charlie."

He nodded, the smile gone. I started for the door and was nearly through it when Mark's voice came again.

"Is it about the cloth for your choir dress?"

"Yes." I turned, trying hard to keep the desperation from showing. "Has it come?"

"I'm sorry—no."

The Ashley home stood on a hill about two miles east of the churchhouse. It was a large, three-story house, built of gray stone. Though it wasn't a mansion, it was by far the largest home in the valley, and only while riding the electric streetcars in Ogden or going down South Temple in Salt Lake City had I ever seen finer homes. There was a large circular drive in front, and the drive from the gate to the house was cobbled with rocks similar to those in the walls of the house. I pulled Dandy up and climbed from the buggy, hesitating only for a breath before dropping the heavy knocker on the tall front doors.

An hour after supper dishes that same evening the family and Peter gathered in the front room to hear Papa read from the Book of Mormon. He chose Alma, and as the ancient lines fell from his lips I sat a little straighter in my seat knowing I had done the right thing by seeing Rachael.

The words of Alma burned into my mind as they never had before: "For they saw and beheld with great sorrow that the people of the church began to be lifted up in the pride of their eyes, and to set their hearts upon riches and upon the vain things of the world, that they began to be scornful, one towards another. . . ."

Vain things of the world, scornful, one towards another. I shifted a little and felt Peter's eyes on me. I smiled across the small room and he smiled back. Papa's resonant voice went on. "And thus ended the eighth year of the reign of the judges; and the wickedness of the church was a great stumbling-block to those who did not belong to the church; and thus the church began to fail in its progress."

Yes, I had done right. I reminded myself of the resolve I'd made as I brought the buggy home that morning. I would not feel sorry for myself, nor would I regret a righteous act.

At length Papa closed the book, saying he'd save chapter five for another night. "Now before prayers, let's make a duet, shall we, Annie?" His eyes shone with his love of music.

I crossed to the piano and, taking up the hymnbook, asked what we should sing.

"Do 'Come, Come Ye Saints'!" Mama suggested. "Katy's been practicing it." She added this quite needlessly, for we hadn't heard anything else from Katy the past week.

"Fine, honey," Papa said as he stood at my side. "That is—if we can get Katy to accompany us."

"Oh, yes, Papa!" Katy's face widened in a smile as she flew to the piano bench. "Now wait for my introduction. I've worked out a new one." She began in a flurry of wrong notes, which brought out large red blotches on the back of her neck. But as she labored over the keyboard the song was at last discernible, and she nodded for Papa and me to join her.

Papa's rich voice blended with mine, and our little family, smiling up at us, listened, knowing each word as they knew each other.

"Come, come, ye Saints, no toil nor labor fear;
But with joy wend your way.
Though hard to you this journey may appear,
Grace shall be as your day.
'Tis better far for us to strive
Our useless cares from us to drive;
Do this, and joy your hearts will swell—
All is well! All is well!"

Our voices fell and Katy finished with the arpeggio she used to end any song she particularly liked.

"Raymond," Papa crossed to Mama's side, "would you pray tonight?" We knelt for family prayer as we had done every morning and evening of my life.

"Anne," Peter called as I followed the family upstairs to bed. "It's early yet. Come out and let's sit a while." He smiled. "There's a moon."

We sat in two kitchen chairs Peter had placed on the porch, and after asking me to the Fourth of July dance (I accepted), he leaned back contentedly in his chair and began to talk about his plans to be a big cattle raiser someday.

"Of course, your Pa does fine, but the growing season here isn't always long enough, and with cattle—well, a person would be on steadier ground."

He went on to talk about the land he was set on buying and of how Papa had approved of his decision.

The moon made soft silver trails across the high, scattered clouds, and the warm wind danced around us as we spoke, brushing the trees above the house, swaying the delphinium at our feet, and lifting a strand of my hair so that it occasionally swept across my eyes. I reached to pull back the straying lock and tuck it behind my ear, but Peter did it for me, his eyes gazing into mine. I settled back against the hollow of his shoulder and closed my eyes.

It was high time I accepted things as they were. Dreams were just that—dreams—empty, vain illusions that kept one from finding happiness if he weren't careful. The pioneer hymn sounded in my ears. " 'Tis better far for us to strive our useless cares from us to drive . . ."

THIRTEEN

Peter drove me to the dress rehearsal Friday evening, and as he helped me from the buggy, he kissed me.

"You get prettier every day."

I smiled at the compliment and hurried from him up the side steps into the churchhouse.

"Well—," Phyliss began as I met her in the hall, "so it's gone that far, has it?"

"Hi, Phyl."

"Don't evade me," she scolded.

"What are you talking about?"

"I saw you out there *kissing Peter*." She bit on her lip. "So that's how the wind blows, is it?"

"Yes," I said evenly, realizing that Mark's door was open and he, standing just inside, had heard Phyliss's comments. "That's how the wind blows."

We went through the program that night just as we would Tuesday evening at the concert. Rachael sat in her chair interrupting only occasionally with brief comments like "Remember to enunciate, girls," or "You're all just singing words—I want you to *feel* them as well."

The evening wore on and finally it was time for the solo.

Mark nodded to me, and as he did so Rachael left her chair to say something quietly at his side. It was evident she hadn't told him about the change as she had promised me she would do, and as she spoke, his eyes darted to mine and his face reddened in anger. He said something then to Rachael and she shook her head in disagreement.

"What's wrong?" Laurie whispered. "Why don't you go up?"

"There's been a slight change in the program," I said.

"Shirley," Mark's voice cut across the sudden stir. "take care of the closing prayer and announcements. We'll call it a night right now. I want to see Anne and Delores in the music library." Rachael followed Mark from the room, her chin a little too high, and as Delores and I got to our feet to leave, questions rang out from the others.

"What's happening?"

"Why are we quitting so early?"

"Is something wrong?"

Delores left without reply, and I thought it best to follow her example. We found Mark and Rachael in the small room off the foyer. Mark closed the door after us.

"So you've resigned! Given up, have you?"

"I haven't exactly resigned—," I began, but Rachael answered for me.

"She hasn't resigned from the choir, Mark—only from the solo, and I think it was a magnanimous gesture under the circumstances."

"Under *what* circumstances?"

"She has no costume and she's not ready."

"Oh, but she is ready! She does the solo magnificently. She has an unusually mature quality, and you *know* it."

"I will not argue with you further about this. We've been through it enough. She's simply not ready."

I felt the old humiliation turn me sick inside. *Not ready.* I would never be ready to sing this solo, nor would I ever sing alone for Rachael or Mark again. They would not be able to hurt that part of me a second time. I stiffened against the door and lowered my eyes as they talked as if I weren't even there.

"I'm the *director* here," he said in a calm voice but with fury in his words. "I cannot conduct your choir if I am to be countermanded on every decision."

"You knew before coming that Delores was to be given this solo."

"Grandmother, please—" Delores clutched timidly at Rachael's sleeve.

"Hush, Delores. I made that clear in my letter."

"And I made it clear that if I came I was to have free rein." Mark threw up a hand, his tone sharpening in warning.

"I have given you that!" Rachael's faded eyes brushed over me. "You've flouted all my rules and my wishes. To give an inexperienced child the Ashley solo—"

"She's obviously no child, and she earned the solo."

"Ah, yes." Rachael laughed. "I know all about your trumped-up audition. Delores didn't even try out."

"*She could have.*" His mouth tightened.

"Grandmother," Delores began again, "you know I declined the audition."

"Just as *I* would have done in your place. How disgusting—to audition for a solo that is rightfully yours!"

"Sister Ashley is right," I spoke at last, and three pairs of eyes looked to me with surprise. "The solo is Delores's. It's tradition for an Ashley to sing it."

Mark's eyes smoldered in his handsome face, and lines of bitter amusement played about his mouth.

"How ironic that you should side against yourself!"

"She's being sensible," Rachael said. "She's lived here all her life, and she knows how my choir is run."

"You were perfectly free to run your choir any way you liked, but when you hired me that changed. You seem to forget that *I'm* paid to run it now."

"You're both forgetting that I have no dress to wear Tuesday," I said. "That settles everything, doesn't it?"

"Yes." Rachael gave me a genuine smile for solving her problem. "You certainly can't sing unless you're in costume. You really are a very sweet girl, Anne."

"That rule is a lot of nonsense," Mark sighed, shaking his head.

"You call it nonsense simply because it doesn't suit your plans at present. But if you'd gone through years with this choir—"

"There's no need to continue," I cut in, knowing that if they didn't stop I would disgrace myself with tears. "I don't want the solo. I wouldn't have given it up if I'd wanted it." As I spoke, I knew it was true. What it had once meant, it couldn't mean again. I looked at Mark, and instead of seeing the relief I'd hoped, his eyes flashed and hardened on me. He had no intention of letting me out of it to placate anyone. "Well," I said in response to his glare, "I won't sing it—I won't!"

"If you didn't want it, why did you accept it? Well? Why did you accept it? Answer, Anne!"

My cheeks flushed. How unfair of him to ask that with these two watching. He knew how much I'd wanted the solo. But as Mama implied, it meant much more to Rachael than it ever would to me. I looked from the impatience in Rachael's face to the dislike in Delores's.

"Well?"

My control snapped. "Because I'd always dreamed of soloing in this stupid little choir." It was out before I'd realized it. I glanced at Rachael as my conscience was pricked, but the comment had not fazed her in the least. She simply wanted me out of the solo spot, and if this was the way I chose to help her accomplish it, that was fine with her. "But it isn't important to me anymore. I won't fight over it!" I fumbled at the doorknob, and as I did so Mark's hand brought me back around.

"I'm not asking you to fight for it. *Just don't give up on me.* I'm asking you to recognize *me* as the director here and to heed my wishes. If you were serious about declining you should have come to me—don't interrupt," he put up a hand to stop Rachael, "and you should have spoken *sooner*. As it is, you *must* sing. It's too late to make changes!"

"Delores knows the—"

"I said, don't interrupt!" he exploded. "Now," he calmed himself again, "I'm depending on you, Anne. Will you stick this out?"

"*I'm not ready*," I cried, my eyes filling with tears. "Please leave it alone."

"Anne, you *are* ready."

I shook my head and tried to tuck the humiliating tears back into the corners from which they had sprung. "Why are you so insistent about having *me* sing? It's just making a lot of trouble for everyone."

"Because," Delores answered quietly, gazing at the floor in front of her, "he'd rather anyone sang it but me."

"Oh, Delores," Mark groaned.

"Well, it's true, Mark. You can't deny that you've fought Grandmother and me all the way."

"I shouldn't have had to fight you. I was brought here to do a job, and as long as I'm in this position—," he brought his eyes back to me, "I will do whatever is best for the choir."

"*We* only want what's best for the choir."

"Then I assure you, Delores, it's best that Anne sings."

"If that were true—"

"It is!" Mark bit off the exclamation he'd been about to make. Then, shaking his head tiredly, he added, "You can't run a choir to show off a family."

Rachael, sitting on a small wooden chair in the corner, brought herself up. "*Young man*," she began hotly. But Delores cut through the indignant voice.

"Then I don't mind, Mark." She reached out to touch his arm with an air of apology. "If *you* feel it's best, I don't mind."

"Now, Delores." Rachael left her corner.

"Grandmother, I want you to drop it. It's ruined for me anyhow. The solo is hers. I wouldn't touch it now."

Rachael gave a sigh of defeat. "Yes, I'd feel the same in

your place, I'm sure. But—,'' she turned to Mark, her voice rising, ''I insist she have a dress, Mark—the color of the others at least. You will not budge me from that decision.'' With that, she swept past me out of the room.

Delores started after her, then paused midway and said, ''If it hadn't meant so very much to Grandmother, I wouldn't have let you give it back to me in the first place.'' She managed a little smile and was gone as well.

So it had happened anyway. Despite my good intentions, it had all come crashing down on my head, and the now hated solo had been presented back to me. I had won, and yet I was the loser here. *Mama*, I wondered silently, *what do I do now?* But her answer didn't come, and I doubted that even she would have one to give.

Mark ran a hand through his hair, his eyes studying the shelf of music he faced.

''Peter will be waiting. I'd better go,'' I mumbled, starting for the door. I was angry with Mark and yet strangely sorry for him too.

''But you will sing it?'' His voice was dry—even curt.

''I don't know,'' I said, not looking at him. ''I would rather you'd left things as they were.''

He nodded, and I left him there alone in the little room.

FOURTEEN

Mama called up to me Monday evening. "You have a visitor, Anne." The door to my room opened and she smiled. "It's Mark Staaton."

"I don't know what to tell him."

"That you'll sing, of course." She picked up my brush from my dressing table and began pulling it through my hair. "You have a dress to wear now, and so there's no reason to make further trouble."

"That dress—," I began hotly.

"It will do fine." I glanced at the closet door where it hung limp and sagging. It had belonged to Vinnie Bacon.

"Ugh," I groaned as I thought of the horrible way it fit me—riding up on the waist and pulling at the shoulders. My eye scanned the faded line that encircled the skirt where we'd let down the hem.

Mama laughed. "It's not that bad, dear. Besides, you have to go through with it. If you don't, what will Mr. Staaton do?"

"He can go to Delores!"

"You know he can't, and anyhow, she wouldn't sing it —not now. She's been injured."

"*I've been injured.*"

"Yes, you have, but *you* know your responsibility to

others." She handed me the brush. "Why don't you change your dress and I'll tell him you'll be right down."

Mama had seated Mark in the front room and ushered the family into the kitchen. As I came down the stairs, I found her and Papa talking in the hall just outside the closed front room door.

"Well, there she is," Papa began.

"You just go have your talk now—," Mama put a hand on Papa's arm, "and I'll see to it you're not disturbed." She gave me her proud-of-her-daughter smile and hurried Papa away with her into the kitchen.

Mark rose as I entered. I thought he looked a little uneasy, and I was glad.

"Hello," I said, trying a wide smile on him.

"Hello, Anne." He took my outstretched hand.

As I read the steady confidence in his eyes that so very clearly had never left him, my heart began to race. The room grew instantly warm, and the wide smile began to crack on my lips, as I realized I hadn't the slightest notion of what to say to him. He made no effort to help me, and my mind floundered wildly for anything—any shred of any conversation. But nothing came. I knew only that Mark Staaton had some curious power over me that I loved and dreaded at the same time.

The lights of the lamps danced in his eyes, as he sat me beside him on the couch. I leaned back stiffly and stared at him, resenting his sureness with me and yet unable to do anything about it.

"I hope you've decided to do the solo." He paused, and when I said nothing in response, he went on. "It's regrettable that you've had to be in the middle of this thing between Rachael and me, and you most likely think I care more for having my way than for your feelings." He stopped again and waited for a comment from me. And when again I didn't speak, he dropped my hand and walked over to a table by the door. He picked up a large box and, coming back to sit beside me, put it in his lap. His lips compressed momentarily.

142

"I suppose I could have let things alone," he said, staring angrily at the box, "but I couldn't let her pull something like that. It isn't good for Rachael, Delores, or the choir, and most of all—when you'd worked so hard on that difficult solo..." His voice trailed off. "Open it." He pushed the box to me. "It's for you."

I looked from the package to Mark.

"Well, open it!"

"I—I don't want to," I said, at last finding my voice. I certainly hadn't expected a gift. It made me feel guilty, and I couldn't think of one reason in the world why I should. All I had wanted to do since my visit to the Ashley home was to give the solo back and get out of a mess I had had no part in making. Mark's stare forced my eyes to the floor, and I said in a weak voice that wasn't without bitterness, "It really isn't necessary."

He took the box from me, tore off the string and brown paper, lifted the lid, and thrust it back on my lap.

"*Now I want you to have this.*" He then added as an afterthought, "*Please.*"

I looked down at the pale folds of tissue. "But what is it?"

"A dress—for you to wear tomorrow night."

A dress! A dress from Mark! But as I began to think with rising pleasure what a thoroughly improper gift such as this might mean, Rachael's one stipulation from which she would not budge sounded in my ears—"She must have a dress—the shade of the others at least—I insist on that!" Of course. The dress simply insured Mark's having his own way with Rachael.

"It's kind of you, but—"

"Look at it before you refuse it." He parted the tissue and spread over my lap the most beautiful dress I had ever seen. It wasn't of silk like the choir costume or even near the same cut. But it appeared to be the same shade of blue, and with the narrow bodice and full skirt, it was the most beautiful dress I'd ever seen. I couldn't help but gasp.

Mark laughed. "So you like it!"

I nodded, not looking at him. "I do, yes."

"Then it's settled?"

"I guess it is." I pressed the huge skirt back into the box. "I'll do the solo." Mark smiled, and it was evident that to him, anyway, the strain in our relationship had passed and we were good friends again. "But I couldn't accept such a gift. Papa wouldn't hear of it. He's very strict." I straightened up. "And besides, there's no need to give it. You see, I already have a dress." I smiled. "It belonged to Vinnie Bacon. It's lovely—," I thought of the hideous rag Vinnie had worn nearly six years, "and will be quite adequate for the concert, thank you." I handed him back the box.

"If you're going to turn it down, you can't do it for the reasons you've just given me." He leaned forward so that his eyes were very close to mine. "I've spoken with your folks just now. Your mother has told me all about the 'lovely,' " he inclined his head slightly on the word, "dress of Vinnie's and both she and your father feel that under the circumstances it would be very proper for you to accept my gift." He held the box out to me again with a smile.

I ignored the smile and, taking the box, got to my feet. Mark stood as well. "Since you're all so set on it then," I said, my head high, "I—I accept it." I extended him a stiff hand of farewell. "And thank you. It really is the most beautiful dress I have ever seen."

"How did he know your size?" Peter glared at me from the kitchen table where he sat with the checkerboard between him and Raymond.

Papa laughed. "You'd better get a move on, Peter. If you don't hurry, this Mark Staaton will sweep my little girl away and right from under your nose."

"Papa! I want it understood that Mark just brought me this dress so I could sing tomorrow. You know very well— you spoke with him about it yourself."

Papa laughed, shaking his head.

Katy came to finger the folds of the skirt. "It's the most beautiful dress I ever saw, Annie. Do you think I could wear something like this in the parade Wednesday?"

"Sure. We'll remake that lavender party dress of mine to look just like this." I tugged one of her braids.

"Now turn around and show them the back." Mama clapped her hands together. "Well, it's perfect, isn't it?"

Raymond gave a short, unenthusiastic whistle and went back to his game.

"I think the cut of that dress—," Papa winked, "may be a little too old for my Annie." He arched his brows at the scooped neckline.

"I'm eighteen this fall, Papa."

"All of eighteen?"

"Bill! It's a sophisticated dress, and not in the least immodest. It's very becoming."

"And very expensive," Peter said drily from the table.

"And very beautiful." Mama smiled, her eyes shining with approval. "Turn around once more, only slowly this time." As I did so, she clapped her hands again. "What a little waist she has! I don't remember *ever* looking like that."

Feeling sufficiently satisfied with the commotion I'd caused, I glided from the kitchen and paused at the long mirror in the hall. An attractive woman with warm dark hair and glistening eyes looked back at me. I gazed for a moment at the sleek-fitting bodice. Tomorrow I'd knock Mark dead with the sight of me and upset his casually confident demeanor forever. I turned away with a triumphant smile and, marveling that Papa should ever let me have such a dress, hurried up the stairs to my room.

FIFTEEN

Tuesday morning I was awakened by the gentle but persistent rattle of rain on my open window. I pulled myself from the warm bed and hurried across the cold floor to close it. The sky was shabby, the low clouds bleak and hazy through the rain. I stood for a moment shivering in the heavy air. Rain was always exhilarating, for when it rained something was happening—something dark and sinister—something terrible in the skies.

I leaned out to feel the moisture on my face, and as I did so, I saw Dell Blaven's old roan tied out front. It was probably much later than it looked if Dell had come to call. Soon Papa's voice would fetch me down to help start breakfast. I jerked the window shut and slipped guiltily back between the covers of my bed. Within minutes I was asleep again.

At breakfast Papa told us Dell and his family were leaving the valley for good.

"But why, Papa?"

"He can't make it here. This valley's just too cold for Margo and Connie, and now something's come up that's finished making his mind up for him." Papa looked up from us to Mama at the stove. "The past week Dell's been battling some kind of disease with his chickens. But he's losing bad. As of this morning more than half are dead. Doc

Sloan says he'll have to kill the others to keep it from spreading."

"There ought to be some way we can help, Bill."

"Emily, what else can we do?"

"Give him another loan. Maybe—"

Papa shook his head. "He's fighting a losing battle. He should get out while he can still make something on his place."

"If he leaves now, how will he get his alfalfa cut?" Peter tapped his fork against his glass. "Did he say?"

"I told him you and I would take care of it."

Peter gave me a quick look across the table. "That might not be too easy. We've got plenty enough to do here. Our own hay's due to be cut, and there are a few personal things I need to get done."

Papa's eyes flicked over the ceiling and back again. "I know very well, Peter. But we have to help. Dell's got to get moved and find work before cold weather starts. I'm afraid that could take some time—more time than he's got." He pushed his chair back from the table. "Now if you'll all excuse me, I think I'll ride over and take a look at those chickens myself."

The rest of us finished in silence, thinking of the shack squatting in the rain just through the fields from our warm kitchen.

After breakfast, while Peter brought in the water for the dishes, I put on a bonnet and shawl and walked out into the sleepy rain, through the willows along the creek, until I could see the back of the Blaven house huddling in the trees. I was sorry about their going. I'd miss them, the children especially, but things would never get better for them here. It was tragic to watch them struggle and lose so often. Maybe somewhere else they would win.

As I watched the cabin through the mist, it looked unfamiliar and not quite real—like an old painting with all the colors faded and mute. Grandmother Carrow had had such a painting hanging on her wall, and as a child I was at once drawn and repelled by it. I shivered and pulled the light shawl tighter around me. The whole scene was so depressing that I turned and, holding my wet skirts out of the damp growth, hurried back along the creek in the direction I'd come.

In the early afternoon the drizzle stopped and the clouds blew away from the sun so that the ground and fields dried somewhat. I stayed inside, helping Katy and Margaret with costumes for their parade the next day, and then, later on, Mama helped me fix my hair into a soft upsweep, copying the style from an attractive model in an old mail-order catalogue Charlie had let me have. It was stylish, like something girls would wear back East. Mama curled the stray ends at my nape and forehead so that when she had finished, I was sorry the girl in the picture didn't look like me.

Peter and I left for the concert early just in case we had trouble with the roads. Mama waved us off, saying the family would come soon after. I was relieved when, at last, I climbed into the buggy and we started down the long road toward town. My hair was fixed as I'd wanted it, the new dress pressed without incident, and despite the rainy weather, I was going to be on time. Now—if I could just sing well.

"That's certainly not the dress Vinnie wore." Phyliss's eyes widened as I met her on the side lawn of the church-house.

I laughed and twirled for her. "What do you honestly think, Phyl?"

"I honestly think I'm glad you won't be standing next to me tonight!"

"I look that good—really?"

"*Good* is not the word, my friend. Where did you find it?"

"Ogden." I smiled to myself. After all, where else would Mark have found such a dress? "A stroke of luck. When I've time I'll tell you all about it."

"Well, it suits you. You look rich—like one of the Ashley clan!"

"Oh, Phyliss, it isn't rich. It's just a *dress*."

"Hmmm." She touched her chin thoughtfully and I thought she had guessed, but she changed the subject. "You know, this is the last concert for me, and the first for you. Isn't it ironic? This is the last time we'll sing together."

"There'll be other times, I'm sure—other practices."

"No, not for me. We have three weeks' vacation after tonight, and I'll be gone."

"We don't have practice Friday?"

"I don't think you've been paying much attention lately. No more practices until the second week in August. So this is it for me."

"Well, you're right about my not paying attention. These practices haven't been much fun. I don't know if I want to stay in when you're gone."

"Of course you will."

I shook my head. With Phyliss gone I'd have only Laurie, and the way things were going with her and Wally, she might not stay long either. "I'm serious, Phyl. Isn't it strange how fast things change."

We went up the stairs and into the church. Inside, Shirley met me and her eyes widened at my dress and hair. "Nice, Anne. Really nice!" She handed us both a program, and as we moved on toward the classroom where we were supposed to wait, she called up to me to go immediately into the chapel. "Mr. Staaton's waiting for you. He wants to go over the solo."

He was standing in the empty chapel below the piano, arranging his music on his stand. He glanced up as I entered.

The expression on his face told me he liked me very well in his dress, and he made a slow perusal of me that caused my cheeks to burn and my pulses knocked crazily. But he said only, "I see it fits."

"Yes!" I turned for him and waited the lavish compliments everyone else had given me. "Perfectly."

He stared a minute longer, then abruptly his jaw contracted and he returned to his music. I stood watching him lay out the numbers piece by piece.

"Well," my annoyance surfaced at his lack of comment, "do you like it or not?"

"I bought it," he said, not looking up, as if that answered my question.

I flounced to the door. "Vinnie's dress is in the buggy," I lied, shooting a defiant look over my shoulder. "I can always change into that."

He gave me a sardonic smile, and his dark head lifted, his eyes flashing to mine. "Maybe you ought to."

"Maybe I will."

He laughed in open disbelief. I studied the bowed head as he worked. He was certainly different from Peter or Wally or any of the other young men I had known. He cared for me, really cared—it crackled in the air between us, and someday, I vowed, someday he'd admit it.

Shortly before eight-thirty we filed into our seats from the classroom. The chapel was decorated simply but elegantly. Baskets of red and white snapdragons and blue delphinium were placed on each side of the pulpit, and a rope of the same blossoms threaded on string was draped along the banisters below the choir seats. Behind us, Rachael's huge flag made an impressive backdrop.

The hall was now nearly filled with people. I strained to see over the congregation but my family hadn't arrived. I couldn't even find Peter. It was just like them, I thought irritably, to be late—tonight of all nights. If they didn't come soon, there'd be no place left to sit.

Finally at eight-thirty Peter came in the rear door carrying Tyler under one arm, trailed by Raymond. The others followed shortly after. They quickly found seats, and as they settled themselves, Papa winked up at me, and Mama smiled supportively. I sat back in my chair. The program could start now.

Mark and Rachael entered together both dressed in black, she in a simple dress with a string of pearls about her neck, and Mark in a suit and slim-fitting vest, white lace shirt, and ribbon tie. Rachael, in a few words of greeting to the audience, introduced Mark as her "most capable and talented colleague," and as she spoke, one would never guess they disagreed on anything—no matter how minor. Mark had a degree in music, she said, from a university in New Hampshire and was hoping to join the faculty at Weber Academy in Ogden soon. No wonder Rachael wanted him for Delores. A professor would fit in well.

"So that you may better acquaint yourselves with Mr. Staaton, may I tell you a little more about him personally? He is the son of Frank and Nina Staaton, both dear friends of our family for years. Of special interest is the fact that Mark was born here in our valley while his mother was visiting my daughter-in-law, Delight. As he was born in my home, we've always considered him a member of the family." Rachael smiled from the audience to Mark and back again. "You'll find our new director a man of his own ideas; and I think as you hear the concert we have prepared for you tonight, you'll agree with me, how very fortunate we are to have those ideas working for us."

The concert began, and both Mark and Rachael seemed exceptionally pleased as we sang from one number to the next. The solo came all too quickly, and as I hurried to my place beside the piano, I began to realize how brave Delores and her sisters before her had been to stand in front of such an immense group to sing. But Mark had insisted I could do it magnificently. I had to remember that.

I nodded for Peggy to begin and smiled over the audience as Mark had instructed me to do. As I smiled I lost track of the introduction, and before I knew it Peggy had paused for me to join with her. Not having the vaguest idea of what note to start on I continued to smile at the audience. Katy waved at me and Raymond pulled a face.

Just below me, Rachael edged forward uneasily in her chair, her eyes darting from me to the piano. Her message was clear.

Play it again. I sent a beseeching look to Peggy and smiled at the waiting hall. As Peggy repeated the introduction, I cleared my throat and readied myself for the beginning note. But again, as she neared that point where I should join her, I felt I couldn't sing.

Suddenly desperate, I looked to Mark and he nodded reassuringly. *Go on*, his eyes told me gently. *You're fine.* You'll do it *well*. But the frowning face of Rachael next to him told me she believed otherwise.

Peggy ad libbed for a frantic moment, and as she did so Rachael's lips parted in a smile. It wasn't a wide, reassuring sort of smile, but a small, furtive one, pleading for me to sing—*sing anything.*

I began then, and as I sang the first notes and my voice came easily, my confidence grew. I saw attentive faces below me, full of admiration and respect. Yes, respect, I thought, respect for the first soloist who did not carry the Ashley name ever to sing anything of importance in this choir.

"He watching over Israel,
Slumbers not nor sleeps . . .
Should'st thou walking in grief languish,
He will quicken thee,
He will quicken thee . . ."

The song struck me as it never had before. My Father in heaven was with me always watching, caring. The emotion of the piece filled me, and I sang as if only I and the notes that grew around me existed—as if the sound and I were one. The final note grew and at last died in resounding silence.

The faces of those below me came into focus again, and in their eyes I saw acceptance and appreciation, and I knew they had shared all the feeling of the piece with me. The tumultuous applause began, and row on row stood, like waves bounding up from an ocean, until everyone in the hall had gained their feet. The old dream, the desire to do this forever stirred within me. I bowed again and again to the roar in the hall, and at length turned back to my seat. But the applause continued. Mark stepped forward and motioned all of the choir to stand. How proud he must be of me, I thought, as we stood, for I was very proud of myself. I smiled warmly at him, hoping to catch his eye. But of course he had a lot on his mind at this moment. Afterwards we'd talk—yes, afterwards. I contented myself with watching the back of his head—the thick curly hair, his strong shoulders, the familiar, easy way he moved with several hundred people watching.

Rachael, too, took her turn bowing. She was radiant. Perhaps I had pleased even her!

"Yikes, you almost had me dying back there." I turned from the congratulations of the choir members to Raymond. "But when you got started—whew! You were good, Anne!"

"Thank you, Raymond."

His was one of many compliments. Most were from old friends who would have congratulated me after any kind of performance, but Phyliss, who never minced words with anyone, told me I was fantastic.

"But the beginning, Phyl—did you notice it?"

"Sure, but you carried it off beautifully. It looked as though you wanted the introduction to be just right and Peggy's first one didn't please you. It was the uppity sort of thing—," she rolled her eyes down toward Delores, "that an Ashley would pull."

Of course it would look that way. Dressed as I was, no one would believe I felt incompetent for even a moment.

I chatted and shook hands for a good fifteen minutes before the crowd began to wane. Mark, still surrounded with people, hadn't even glanced my way. I felt bereft. It hardly mattered that everyone else liked my performance.

What if *he* didn't! If he didn't come up soon, I knew I would have to leave. Peter was waiting at my elbow, but though I stalled and stretched every little conversation to the limit, Mark didn't look up.

"My child, you sang well." Rachael touched my arm, and before gliding back to her little group below with Mark, she said, "You can be proud because *that time* you felt it." Her smile seemed slightly malicious, but I called a thank you after her as she moved away.

"Well, I guess we can go now. Your folks are waiting," Peter urged.

"In a minute." I gathered up my things and searched the floor with my eyes, anything to give Mark more time.

"Have you lost something?" Peter scowled.

The hall was nearly empty now, and if Mark couldn't leave off talking—I smoothed my hair and gave Peter my hand. We moved down onto the landing, passing within inches of Mark.

At the wagon Papa gave me a hug and told me I looked as pretty "as all get-out." He thumped my nose. "And you sang all right, too!"

Mama hugged me too. "Your father and I are proud of you, dear, and not simply because you sang so well."

The family piled into the wagon, and as they pulled out, Papa hollered back to us, "Take your time coming home, kids!"

As we walked to the buggy I brushed a tear from my eye and took one more lingering look at the church. The large doors opening onto the front stood open, and as I watched, Mark, with Delores clutching his sleeve, emerged from the chapel and started down the steps.

"Now what?" Peter asked, turning to look back with me.

"Nothing." I pulled on his arm. "Let's hurry, shall we? Race you to the buggy."

"Anne," Delores called, "wait a minute!"

I dove into the buggy as Delores called again. "Jump in,

Peter. Let's go," I whispered frantically, and leaned out to see them coming—both of them together.

"What's the matter with you? You heard Delores."

I shrank back into the shadows. "Peter, get in."

"Good evening, Mr. Tate." Delores's voice told me she was smiling.

"Good evening, Peter," Mark said at her side.

Peter, standing below me on the ground, inclined his head. "It was a nice concert."

"Wasn't it?" Delores began. "And Anne, you did well. Such a surprise. Grandmother is ecstatic!"

"Thank you." My reply was wooden.

"You did extremely well." Mark joined her. "But then I never had a doubt. Your talent is wasted on this valley. You—"

"I'm sorry about all the trouble," Delores cut off the compliment, sounding surprisingly genuine. "It was just that when your fabric didn't come, we were kind of stuck and—"

"I know." I tried not to sound cold though I felt like winter. "I understand."

"I hope you do," she said, tilting her head until her curls rested against Mark's shoulder, her eyes lustrous and large. In the dark she was very much like a cat.

"I know the solo meant a lot to you," I half-apologized, knowing her attitude was in part because I had taken the solo from her.

"Oh, it did, of course, at first," she said, "but then Mark—," she gave his arm a squeeze, "Mark helped me see how *unimportant* it was."

I nodded at them both. Mark shifted, I thought uneasily, though of course he was never uneasy.

"It's late," he said, "and with the big Fourth of July celebration tomorrow . . ."

"Yes, these two sweethearts seem in such a hurry to get away, we'd better let them go. But I just wanted Anne to know how I felt."

"Well, thank you." I moistened my lips and forced a smile.

"And I wanted to tell you, Anne, how very pretty you look in that dress."

"Delores—" Mark's voice was suddenly harsh.

"It's lovely, don't you think?" She ignored his interruption.

"Yes, it's the most beautiful dress I've ever worn," I said.

"Oh, really? It's not that grand, but I am glad you like it." She laughed, and the sound of her laughter cut like glass, for I knew in that statement she meant to tell me something. Mark hadn't purchased the dress in Ogden at all. It was ordered and cut and made especially for the *Elijah* soloist in a fabric and design more elegant and costly than the others but in a matching color. The dress was to have gone to her—to Delores.

They said goodnight, and as Peter came around and climbed in beside me, he put his hand into mine. It was a warm hand, a steady hand, and I felt so grateful for his friendship that I reached a kiss to his cheek. Then I collapsed into tears upon the buggy seat.

"Anne, don't, honey." He pulled me gently to him.

SIXTEEN

The Fourth of July was one of the most exciting holidays in Ashley, because we celebrated Independence Day and the founding of our little valley as well.

From the moment we crawled out of bed on the Fourth, our house was filled with excitement and activity. There was a picnic lunch to pack and chores to get done before the Founding Fathers parade started. And always there was a minor emergency of some sort—such as Raymond changing his mind about the costume he had chosen to wear.

Four years ago, Mama and I had spent many hours remaking a black jacket of Papa's into a long Abraham Lincoln coat. We had fashioned a long stovepipe hat and even a lamb's wool beard that we'd carefully dyed black, but then, just before parade time, Raymond announced that the beard hurt his face and he wanted to be Jim Bridger instead.

Lincoln was hung in a closet and the house was turned upside down as the family searched every drawer and closet for frontiersman trappings. Minutes later Raymond emerged wearing a coonskin hat and various paraphernalia falling from his shoulder—Katy's white fur mittens, a fur collar from Mama's winter coat, and two stiff beaver skins that had hung in the barn a decade or more. Around his waist he'd strapped Papa's hunting knife and a broken deer antler threaded onto a piece of twine. He looked more like a tattered Hec Bailey (the valley's drunk) to me, but as he swaggered to the wagon, it was obvious he had found his role.

After the parade and speeches, while many were equipping their booths on the sloping stretch of lawn between the school and church, we children (for Mama and Papa were usually involved with the high priests' ringtoss) would take our lunch down into the hollow that followed along the river. Here we'd spread a blanket at the bank and have a little picnic with our feet dangling in the water. There were always other groups that ate in the hollow too, but we had the most fun, we were sure.

After lunch, we'd search out Papa and he'd give us each a quarter. From then on we were on our own. We had the entire day to roam about the booths, playing the games and trying to win one of the alluring prizes strewn across the booth fronts. We could also buy homemade pastries, ice cream, candy, or even funny hats or tiny wooden dolls. And when we tired, there was a ball game to watch or a watermelon bust to join.

And then in the evening about eight-thirty, the dance in the basement of the church would begin. When we didn't have dates, Phyliss and I would go together and join the long line of girls sitting along the stage. If we sat all night, which sometimes happened, we didn't mind too much. It was fun just to be there and to watch the bright summer dresses swirl by.

Finally, beginning at ten, Brinton's Mercantile sponsored a fireworks display. For thirty minutes the sky glittered—"streaming," as Katy put it, "with dripping flowers." July Fourth was the highlight of every summer.

But this Fourth of July I didn't get up when Papa called. I would stay in bed, and perhaps the family would think me ill and leave me home while they went to the parade. And

Peter, too, would learn without my having to tell him that I couldn't go to the dance with him as planned. I had only to lie still and pretend sickness. No, I reasoned, there would be no pretense about it—I was ill. I could no more bear to get up than I could fake a jovial attitude today.

"Annie!" Katy, dressed in sunny yellow, came into the room. "Everyone's waiting for morning prayers, and Papa says I'm to get you—even if I have to yank the covers off."

"Leave me alone." I turned away from her. "*Please*, Katy."

"But I can't. You've got to come or we'll all be late." She tugged at the blankets which I held firmly over my shoulder. "Annie, let go! Get up! Papa said!" When I still held to my covers, she ran from the room and clattered down the stairs. Seconds later I heard her returning with Mama.

"And I said we were all waiting, too!" she whispered as they entered together.

"Thank you, dear, now run along. We'll be right down." I felt Mama's eyes harden on me. "Anna Jeanette! We're *waiting*."

"Mama, just let me sleep."

"Now it's the Fourth of July, and if we're going to play all day, we've work to do now."

"I'm not feeling well. I don't want to go to the celebration—or to the dance tonight."

"After your success last night I'd think you wouldn't miss it. Are you ill?"

"No. I don't know. I'm tired. I didn't sleep until dawn."

Mama crossed to the bed and pulled the blankets back. "What's the matter? You were so happy last night. You and Peter didn't fight, did you?"

"No, honestly. I just don't feel well."

She gave my shoulder a pat. "You go ahead and rest then. I'm sure you'll be feeling better before it's time to go."

"I don't think so, but thanks, Mama."

She left me, closing the door softly behind her. I turned over on my back and stared at the rose-papered ceiling.

"You're not serious about missing the dance." It was midafternoon when Peter came into my room. I was curled up in the corner chair, my head in my arms, and the sound of a voice in the deathly silent house so alarmed me that I cried out.

Peter frowned, catching sight of the tear stains on my face, and walked to the window, apologizing for coming up so quietly. "I thought you might still be resting, Anne, though I can't for the life of me understand what's the matter. You should be triumphant today, and I'm not going to let you miss out on all the compliments that are floating around the celebration about your solo. Pull yourself together and let's go to the dance and have some fun."

Peter had that look in his eye. He wasn't going to take no for an answer. Too tired to resist, I finally nodded assent. His face registered shock, as if he'd expected to do battle. Then he smiled.

"Well, good—I'd like to get there a little early. I'm helping with the dance, and Charlie's asked for a hand with the fireworks right after. We've got to set up, too, so if you could leave by seven-thirty?"

"That's hours off—yes, of course." My dress, an altered formal gown of Mama's, hung in the closet in readiness for this very occasion. I had little to do but bathe and somehow fix my ravaged face. "I'll be ready, Peter."

But it was a long time later before I was able to move from the chair to lay my dress out on the bed. Even its old-world beauty couldn't shake me from my depression. I caught sight of my face in the mirror and felt ashamed. Peter was right. My mood was unreasonable. I'd known Mark scarcely two months. What did it matter if I were only a pupil to him? It did little good thinking about the hike when he had swept me from near death to the safety of his arms, or the moments by the fire, or outside the church-house when he'd so graciously returned my music folder. It was clear I'd misread him all along. The gallant fight to keep my solo for me had been nothing but a statement of independence from Rachael and her manipulations. It had little to do with me. And the dress—I could just hear Mark talking Delores into giving it up as a gesture of kindness for the "poor Carrow girl" who never had much of anything nice.

Well, it wasn't true, and I'd show them both. I turned to the lovely dress on the bed and closed my burning eyes. I owed Peter. He was in charge and counted on me as his date. And I owed something to myself. I would smile and laugh with lightheartedness tonight and dance the evening and my cares away. This was a victory celebration, one that should be memorable. And if it killed me, I was going to look the part.

With determination I bathed and cleaned my face. Later, with the mail-order catalog open before me, I created, all by myself, a daringly up-to-date hairstyle that could rival any Ashley. When I'd finished, my hair glistened in a soft dark cloud about my shoulders with a section swept into a soft, satiny knot at the crown.

I slipped on the dress, a pale wisp of voile over an apricot underskirt. The soft, gauzy material encircled my shoulders in sheer, breezy ruffles. The waistline tucked so narrow that I could scarcely breathe, and the skirt swirled about my feet.

I stood at the mirror while Mama did up the many buttons at the back. It was like coming into womanhood, being able to wear her dress. For years I'd tried it on repeatedly, only to find it too large. But now it fit like a glove. The slight alterations she'd made had only enhanced and updated the style. The color made my skin glow and darkened my eyes to a charcoal hue. I laughed, surprised at the picture I made in the old dress suddenly turned new again. Yes, I could shut myself in and cry forever, but what would it really change? Nothing!

Peter too had taken special pains with his appearance.

His hair was brushed back from his temples in expertly cut layers, and he wore a new dark suit. The color brought out the vivid blueness of his eyes. His shirt, freshly starched, gleamed against the deep tan of his face, and I couldn't resist telling him how stately he looked.

"We do look grand." He bowed his head at the compliment. "But under all the finery, Anne, we're still just us, and we'd do good to remember that."

"Just us?" I challenged. I ran to the buggy, not wanting to hear his reply. My bolstered spirits were still too fragile for a duel with Peter.

He was occupied so long with setting up Charlie Brinton's fireworks that the dance was going strong when we arrived. It took me only a moment to discern that Mark was not there, and I was almost glad. Delores swept around the floor with someone else, and I knew that if Mark were present, she'd be with him—only with him. As the evening wore on, I became more at ease. Peter had been right. Everyone was full of compliments about my performance, and I had so many of the men ask for dances that even Peter had to stand in line. But during one rare dance with him, the bishop approached with a worried face. There was some sort of problem with the refreshments, and would Peter come and help out?

I took the opportunity then to slip outside for some air. I felt light-headed with success, and every time my hurt over Mark surfaced, I squelched it and replaced the gnawing ache with something nice someone had said. My eyes stung with gratitude at everyone's kindnesses to me. My dress and hair had caused so much commotion that Wally Brinton had teasingly asked if Papa had come into money.

I fairly skipped down the steps, past a few lingering couples, and lit out across the sloping lawn toward the star-dusted trees. The canyon winds were blowing, and I let my skirts and hair fly. There was time enough to freshen up at the cloakroom mirror, and anyway, my appearance hardly mattered. Mark wasn't here.

"Not too far," a voice sounded behind me. "Dragons come out at night."

I laughed, incredulous at the attention I'd received from the male half of Ashley, and turned to see a figure coming across the grass, but the lights of the open doorway were behind him and I couldn't distinguish his features. "Who is it?" I paused, but when there was no answer I turned and resumed my flight to the river path.

I hadn't gone far when a hand caught my elbow. "I'm not joking." His tone was harsh now. "You shouldn't be walking this far away by yourself. It's late."

Mark! I stood a moment wondering where he could have come from, agonized by the sudden thumping of my heart despite all my vows of indifference.

"You needn't worry, Mr. Staaton." The breath was wrung from me. "There isn't a soul in Ashley who would do me harm, but thanks for your concern." I shook my hair carelessly, letting it cascade in the breeze, and tried to ease my arm from his grasp, but his fingers remained where they were.

"What's this 'Mr. Staaton' business? You're angry." He seemed actually surprised. "Why?"

"Angry? Not at all. I'm having the time of my life." I stepped backward. "Isn't it the most delightful dance?"

"Don't evade me, Anne," he pressed, and his hands, burning where they touched, drew me to him.

"Let go. Oh, please!" I panicked. As his hands fell away, I fled deeper into the trees. I was thankful that he didn't follow. I stood at the bank of the river and plopped rocks into the swirling water, and battled with the tears that scalded my eyes. How was I ever to make him think I didn't care, when at his slightest attention I lost all thought and poise? I listened to the cooling, soothing sounds of the water, the rustling trees, distant music floating on the night air, and the eventual slowing of my heartbeat, until, afraid that I'd been away too long, I turned back.

Mark stood on the path just twenty feet away, and I

163

wondered how long he'd waited there, watching me. I had to pass by him. At my approach, I smiled and caught my skirts to move past him. But he stepped off the path, leaving the trail for me, and, turning, walked back through the dimness at my side.

"Dance with me," he said as we came out of the trees.

I glanced away from the shadowed planes of his face, an alarm shrilling beneath my speeding pulse. "Thanks, but no—I'm here with Peter."

"So what?" His head jerked around and I felt his eyes searching mine. "You've been dancing with everyone."

"How do you know? You haven't been around, have you?" I turned to sweep up the hill and away from him, but my skirt stopped me short. It had caught on a twig, and tug as I might there was no undoing it.

"Let me." Mark stooped, but he couldn't seem to get me loose either. He sighed as he worked with the hem. "I've been watching from behind the keyboard of the piano. Molly Klemons was late coming so I filled in." He stood up. "I would appreciate a dance, Anne. I've just saved your pretty dress and you owe me, don't you?" I stared up at him, confusion fairly swamping me. How could I dance with him? I would surely betray my feelings. Oh, where was Peter? I looked toward the lights of the church, at the couples strolling about us on the lawns.

"Come on, Anne," he murmured, his tone light and bantering. His hand lifted my face to his. "Whatever I've done, forgive me and let's dance, ummmm?"

It was ridiculous. He was charming me back to a good humor, after all he'd done, though I knew well enough the dance meant nothing to him except as a way to make us friends again—friends.

He took my elbow and propelled me up the slope with him, taking my lack of comment for assent.

Delores was coming down the steps as we approached the church, and I slowed my pace, half afraid that his seeing her would result in a cancelling of our dance; but he only urged me on, murmuring a "Good evening" to her as we

164

passed. Inside, he whirled me out onto the floor and expertly guided me through the crowd to the raucous rhythm of a polka. His hands held my waist, and my arms stretched upward to curve around his neck, my fingers in the lustrous thickness of hair at his nape. I couldn't help it. I enjoyed myself with a passion, laughing and thrilled as the dance ended.

"Don't run away." His hand caught my wrist, and his long fingers entwined through mine.

"I wasn't going to."

"Weren't you?" he mocked, standing tall and lean above me. He coughed, then laughed, admitting he was out of breath himself. "Let's hope the next number is a slower one." At his words the orchestra began a lilting introduction to a waltz and Mark sighed his appreciation, his hand at my back fitting me so closely to him that we moved about the old hall as if we were one. He bent and swayed me with such ease and polish that I could scarcely believe it was I in his arms.

I sighed, and my eyes skimmed over his shoulder at the line of girls sitting against the wall—there were Laurie, Shirley, the Carter sisters . . . Phyliss whisked by in Aaron Thompson's arms and I smiled at her huge stare; then, looking up into Mark's eyes, I told him how beautifully he danced.

"I owe it all to my lovely partner." His lips turned into my hair, and his hands tightened, sending thrills up my spine. "Now, where were you all day?" He pulled back slightly to look down into my face. "I did see your family, but no Anne. Raymond said you've never missed the Fourth celebration before."

"Don't listen to Raymond. I wasn't feeling well."

"So I understand," he murmured. "And to whatever prompted your quick recovery, I am grateful." We swept past the main double doors, and Delores, still standing there, sent me a poisonous look.

I spoke my thoughts aloud. "She's waiting for you."

"Who?" he asked, a slight withdrawal in his tone.

"Delores." I licked my lips, wishing I hadn't said anything. Mark looked about to see her and shrugged, his steps continuing faultless. "Maybe."

"She's beautiful, isn't she." I had to say something, things had grown so awkward between us.

But Mark ignored that. "How old are you, Anne?"

"Eighteen this September."

"Then you are just seventeen." He said it almost sadly. "Delores said so yesterday and I thought . . ." His eyes flicked to the door and back.

"Sarie Bennett's my age, and she's married and already had her first baby."

"Oh, I know out here that's common enough, but it's still awfully young."

"It is not!"

"Don't go flying off the handle, Anne. I can assure you last night and at this moment, you look and act like a disconcertingly mature woman. That's why I was beginning to think Delores had had me on and you were older."

"I am. I'm nearly her age."

He shook his head. "Delores is—," he grimaced, "well, she's lived away from home and traveled a lot. Besides, she's nineteen, and two years can make a world of difference." There was a hint of regret in his tone, and again his eyes traveled back to the young woman at the door.

"I'm sure it can." I stopped so suddenly that for once Mark was caught off balance, and I pushed away from him, tripping slightly. His fingers reached out to my elbow and he pulled me back against him, his face breaking into a smile.

"The dance isn't finished, Anne. You ought to see the sparks flying from your eyes, as if I've accused you of some crime. There's nothing wrong with being young, and anyway, time's a sure cure." Despite my wooden resistance, he pressed me into his arms. Suddenly I felt him stiffen. "Forget it. Peter's heading this way, and by the look in his eye I'm not likely to have you long."

Peter cut in, and Mark, giving a little bow to me, walked

166

away, his long strides taking him to Delores, just as I knew they would. Peter had scarcely taken me in his arms when the music ended and the orchestra leader announced intermission time.

"You went outside, huh?"

"Yes, for a little air. You were busy, remember?"

Peter nodded, his mouth clamped into a disapproving line. "I want you to see the floor show, and afterwards you owe me the next five dances. I'm running the spotlight, but you stay inside!" With that firm directive, he led me to an empty chair. Everyone was seeking a place to sit down, and the bishop was announcing the upcoming entertainment. "Here comes Phyliss. You can visit with her."

"Peter," I began, bristling at his possessive attitude, "you've been occupied during a lot of the evening. I can't just very well sit and watch."

He lingered a moment, his eyes on me, and then without any kind of reply he went off to run the spotlight.

Phyliss daintily adjusted her billowing yellow skirts and sank into the chair next to me. "Did you see me dance with Peter?"

She resisted a smile and stuck her tongue in her cheek. "Twice! He was even polite, Anne. Almost—not quite— but *almost* nice. He hasn't liked all your popularity, you know." She caught her breath. "Anne, how on earth did you manage to get a dance with Mr. Staaton? I didn't think he was here and the next thing I knew you were in his arms."

The remainder of the evening was full. It was a far cry from previous years. I danced and traded about, not even able to sit down once. It relieved me to see Mark dancing with a good many other girls besides Delores, though she was obviously his favorite. Frequently I'd feel his eyes on me, and I, determined not to show my unease, would smile brightly across my companion's shoulder and nod as if it were the most natural thing in the world to have his attention.

With only three more dances until closing, Peter went

off with the bishop again, reminding me that the last dance was his, and I stood with Wally Brinton below the stage, gratefully getting my breath. Suddenly Mark approached.

"I'd like to claim Anne. Thanks." He slapped Wally's shoulder; then, sliding his hand down my bare arm to my wrist, he drew me out onto the floor and into the circle of his arms. He didn't wait for Wally's reply.

As our feet moved in time he cocked back his head, his eyes looking deeply into mine.

"You could at least smile at me, and pretend to be enjoying yourself."

"Oh, I have been."

"I know you *have been*, but now you're with *me*, and those big eyes of yours look far too serious." His gaze narrowed. "I wonder why."

Why are you so different tonight? Why all the attention? It was baffling. But I only shook my head.

"Something's troubling you, and you might as well tell me." His voice had that low, smooth quality that made me nervous, and I found myself babbling.

"I just don't under—" I stopped, horrified that I'd very nearly told him. I dropped my eyes, my face growing warm under his close scrutiny.

"Go on, Anne. You just don't what? You can't start and not finish. It's against all the rules."

My legs began to tremble. I was no match for this man. Last night he'd been aloof, uncaring. Tonight, at this moment—the look in his eyes, the way he held me—I could swear his attentions were those of an ardent suitor. He was courting—at least he seemed to be. Unable to stand it any longer, I lifted my head and looked straight into his mocking gaze.

"All right," I stiffened in his arms, "why are you being so nice to me?" It sounded inane, blurted like that, and I felt my face redden.

"And why shouldn't *I* be nice to *you*?"

"You know what I mean. You're completely different tonight—so—so—"

His lips brushed across my temple and he chuckled softly against my ear. "Your mirror should tell you the answer to that, Anna Jeanette."

I caught my breath and looked at him.

"Now what's wrong? Don't you believe me? It's true—you're lovely!"

"Didn't I look nice last night?"

He bent his head, his eyes inches from mine. "You know very well you did. You were every bit as beautiful."

"But you were so awful, weren't you?" My voice wavered. "I wanted so much to please you. After all the trouble with Delores and Sister Ashley, I wanted to . . ." My eyes misted at the memory, and I closed them quickly.

"Annie. So that is why you were so upset earlier." His voice was tinged with gentleness. He adjusted his steps to a change of tempo and swept me to a less crowded corner. "You did please me, Anne, and I thought you were very much aware of how well you'd done. Everyone was swarming around you to say so."

"But you—you didn't say anything!"

"Yes, well—the performance was scarcely over and Peter was there, dogging your heels, and—" He grinned a little lopsidedly. "I just don't know. You didn't seem to need praise from your teacher. But if I acted a bore, don't feel bad about it!"

I smiled in relief. His words made little sense, but I felt immeasurably better. Whatever had happened last night, Mark hadn't meant to hurt me, and it was silly to worry. I was in his arms, and he was being so enchantingly attentive. What else mattered?

"Are you staying to see the fireworks?" he asked after a moment.

I nodded happily. "Oh, we never miss the fireworks!"

"We? You and Peter?"

"Well, yes. Peter comes. But I was talking about the family. Mama and Papa bring the wagon into town and make up a bed for the children in the back."

"Sounds fun. You have a very special family."

"I'm so glad you think so, Mark."

His lips curved wider at that and his eyes glinted with satisfaction. "And I'm glad that at last you're back to calling me 'Mark.' "

Aching with happiness and feeling more alive—vibrantly alive—than I'd ever dreamed possible, I closed my eyes as we finished the dance in silence, the strains of music filling my head like a drug. I was in love. No matter how much I'd wanted to deny it, I loved him. Mark Staaton meant everything to me.

I wanted at once to weep and to laugh, to tell the world and to keep it forever my secret. I gave up pretending indifference and let my eyes shine and my heart sing. As I nestled against Mark's shoulder, I naively believed that what I felt so strongly, he must surely feel too.

When I opened my eyes we were near a small open door at the back of the hall. I stood a moment, locked in Mark's embrace, and then he gently led me onto the narrow landing. In the cooling darkness he drew me close again, folding me against his chest, his eyes glittering like the night, his mouth hovering barely above mine.

"All night, *all night long,* I've wanted to kiss you." His lips came down once—twice—three times in a soft caress, and then he whispered my name, and his hands crushed me to him while his mouth took full possession of mine. His skin smelled of soap and starch and a male fragrance that made the night reel about me. Star fields swam over our heads in a whirling dance of their own, music falling about us as if from the heavens. In all the world there was only us.

"I'd better get you back inside, Anne." His tone was rueful, as if returning was the last thing he wanted to do. He gently hugged me against his shoulder, and I sighed.

Reluctantly, with the imprint of his kiss still burning my lips, I followed him into the dance hall, just in time to bow my head for the closing prayer.

"What? Were you getting more air, Anne?" Peter's quiet voice broke my reverie. "The last dance was *mine*. I *did* bring you." I cringed, remembering my promise to him.

How could I have been so carried away as to forget that? I hadn't done a thing to please him tonight—and now . . .

"Peter!" I cried, reaching a hand to his sleeve. "Honestly, I completely—"

"Forgot—I know! I saw you come in."

"Oh, I'm sorry," I stammered, trying to think of a way to put it right with him. "The time just got by us. It wasn't deliberate. Please understand."

"I may have been involved a good deal tonight," he muttered, shooting a challenging gaze to Mark, "but Anne came with *me*—and I'm sure you knew that. We have a tradition, Staaton, that no one breaks. A girl gives her escort the last dance of the evening even if she does find someone else's company more to her liking."

"Peter," I tugged on his arm. "I'll make it up—"

"It was my fault," Mark cut in, stepping closer to Peter.

"Of that I'm sure. See to it that she finds her parents' wagon. They're out front waiting for the fireworks to start." Peter spun about, and I watched the back of his head until he disappeared into the crowd.

"Come on." Mark led me to a chair and I fairly dropped into it.

"How could I have done such a thing?"

"He'll get over it."

"But he won't. You don't know Peter. It was a terribly wicked thing to do. Oh, Mark, I should never have gone out there with you!"

"Now don't go regretting that. I think it's for the best, Annie. You're too young to tie yourself down to Peter like you've been doing. Everywhere I go I see you with him. It isn't wise. I don't see why your folks don't insist that you play the field a little. Believe me—"

"Play the field?"

"Go out with lots of men. Have some lighthearted fun. Don't let Peter ruin your youth, Anne."

He slipped an arm about my shoulder and sat down beside me. "Now smile, and let's go find a place to sit where we can enjoy the fireworks."

"Us—together?"

"Sounds good to me." Dark fire leaped in his eyes, and he pressed my fingers to his lips.

We moved through the thinning crowd to the cloakroom. As Mark helped me on with my wrap, I turned to see my reflection in the big mirror. My hair was tangled and wild looking, my face flushed. I wanted to cry. No wonder Peter was so angry.

"Why didn't you tell me my hair was such a mess? Oh!" I wailed, dragging my fingers through its heavy masses, pushing at the misplaced pins.

Mark's face appeared over my shoulder, and he stared with me at my reflection and laughed, shaking his head. "I see I did do a little damage, Annie, but I'd never call your hair a mess." He tugged at a curl. "Lovely disarray, maybe."

I frowned at his compliment and he gave my shoulder a squeeze. "Cheer up! It isn't the end of the world." For him it wasn't. He seemed to be in higher spirits than ever.

As we moved up the short flight of stairs to the entry, I remembered Delores standing there watching us dance.

"I wonder how Delores will feel if she sees us out watching fireworks together? I can't stand the thought of making any more people unhappy tonight."

"Stop worrying. What would you have us do? Live our lives to make others content?" Mark's hand came over mine on his arm, and he sighed. "Delores knows better than anybody that I'm just marking time here. She might not want to believe it, but I've told her repeatedly that at this point in my life I've no intention of getting serious. Listen! The fireworks have started." Distant pops broke through the night and Mark grinned. "Let's get out there!" Though he urged me on, I hung back in the shadows.

His lightly spoken words had knifed through me. No intention of getting serious . . . marking time . . . My voice shook as I spoke, but there was no helping it. "You're not going to be staying here then?"

"Not forever." His smile did nothing to reassure me.

172

"Rachael offered me this job knowing I was waiting for a position at Weber Academy. No matter how generous she is, leading a choir doesn't provide a living." He cocked a brow. "Clerking doesn't help a lot either."

"No. No, I guess it doesn't." I dropped my hand away from his sleeve and moved up the stairs ahead of him. The hall was empty, the music and laughter gone. Where was the magic now?

Mark paused on the landing, frowning. "Something wrong?"

"Would you just go ahead? Go on. Please." I averted my head from his searching eyes. "I can find my own folks, thanks."

"You're a generous girl, Anne," he said with exasperation, "but when it comes to courting, you must think of yourself. Forget this thing with Peter."

"It's not Peter." I half-laughed, but my voice was ragged, and I looked beyond his shoulder to see a dazzling rocket splinter the sky above the park. *Playing the field*. Was he doing that with me?

"Then what is it? Tell me and be done with it." Closing the distance between us, he bent toward my lips.

"Don't!"

"*Whoa*!" His fingers ensnared my wrist. "If it's not Peter—"

"It's you," I rasped. "You! Don't you know what you've said? You've ruined—ruined everything."

"You'd better explain that." Mark's light tones were gone, and he was angry.

"All right," I flared. "Yes—I let you kiss me out there like—like *no one* ever has in my life! And now, *now* I find you were just playing the field—having some lighthearted fun—marking time! How stupid of me. I should have known a philandering easterner would think no more of kissing a girl than crossing the street. How stupid!" I choked off as a bitter torrent of tears flooded my face. Then, hating myself for crying, I stomped my foot, my fists flying to brush the tears away. "I'm no wanton," I tossed my head at him, "or didn't you know that? I don't go around kissing just anyone!"

"Hush!" Mark seized my shoulders and gave me a hard shake. "And I'm no philandering easterner, and you know that!" His grip tightened. "Our kiss, Anne, meant every bit as much to me—"

"Oh, sure." I twisted desperately in his hold. "A nice diversion, right? A change from Delores, anyway. Let go of me—and don't you ever come near me again, do you hear?"

"Dang it all, Anne, hold still and listen! I don't think you understand—"

"I do, *perfectly*. You're slick—all that whipped cream charm and personality." I sobbed, blind to anything but the fact that I'd been tricked into caring, tricked into loving him openly with my whole heart, and all the while he hadn't meant any of it. I broke free of his arms and ran toward the door, but Mark was there in a blur, barring my way.

"You're not going anywhere until we can resolve this."

"I don't want to! You're not worth it, and I don't care—"

"That's enough!" He jerked me against him, the cords in his neck pulsing, his face set like granite. "You're wrong, Anne. You've jumped to some completely false conclusions, and I'd like an apology. Right now!"

"An apology? *From me*? Go back to Delores. If she'll put up with that kind of commitment from you, you deserve each other. Now, kindly let me pass!"

Abruptly he let me go and stepped aside. I ran headlong down the stairs, the bursting fireworks and echoing cheers of the crowd making a mockery of my shattered world.

SEVENTEEN

The weeks following the dance were lonely ones. I was relieved that the choir practices had stopped for a while, but I missed the excitement of something to do, of dressing up and seeing people—seeing Mark. Things between him and Delores had mended, and though Raymond told me Mark still slept behind Charlie's store, each Sunday he sat with the Ashley family, and it was soon evident to everyone that despite what Mark had said, there would be a wedding in the not distant future.

The passing of July found the Blavens gone, and their little place looked more forlorn and ragged in its deserted state than it ever had with the boys jumping onto the roof of the house, banging the doors, or tearing at the gate.

"If I had the money, I'd buy the place from Dell," Papa often said, but Mama on hearing him would shake her head.

"Bill, we need close neighbors, and you've got more land now than you can handle."

We all missed them terribly—Mama her visits with Margo, and Raymond missed the boys who had so faithfully copied his antics, and who could so easily be maneuvered into helping with chores.

"My heck, you've been mopey lately," Raymond growled one morning as he and I washed windows outside for Mama. "What's got into you?"

"You should talk," I replied crossly. "Now go into the house and get some more towels."

"And you've become as bossy as Peter. *You* get the towels."

"How can I when I'm up here?"

"Simple. Climb down." Raymond stalked off around the side of the house and left me high on Papa's rickety ladder.

"Raymond, you come back here! I can't move or I'll fall. *Raymond*—you've got to hold this thing at least." But he didn't return, and I, in a huff, teetered down the rungs after him. "You come back here you little snip!" The ladder rocked precariously. "Oh, *help*!" I let my weight fall against the ladder until it steadied. "Darn him!" I eased down the final rungs. When I felt the earth under my feet, I tore around the house in Raymond's wake, nearly running into him returning with Mama.

"What's going on out here?"

"Annie swore at me, I told ya'. "

"Hush and let her answer."

"Swore? I did no such thing. He left me on the top rung of that ladder. I—I nearly fell off!"

"Raymond?"

"Well, she told me to go." He was defiant. "She said, 'Raymond,' " his voice rose in imitation, " 'go in the house and get some more towels.' And I did, and then because I left her like she told me, she started yelling her head off and she swore."

"Anne?"

"I didn't, Mama. Honest!"

"All right, you two—," she shook an angry finger at both of us, "I don't want to hear another cross word. Now get going on those windows." She waited for Raymond and me to begin the job again and then left, lecturing about how brothers and sisters shouldn't quarrel—when she was a girl, *she* never did.

"Thanks, Raymond," I whispered sarcastically. "To say that I swore. I haven't ever, you know."

"Oh? Well, you did then. I heard you say clearly, 'heck.' But it wasn't heck, I can tell you."

"What I said was 'help!' " I exclaimed. "If you wouldn't have been so all-fired ornery, you'd have listened better. It was *HELP!* The ladder was falling!"

Raymond nodded. "Yeah, sure."

"Well, it's the truth. I just wish everyone would leave me alone."

He jumped off the ladder. "Your wish is granted." He bowed, flinging his right hand nearly to the ground, and left me to wash the windows myself.

I didn't bother to call him back.

My irritable attitude didn't stop with quarrels with Raymond. I was short with everyone in the family, and though Mama and Papa both spoke to me about it and I had resolved time and time again to be better, I couldn't seem to help slipping back into my horrible depression and lashing out at the people around me.

Sundays were the hardest to get through. I'd try to avoid Mark and Delores completely at church, but it was never any use. I was constantly stumbling into them before or after meetings. And the empty dullness I carried inside would literally sharpen to acute pain every time I met them and received one of Mark's grim looks or saw Delores giggling so foolishly on his arm.

And so if I wasn't biting my tongue off trying to get along with the kids, I was upstairs in my room staring at the expensive blue dress and hating it and Mark at the same time.

But the more I tried to convince myself my feelings for

Mark were dead, the more I thought I'd never be able to cope with life without him. I prayed night and morning that the Lord would take away the anguish. But He didn't seem to hear me. I no longer felt young and carefree. I had aged —if not my body, then my spirit.

One afternoon early in August, Peter knocked on my bedroom door and asked if I'd like to go for a ride with him.

"I don't know, Peter, I—"

"I won't take no for an answer." He settled himself against the door jamb and frowned good-naturedly.

"Well, then," I said slowly, knowing this ride was inevitable, "I'd better get some shoes on."

He drove me out to see the land he'd been thinking of buying. It was a relatively small spread up against the foothills adjacent to the Jared Miller farm.

"It's lovely, Peter."

"Well, it's not a lot, but there's plenty of room for a nice house, a good-sized garden, and pasture enough for a small herd."

Not knowing what else to do I nodded.

"Through the scrub oak there, you can see both of the Miller homes. We'd have close neighbors."

We again! I didn't reply, but followed Peter's finger until my eyes found the two narrow houses and the road that led up to the cemetery.

"You wouldn't be awfully far from home, and no further away from town than you are now." Peter took my hand and led me up a grassy rise. "The house'll be here. Look at that view. After chores, we could sit out on the porch and watch the sunsets." He stretched his arms over the valley, which sloped gradually below us. "Do you agree, Annie?" His clear blue eyes looked into mine, and I was suddenly struck with the notion that Peter knew very well I didn't love him—that despite all his pretensions to the contrary, he'd known it for some time.

I let my eyes slide to the wheat growing in the valley beneath us. What did I want? The pain for Mark twisted inside me. I couldn't hurt Peter—not like I'd been hurt.

"Well, Anne?"

"Oh, Peter," I began carefully, "I'm just so confused. I wish we could talk about this later—when I know what I want."

He heaved a deep sigh, the scuffed toe of his boot digging into the black soil. "Anne, I've waited all summer. It's August. We don't have much more time before cold weather starts. You could moon like this forever."

"I've not been mooning."

He shook his head angrily. "Blast it, Anne, be honest, will you? You've forgotten whose girl you are!"

"I've never been anyone's girl, Peter Tate. Just because *you've* been assuming things doesn't mean I have. You know, you're always saying *we* and *us* like we're engaged or something, and you've never even *asked* me."

"All right," he pulled me into his arms, "if that's what you want. Will you marry me?"

"Don't! I'm not trying to force you into proposing. I just want you to *stop assuming—stop pushing*. If you don't you might get an answer you won't like." He let me go, his jaw clenched.

"I will not wait forever, Anne."

I moved away from him feeling shaken and guilty. It was some time before he left the rise and joined me in the buggy. When at last he climbed in beside me, he started the horse homeward without so much as a word to me.

When we arrived home, Phyliss and her brother Cage were sitting on the lawn. Their father's carriage, laden with bags and boxes, stood nearby, and jutting up from the back seat, I could see the purple-tasseled umbrella I'd given Phyliss last Christmas.

"Thank goodness!" She waved a hand and ran to meet

us. "We'd begun to think you'd forgotten, and I was afraid I wouldn't get to see you before I'd have to leave. How are you, Peter?" Her eyes brightened but he didn't answer.

I jumped out of the buggy beside her and Peter moved off to the barn. "Phyliss I'm sorry! I didn't realize it was so late. Thanks for waiting."

She cast a puzzled look after the buggy. "You know I'd wait anyhow, job or no job."

"You look good, Phyl, but I don't know if I like your dress. You look *too* grown up."

"No more so than you looked at the concert." She sighed. "I suppose it's inevitable."

"I suppose. I can't believe you're really going away. I think it's the worst thing you've ever done to me."

Phyliss tipped her head to one side. "We never did bring out the best in each other, so I guess it's all for the best. We can both become the adults we should be now that we'll be apart."

"Oh, Phyl—Phyl!" I thrust my arms around her, and we hugged each other tightly. "I can't stand it—I'm going to miss you so much. You'll write often, won't you?"

"Of course," she said, blinking at me. "You too, huh?"

I nodded, knowing how unlikely it was that either of us would keep our promise.

"Well, Anne, what more is there to say?" She wrinkled her nose at me and shrugged. "Come on, Cage."

And then she was gone. I waved until I couldn't see her anymore. Then, turning to the house, I went up to my room and wrote a formal note addressed to Miss Shirley Green. I was resigning from the choir.

Friday morning Raymond was going into town to pick up some wire for Papa, and he would deliver my note for me.

"Do I say anything special to her?"

"No, just give her the note."

"Okay, but I think you're crazy to resign now that you're the star."

"And while you're at Brinton's store, would you give this to Mr. Staaton for me?" I handed him the box.

"What's in it?"

"That silly blue dress he gave me for the concert. If I'm leaving the choir I won't be needing it."

"He won't like it, Annie. Do you have a note for him, too? I don't want him mad at me!"

"No, but tell him it was a really pretty dress, will you?"

"Sure thing. He's a nice guy."

I snipped beans on the porch until Raymond returned.

"Well?" I called as he drove the rig past the front lawn.

"Well what?"

"Did you deliver the note, and did you give my dress to Mr. Staaton?"

"Yep."

"Did either of them say anything?"

"Shirley said she was sorry to lose you, and she hopes you're not ill or something. I told her you just had to get out. When you're at the top, where else can you go?"

"Raymond, did you?"

He laughed. "Thought that would get a rise outta you. No, I didn't say anything like that. Just said you weren't sick, and she'd have to ask you for reasons." He began to whistle and headed the horses for the barn.

I got to my feet. "And Mr. Staaton? Did he say anything?"

"Under his breath, he did. And this time I'm sure it wasn't *help* I heard. I told you he wouldn't like your giving it back. What's he gonna do with a dress?" He resumed his whistling and as he left, shot me a sidelong glance.

I went back to my beans.

Later, after Raymond had unloaded the wire and pastured the horses, he returned to sit beside me on the porch.

"If you've got an extra knife, I'll help finish those off."

He took a handful of beans and began to snip them with me. "I got a secret. Want to know what it is?"

I gave him a quick look and wondered if he knew my feelings for Mark.

"Well, do you want to know? I could always tell someone else."

"No, go ahead. I'm listening." Not thinking, I put another bean in my mouth. By this time, they had begun to taste thick and waxy.

Raymond glanced behind us into the house and whispered, "I've found myself a pet."

I finished the bean I was chewing and relaxed considerably. "Oh? I thought no dog could replace your Ivan the Terrible." Ivan had died less than a year ago, and when Papa had suggested he get Raymond another dog, Raymond declared he'd never have another.

"No dog can. It ain't a dog I got."

"Then what? Some stringy tom cat?"

"Heck no. You'd never guess—not in a million years."

"A frog then?" I was tiring of the game. "A pig?"

"No, no, no! I'll give you a hint. I call it Caesar. Great name, huh?"

"Yes, great name. Now what is it?"

"That's cheating. You've got to *guess* it."

"I'd like to Raymond, but I haven't got a million years. Now I'd better take these beans in to Mama."

"C'mon, guess, Annie!"

"Why not let me think on it a while?" I got to my feet and started up the steps. "Thanks for delivering those things for me."

Raymond nodded his head dejectedly. And so before closing the door I made another try.

"A rabbit?"

His dark eyes twinkled. "Wrong again!"

That evening I decided I needed to walk. The days had grown noticeably shorter. It was just after eight, and yet it was growing dark. Tonight the practices for choir were beginning again, and had I still been a member, I would be walking up the steps to the churchhouse about now, braced for my first glimpse of Mark.

I was glad I had resigned. Why torture myself more?

As I walked, I pulled a stem of peppermint from the ditch bank and placed it in my mouth. So much had happened since the afternoon in May when I'd lain here watching the high blue sky of spring.

Tonight, too, the sky was high and clear, but pierced with the first stars of evening. I sat down on the ditch bank awhile, sniffing my sweet stem, and watched the line of mountains darken in the west. As the sky above me dimmed, I tried to imagine myself married to Peter, and the two of us gazing at this same sight on our own porch. The idea wasn't all that repulsive, I mused. Peter was charming when he chose to be, and handsome. Phyliss always said he was handsome, and he was a good man. My folks liked him—especially Papa. That meant a lot.

I left the bank of the canal and walked through the willows at the far end of the orchard and along the creek.

At length I stood staring at the back of the Blavens' barn. It was so very black! Why? And then I saw them— orange spikes shooting skyward. The place was ablaze—on fire!

The sharp flames licked and snarled up the sides of the barn in the twilight, and the slender amber tongues reached out, slapping at the surrounding trees and running along the ground to the house. And in the midst of the violent light a dark, hunched figure moved.

As I had done nearly a month ago, I turned, holding my skirts, and ran for home. But tonight was different. There was no rain to haunt the place, to streak the sky a mournful gray, or to quench the fire.

"Papa! Someone, quick—fire!"

EIGHTEEN

We fought the blaze and choking smoke for hours but only succeeded in saving a portion of the hay from the barn before the structure collapsed and fire consumed the rest. The hutlike chicken coop burned entirely, and most of the house was gone as well. The few walls left standing were black and warped, and the trees above them twisted and shriveled.

News spread, and before morning carriages and wagons filled with people came to stare at the ugly ruins and to shake their heads tragically.

"I reckon that about does him in, and poor Dell doesn't even know about it."

"Where's he gone? Anyone heard?"

No one had, but Dell had promised to write Papa.

At breakfast Papa scarcely said a word. He ate solemnly, frowning at his plate, his eyes red and puffy from the smoke and underlined with fatigue. Mama, looking just as worn, worked over the stove—her eyes red as well, but not from the fire. Dell had left his property in our care. Papa was to have sold it and forwarded the money. But it was doubtful now there'd ever be a buyer.

"Even if I knew where he was, I couldn't write him that everything's gone," Papa said suddenly into the dismal silence that surrounded all of us that morning. "I just couldn't."

Mama left the stove and caught Papa's outspread hand in hers. "But *everything* isn't gone. The land's untouched, isn't it?"

"Of course," Peter agreed. "The buildings weren't worth anything. It's the land that's important."

Papa shook his head. "The hay crop—"

"That's the only damage. And we've lost that much ourselves a lot of times. Remember all the potatoes that rotted out one year." Peter smiled at me. "We take chances. Sometimes we lose." He shrugged his shoulders and began on his third helping of hotcakes.

Papa scowled at him. "Dell loses most the time, I'd say."

"If he does, it's because he lets it happen. He's a weak man."

"Now, Peter—"

"I mean it. That fire was just carelessness. I found a scorched lantern in the ashes of the chicken coop, several stubs of matches, and this—" Peter pulled himself from his chair, and taking a small silver tin from the shelf above the stove, returned to the table. "Ever seen it before?"

Raymond suddenly spilled the syrup he was pouring, and I saw that he knew with me who'd caused the fire. It hadn't been Dell's thoughtlessness, I was sure.

I waited for Raymond to tell about the matches and the person who always carried the little tin bulging in his front shirt pocket, but he didn't. Instead Raymond finished the hotcake on his plate and gulped his chocolate.

"More eggs?"

"No thanks, Ma. I'm full up." He pushed his chair into place, asked to be excused, and hurried out the back door.

I left the table as soon as I could and went out back to find him. But the yard was empty. I knew that I'd have to tell what I'd seen, and soon. If Chester wasn't stopped he might start another fire. I waited until I had the chance to speak to Papa alone.

"I'm sorry I didn't tell you right off, but I wanted to talk to Raymond about it. Chester's defenseless. They won't lock him up, will they?"

"I can't say, possum, but just the same it's a problem we've got to face. Hec, killing himself with drink—his boy, a grown man with a child's brain, living like a wild thing." He rubbed a hand through his hair. "It's a problem we've all got to face."

I rode in with Papa to tell the authorities of the hunched figure I'd seen moving about the fire. As we spoke to Brother Todd, he thumped his wide fingers on his desk and nodded his head at us, like he'd known it all along.

"In recent months I've had complaint after complaint about Chester. I don't know what's gotten into his head. He killed two of Ted Sorenson's chickens last week—right there with Vivian waving a broom at him. Snapped their necks —," he snapped his big fingers to illustrate, "with that smile on his face."

I didn't believe it about the chickens. We were a small community, and folks sometimes spun tales to add a little flavor to their routine lives. Chester wouldn't hurt anything deliberately. But when Papa and I returned home we found Raymond out by the pump in tears.

The pet he'd found had been a chicken. It was one of Dell's.

Papa was a little angry. "Those chickens were diseased, Raymond. They were all to have been killed."

"This one was fine," Raymond cried, "just fine! I found it walking around like normal down by the creek. It was a tough chicken, I tell you." He pushed his bottom lip forward. "I'm gonna get Chester."

"But you don't know it was Chester."

"I do too." He made a fist. "We had a tree hut up the creek. Chester got into some kind of trouble in town so I said he could stay at the hut and take care of Caesar for me. How stupid! That big ox killed him."

"Why didn't you tell us Chester's been there with you, if you knew he was in trouble? That could've saved Dell's place. And this morning, did you try to warn him?"

"He was my friend," Raymond said. "I didn't think people knew him like I did." His face suddenly darkened. "But I was wrong, Pa. I'll find him now and lock him up myself. He knows what he's done."

"Maybe he doesn't," I said. "He's certainly seen many people wring a chicken's neck before."

"But this wasn't a chicken to eat, Anne. I explained that over and over to him. This was Caesar—*my* chicken. Besides, Chester's smarter than any of you know. He plays dumb a lot of times; then people don't punish him. He told me once he *likes* to feel things break."

There was no convincing Raymond. After the noon meal he set out in search of Chester.

"I'll make him come in, all right." He pulled his cap low over his eyes. "He does what I tell him to do."

As we were clearing up the dishes, a dust-covered buggy pulled up out front and Sister Andrews from the Relief Society stepped out to knock at the door. She'd come to ask Mama to make something for a benefit that night. "It's going to be for the Blaven family. Tragic news—that fire. We thought if all of us pitched in we could give them a little something to get them on their feet."

As she spoke a look passed between Papa and Mama, and I knew this was an answer to their prayers. The letter to Dell wouldn't be so gloomy after all.

"And there's more," she gasped for air and rushed on, "the bishop says anyone who will buy the Blaven property has his guarantee that fifty men will help cut the lumber and raise a new house and barn. Think of it!" She clapped her calloused hands together. "My Ken says with an offer like that, he's tempted to leave the gristmill and move out here himself."

Just before the family was to leave for the benefit that night, Raymond returned empty-handed. "He's cleared out. He knows I'd be after him."

All of the family went to the benefit but me. I didn't feel up to facing the choir members yet, especially since last night's practice would still be fresh on their minds, and they'd be wondering why I resigned. And neither could I bear another silent encounter with Mark.

When the wagon pulled out, I turned back to an empty house. Except for Peter, who'd stayed in the fields to finish up the water turn, I was alone.

I sat at the chair by my bedroom window and stared out into the gathering darkness, part of me wishing I'd gone with the family, and part glad I'd stayed home. Everyone had long since stopped coaxing. Peter, too, had stopped bothering me since our little ride. He didn't even speak nowadays. I'd gotten my wish. Everyone left me quite alone —just as I'd wanted them to do.

I lighted a lamp and began looking through the box of books Margo Blaven had given me just before she left. Mostly they were novels that Papa didn't much approve of: *Wuthering Heights, The Blithedale Romance,* and several of James Fenimore Cooper's tales, *The Deerslayer, The Last of the Mohicans, The Pathfinder,* and one I thought Papa might like after all—*The Pioneers.*

But none seemed to interest me at the moment.

Suddenly I got an idea. I'd been very uncomely lately and ornery to everyone, especially Peter. I'd fix up in my best dress and take him some supper. It was the least I could do.

After I'd changed into my ruffled pink print and brushed my hair, I felt much better. I slipped into Mama's room and dusted my cheeks with her rouge and ever so slightly colored my lips. I found her lavender shawl and threw it about me. Then, hurrying downstairs, I wrapped in a dishtowel a large piece of cake and two legs of chicken along with half a loaf of sliced and buttered bread. With the food in one hand and a lantern in the other, I set out for the canal.

Not knowing exactly where Peter would be, I headed for the fields on the other side of our headgate.

The air was still heavy with the acrid smell of smoke, and the thought nagged that I shouldn't have worn my nice clothes—especially Mama's shawl. As I walked into the orchard I regretted it even more. The smoking ruins of the house had filled the orchard with a bluish haze that showed in the lantern light all about me. I hurried through the trees trying not to breathe too often, and when at last I emerged at the canal, I was relieved to find the air clear, though Peter seemed to be nowhere around. I stood for a moment on the bank and called at the top of my voice but there was no answer.

Obviously, if he were anywhere near he'd see my light, if not hear me. I turned back toward the orchard and, hating to wade through the smoke again, decided to follow the canal upstream to where it met the creek. Peter would be nearly finished, I was sure, and he was probably up there right now rerouting the water. Following along the bank, I held my lantern high and began through the long grass toward the main headgate. The stars had come out, and it was really a very pleasant evening to walk.

I must have gone more than half the distance before I realized that Parry Thomas took the water after Papa. He lived below us, and so Peter wouldn't be up here at all, but below the house in the south field, turning the water back into the canal. The night had grown so dark, and already this surprise for Peter had been such trouble that I turned back toward home regretting even coming out in the first place. I could run into a skunk and get sprayed and have to bury my clothes—Mama's shawl could be ruined.

I heard a rustling noise in the grove of willows ahead of me and stopped still—my ears straining in the darkness. No one knew where I was, and ours was the only farmhouse around.

"Animals," I said aloud, startling myself with the sound of my voice. *Like wolves*, something within me said. I grabbed at my skirts and began hurrying along the canal. My ears, now attuned to all the night noises around me, seemed to hear strange sounds on every side. I deliberately slowed my pace. I was not going to frighten myself. I began to hum a hymn as I walked, but I realized that the allegro tempo I'd begun was a little too fast for "Abide With Me; 'Tis Eventide." But I sang it allegro just the same, and with the racing tempo of the song, my heart began to hammer in my ears. The lantern flickered. It was going out. I began to run—a lantern in one hand, a bundle in the other, and both occupied hands trying to cope with a too-full skirt that kept catching in the growth. I hadn't gone ten yards before stumbling on my dress and tumbling headlong across the bank, dropping the food and the lantern as I went. The light snuffed out as it rolled into the canal, and the food fell over the bank and down the rise into the darkness. I searched madly for a moment, wetting my sleeves up to my elbows in the inky water, but it was no use. The lantern was gone.

I sat up, peered into the blackness about me, and tried to collect myself a moment by thinking sane thoughts. It was foolishness that had gotten me into this mess. I had frightened myself, and by being so childish, I had lost the lantern. Without the light I'd have to go even slower.

My eyes adjusted to the dark, and I felt considerably calmer. I picked myself up from the bank and fumbled around until I found the food; then I began again along the bank, picking my way in the hazy starlight.

I had almost forgotten my fear when unaccountably my heart began to pound again. My eyes searched the growth below the canal bank. I was *certain* I heard the same snapping noises that I'd heard that day months ago at the ward outing. The memory of that other scare came rushing back—five sharp snapping sounds in succession. There it was again—one—two—three—four—five. And it wasn't coming from behind, as the little animal sounds had done, but in front and to the right. I was nearly back to the orchard. As I stopped to listen, I was sure the snapping was coming from the apple trees, and to get home I had to go back through those very trees toward whatever was waiting there.

Remembering the fright I'd had at the outing made me

shiver. If I'd heard the same peculiar sounds both times, I wasn't imagining it.

"Oh Peter," I whispered, clutching the bundle of food close. "Please come and find me."

I moved toward the trees as quietly as I could, but to my own ears each step made an awful commotion, and as the edge of the shadowy trees loomed just ahead, I began to smell the smoke again. Without the lantern, how could I see at all? I'd have to go another way.

Cutting through the fields just after the water turn would sink me up to my knees in mud, and if I had to run—

I had only two other alternatives: either follow the canal upstream to the headgate and along the creek, or follow downstream until it crossed under the road and walk home by way of that and the lane. *And what if the snapping follows? You'll only be further from home and help.*

The warm kitchen was only minutes through those trees. I began down the grassy slope, ignoring the snapping that had begun again. I'd keep my eyes ahead and, hurrying one step at a time, I'd be home—home—before I knew it.

The smoke met me full in the face. On all sides a strange filmy blackness pushed through the trees, fading and twisting the trunks into ugly distortion. They seemed to sway and walk toward me, reaching sudden arms that whipped my face and tangled my hair.

I was well into the trees when I stopped suddenly. A low gurgling sound crackled through the smoke—laughter! I had known it would come, just as it had before—that other time when this same terror had stalked me—the sun, high in a spring sky then, and several hundred people only feet away.

I ran, flinging blind arms in front of me, fighting the limbs, the dangling apples, the smoke—too senseless now even to drop the silly bundle of food.

Again the hideous laugh, the labored breathing. I knew that if it was human laughter it came from a demented mind. And I knew only one such person—someone who exulted in fires, in strangling chickens, and in the feel of something helpless snapping in his huge and gnarled hands. One of the swaying shadows that surrounded me was Chester, and—heaven help me—I couldn't see *to see*.

He was close now—panting just behind or somewhere to the side, or perhaps just ahead—panting and dancing in the swirling blackness.

The trees tore at my arms, shredding my sleeves and skin. Mama's shawl yanked from my shoulder, and the uneven ground rose to trip me again and again. The familiar orchard had vanished—and in its place was a cavern. Echoing through smoky corridors cackled the incongruous laughter of an old child grown mad.

When at last the large hand found my face I didn't even bother to scream.

NINETEEN

Far down in the valley yellow lights blinked into the moonless night and dogs barked, splitting the summer stillness. Couples strolled hand in hand about the starlit lawns of a little church, and inside the bright, gay hall, Papa and Mama danced and sang—forgetting for a while the stabled animals, the unhitched plow, the darkened fields.

I tried to fight him off, screaming that I was *"Anne Carrow, Raymond's sister*—your friend. Chester, don't—*please."* But he was not the dull and childish boy-man I'd known. He exuded only animal-like grunts to my pleas, and increased the power of his hands, which finally succeeded in pushing me to the dank earth at his feet. I lay trembling and beaten, too exhausted to resist any longer, engulfed by a cold wave of hysteria.

I suppose I had always feared Chester somewhat—the knotted hands and misshapen head. But more than strength and ugliness had produced the fear. What really lay in the soul behind the transparent eyes? How strongly did he feel those urges and drives natural to a man?

The dark bulk knelt beside me, heaving laughter. His burning hands came down on my face—fumbled downward.

If I hadn't been screaming before, I began now—again and again—and even when the splayed fingers smashed themselves over my mouth I screamed—screamed until the nauseous blackness took the terrible din of my voice from consciousness.

I awoke to the sound of crickets, shrill in the grass about me. My head hurt, every bone felt bruised, but I was alive. My clothes were intact.

I had been dropped in a heap, my head and back scraping against a tree trunk at the very edge of the orchard. I lay still, trying to focus my eyes. The shadow of the barn leaned against the sky only yards away.

Chester squatted on the ground nearby—eating the food I'd wrapped for Peter. His jaws worked noisily, spewing bones and tearing the chicken flesh as if he hadn't eaten in days.

I eased away from the tree and straightened my sore legs. If I were very, very quiet . . . I got to my feet. The ground swayed and then steadied. I fixed my eyes on the barn and, with all the strength I could find within trembling legs, began to cross the soft turf.

But Chester had heard. Snorting, he lunged about, his arm nearly reaching me as I ran.

I threw myself forward, screams searing my throat. He was so close, and I, too weak. His hand came down on my head, hitting me to the earth. I felt his weight sprawling behind. I clawed the dirt and pulled to my knees, but his fingers closed about an ankle. I turned and kicked at the hand that tried to jerk me to him, kicked at the pale head streaming with sweat. I hadn't realized I was free until the splintered wood of the barn hit my hands. I shoved myself around the corner to Peter's room. The window was dark.

"*Peter! Somebody!*" I pushed in the door—empty. I ran from his room into the void of the barn and under the loft. My feet stumbled over the ladder. The loft! No. There'd be no escape from the loft.

Outside Chester banged furiously on the barn and shook

the big doors. I thrust myself against the far-side wall and worked my way to the very back. There I lay flat against the straw behind the buggy, praying my heart would be still and not betray me.

One of the big doors jerked open. Against the lighter dark outside, a black form filled the doorway. It spoke my name. I pressed my face and body closer to the ground, willing myself a part of it. I heard only a soft step and steady breathing. The ladder rattled.

Yes, go up the ladder. But it flung back into place. Silence again. I lay a long while, my face down, straining my breathing into nothingness.

And then he was there. I felt his eyes above me—the huge body bending down—

Not waiting to be dragged from under the buggy, I stood, screaming, and fought with dying strength the sure arms that shook and then pulled me to him. It was no use—I'd lost.

"He's gone, Anne—darling, listen to me. You're safe!" The words, fragmented as they seemed, at last penetrated my hysteria. "Stop it, Anne. I'm not Chester. He's gone." I clung, sobbing out my terror, until at length the horrible convulsing stopped, and I was able to breathe and think again.

"There now," the gentle voice said against my hair, "that's better." He lifted my chin and briefly touched my lips to his. "I'll take you to the house."

I don't know just when I realized it was Mark and not Peter who walked at my side, helping me find my way back to sanity, but when we came into the light of the kitchen and I saw his troubled face, I didn't question it. Not how he'd come to be there or why he'd come. It was as it should have been. A miracle—just like that other time when he had pulled me to the safety of his arms. But now he didn't put me from him. He took me into the front room, and after putting me on the couch and lighting the lamp, he returned to hold me, shivering, against the crook of his arm.

"Cold?" I shook my head, though my teeth continued

their chattering. "Close your eyes. I'll try and round up a blanket and some bandages."

"No, please don't go."

The arm tightened around me. "I'll stay, but something needs to be done to your head. You have an awful gash, poor thing, and your arms are raw."

Exhausted, I shut my eyes and settled against him.

I must have dozed, for when I opened my eyes the lamp was dim and I was lying on the couch, the blanket from Raymond's bed thrown over me. For a terrible instant a haze seemed to dance above me. "Mark?"

He came in carrying a pan of water, with a towel over his shoulder. "I'm not much good at doctoring, but I suppose washing can't hurt." He stopped abruptly, frowning. "What's wrong?"

"I can see it again." My voice rose in fear. "Look, Mark, smoke!"

He turned up the lamp. "See, Anne," he smiled, "no smoke."

After cleaning the cut on my forehead and washing the streaked blood from my arms, he pulled a chair opposite the couch and settled back. "Feeling better?"

He waited then, relaxed in his chair, for me, in my own time, to tell him about it.

I told him first about the terrible laughter and the queer snapping noises. "Chester chased me before. It was the day of the ward outing—don't you remember? I'd hurt—"

"Your shoulder, yes." His face darkened. "You didn't tell me then that you'd been chased."

"Well, afterwards I thought I'd probably just imagined it. There were all those people around, and I couldn't believe someone would really be chasing me."

"But you heard the snapping then?"

"Yes, and that laughter. That time, I outran him. Tonight—," I closed my eyes, "he just kept coming—I couldn't see, and then he—" I began to cry a little, the tears slipping out of my clenched lids. "He caught me. He forced me to the ground and—" My voice broke on a sob. "I—I don't know *what* he did to me then."

Mark found my hand and held it in his. "Anne, listen to me. I don't think Chester would know how to hurt you that way." He put my fingers against his lips. "If he had, you'd know it. Your clothes would be torn, for one thing. He just roughed you up a little." He blotted my tears with the towel.

"When I came to, he'd dragged me to the edge of the orchard and dropped me. At first I thought he'd gone, but there he was, gulping down the food I'd been taking to Peter. I tried to slip away, but he chased me to the barn. No matter what I did I couldn't get away from him. And then, out there—" A chill ran through me as I remembered lying with my face against the straw, believing Chester had come again. "Mark, how on earth did you happen to be out here?"

"I had to see you, Anne—and you know why. We've got to straighten this out between us. I stopped in at the benefit hoping you'd be there, but Raymond told me you'd stayed home. So I rode on out. The kitchen light was burning but no one answered the door. At first I thought maybe you didn't want to answer, and if you felt that way I couldn't blame you, but I kept pounding anyhow. I was going to force you to hear me out. I hollered and eventually walked in. The place was deserted, and I began to wonder. I thought I'd have a look around. I was behind the house when I heard you scream for Peter. Some help he's been. Where in the deuce is he?"

"Watering, I guess. He didn't know I was staying home. He's been in the fields all afternoon."

"Then you should never have left the house, Anne. I've warned you before about walking at night! To hear you screaming and then to find Chester beating the barn down . . ." He shook his head. "That poor boy's sick, and after tonight I'll see to it he's locked up. Next time, let Peter come in and eat!"

I nodded. "I will—I promise."

"Anne," Mark brushed a finger lightly across my forehead and studied me a long moment, "why did you quit the choir?"

I shrugged beneath the blanket. "Phyliss had gone. I couldn't see any reason to stay."

"It was me, wasn't it? You shouldn't have quit. You ought to keep up your singing, and I've brought back your dress. Please, I want you to keep it."

"I suppose Delores won't take it back now that it's been used?"

He started out of the chair as if I'd hit him. "Where did you hear that?"

"Did it belong to her?"

"In a way."

"I see."

Mark's hand closed around my arm. "But you don't! When I'd finally convinced Rachael that you were doing the solo, she canceled her order, and in her place I bought and paid for that dress. *None of it had anything to do with Delores.*"

How silly and trivial it all seemed now, unimportant and long ago. "I'm sorry," I said, "for being ungracious, and I'd love to have it back, thank you."

He smiled down at me. "Anne, I know how I must have sounded at the dance, but I've never played with your affections. You misunderstood. I was talking about my position with Delores. She seemed to be forever man hunting and . . ." He shrugged. "That isn't important. Just know that I wasn't referring to you—not at all." He leaned and brushed his lips over mine. "Now that's *enough* talk. You sleep. Your folks should be home soon."

"Did you know you have a bruise on your cheek, Mark?"

"Have I?" He touched the dark spot. "You've got a pretty good left swing!"

198

The back door slammed, and seconds later, Peter strode into the room. He stopped short, frowning at me in Mark's arms, and said half under his breath, "What the devil are you doing here?"

TWENTY

The next morning Mama thought it best that I stay home from Sunday School, though I was really feeling almost normal. I suppose I looked a lot worse than I felt. The jagged tear beneath my hairline was surrounded by a pale bluish tinge, and down one side of my face, I discovered a series of tiny scratches that had reddened in the night. My shoulders were covered with bruises, and below my elbows my arms were gouged. In two places the cuts ran deep and had to be bandaged, as did my forehead.

I was afraid I'd have scars, and I said so to Raymond as he sat on the edge of my bed buffing one of his Sunday shoes. He'd come, I think, to give me company while Mama hurried to get the family ready for church.

"Scars are kind of nice to have." He worked the soft rag over the gleaming black toe and smiled at his reflection. "They give a body character and show you've lived!" He held up the shoe. "What do you think? Great shine, huh?"

I smiled at his efforts to cheer me up. What a good little brother he was!

Last night after hearing my story and the account of snapping sounds, he told me that it had become a habit of Chester's to sit poring over his own hands, pushing and pulling the knuckles till they popped in their warped joints. (Raymond pulled unsuccessfully at one of his own knuckles.) He reassured me that when he'd rounded Chester up, and he'd do it soon, he'd "even up the score" for me.

"Caesar was one thing," he narrowed his eyes at me, "but my sister's another. No one can do that to you." Then he added that I could forget the whole thing. "Now, leave the worrying to me, Annie. I'll take care of everything." And I supposed his vigil at my bedside that morning was to hurry me along to a thorough mental recovery.

Not that I needed one. It was strange. I felt as though it had all happened to someone else. I was fine, and feeling much happier than I had in weeks.

"Well," Raymond said, pulling on his shoes, "guess I'd better go. Maybe you'd like to look at my bug collection while I'm gone? No? Well, see you later."

After the men and children had gone to church, Mama helped me curl my hair and I put on my long-sleeved yellow dress. My face looked passable with my hair combed over the bandaged gash, and the sleeves covered my scraped arms. It was good to be up.

I helped Mama prepare dinner, and when the family had returned, we sat down to an exciting meal together, the children telling in turn what they'd learned in Sunday School, and Papa telling of the great success of the benefit the night before.

"And the *best* news yet," Papa beamed across the table at us, "I've sold their land! After Sunday School I received an offer. Tomorrow, I'll transfer the deed and it'll be done."

We all clapped over the Blavens' turn of fortune. If only they'd write now, so Papa could tell them about it.

When we finished the meal, everyone but Mama and Papa went out on the back lawn.

Peter stretched out under a tree to snooze, and Raymond tumbled about on the lawn with the kids. Katy, leaving the game, went chasing an elusive Monarch, her braids flying.

I sat in the swing—drifting back and forth to the creak of

the rope, listening to the faint clink of dishes being done in the kitchen, and glad Mama had sent me out for sun.

It was a warm-winded day, and the valley air was sweet with the mixed fragrance of blossoms and sage. Mama's marigolds and four-o'clocks nodded sleepily in little rows against the house, and the leaves rustling in the trees made softly changing patterns of light and dark in the shade across the grass. The green valley and vivid sky seemed at that moment eternal—forever safe from the distant intrusion of winter.

"Anne!" Raymond called, kneeling in the grass. "Someone's coming. Look, a buggy!"

I watched the little rig come down the white lane, knowing before I could see him that it was Mark.

Raymond shot across the lawn with Margaret and Tyler trailing behind. "It's Mr. Staaton!" Raymond waved. "I bet he's come to see you, Anne." He grinned and threw Tyler upon his shoulders and piggybacked him out to the buggy.

I crossed to the edge of the lawn after them. Mark swung out and tied the horse to the fence.

"Hello, Mark. What a nice surprise!"

He came forward, the sun on his face, and a shock of hair spilling above one eye. "How're you feeling?"

"Fine," I said, lifting my shoulders. "Fine!"

"Are you really?" He took my hands in his and looked at me with such an expression of concern, it knocked the breath right out of me.

"Hey, Mr. Staaton. Look at this." Raymond swung Tyler from his shoulders, turning the small body in a somersault as he did so. Tyler sank back giggling in the grass.

Mark laughed and arched his brows—impressed for Raymond's sake—and turned back to me.

"Do you think you're up to a pleasant ride?" He gestured to the buggy. "Mrs. Brinton packed a little chocolate cake."

"My favorite," I said. "Let me tell Mama." I hurried

into the house. He's come courting, I thought incredibly—courting *me*!

When I came out of the house Peter and Mark were talking together by the buggy. As I approached they stopped abruptly, and Peter left without a glance at me.

"I'm ready." Mark's face seemed a little grim.

"Something wrong?"

But he didn't answer. Instead he took my arm and handed me into the buggy. Stepping in beside me, he shook the reins once over the horse, and we moved out of the yard and down the lane.

The children resumed their play, and their laughter fading behind us became the gentle music of the wind sweeping over the fields—Papa's lush alfalfa, and the open meadow dotted with silent cattle.

"It's a beautiful day, isn't it?" I said at last into the silence.

Mark's eyes flicked over me and returned to the road. "Yes, beautiful." His tone wasn't kind.

I leaned back and watched the fence posts move past us. A violet-green dragonfly perched a moment in the air, his bulging black eyes mocking me, and darted suddenly over the horse and into the sky.

I looked at Mark's profile. If he chose to be glum and ruin our ride—that was just fine with me. I was not going to be Miss Sunshine today. I fixed my eyes on the unwinding road, the afternoon's magic limping away.

At the end of our lane, instead of turning the horse onto the main road, Mark headed him down the Blavens' lane. I looked at him in surprise.

"Look, I don't know *what* Peter told you," I began a little shyly, "but I think it's very unfair to be angry when I don't even know why. You ought to at least let me defend myself."

"I'm not angry." He snapped the reins again.

"Oh, no? I thought this was to have been a pleasant ride."

He grunted and hurried the horse. We rounded the bend, and the charred house and trees came into view. It was ghastly—the dead black of everything in the midst of so much living green.

Mark drew the horse to an abrupt halt at the bend, staring at the ruin ahead. "What's Peter Tate to you?"

I was taken aback and stared at him incredulously. "Peter?" Darn Peter, I thought, feeling the old knot of discomfort growing beneath my ribs. "He's, well, a friend I guess. A good friend."

"He obviously feels you're much more than friends."

"Peter's a great assumer," I said quietly.

Mark said something inaudible, and the little buggy gave a sudden jerk beneath the reins and lunged down the lane toward the house. The jolting buggy brought out the soreness in my legs and back. I gripped the arm of my seat and tried to hold myself rigid from the rattling springs— and was growing angrier by the minute.

When at last Mark stopped the rig in front of the blackened house, I slipped from it without waiting for him.

"Well?" I whipped around and faced him. "Why have we come here?"

"I hadn't seen the place," he said, lifting himself from the buggy. He rubbed the dust from his jacket sleeve and frowned down his nose at me. "I thought that if this is where you were going to live, I ought to."

I moved away from him. "And what does that mean?"

"You tell me!"

Why was it always so hard lately even to get along with people? I hadn't done anything to Mark, and here he was, on our ride that was to have been so nice, shouting at me. I turned on him. "I don't know what you're talking about. Now it's obvious your change of mood was caused by something Peter said. *What?*"

"Don't tell me he hasn't told you!"

"Told me what? Mark, for goodness' sake, tell me or take me home."

"He's bought this land for the two of you." Mark moved close, his eyes hard on me. "He tells me you will be married sometime this month. You," he lowered his voice, "you don't act much like an engaged lady."

"But it's not true, Mark!"

He shrugged. "He says it is."

"Well *I* say it isn't. I told you. Peter's a—"

"Great assumer, yes. But to buy a stretch of land on an assumption?"

"I've never told Peter I'd marry him. If I've told him anything, it's been to stop his pushing. He can't goad me into marriage. I don't know where he gets the notion—"

"You think you're blameless?" He laughed, taking my elbow solidly. "I think you need to do a little housecleaning. A man doesn't fall for a girl uninvited." The pressure of his fingers on my elbow made me wince. Furious, I shook off his hand, reminding him that I had not yet fully recovered from my bout with Chester, and I hardly needed another bruise.

"And what" I said, with my voice rising uncontrollably, "what does *any* of this have to do with you?"

He studied me coolly a long moment as I shook beneath his detached gaze. Yes, he was meddling—prying where he had no real right. "It isn't your business, is it?" I scoffed. "So why should I answer to you?"

"You know very well why!" Hands at my back pressed me solidly against his muscled length, and his mouth punished mine. His kiss had none of the gentleness of the night before, and when I pushed from his arms I was, I told myself, enraged. But I hadn't made a move to resist him, and I feared my lips had responded to his.

We stared at each other for some seconds, and when an apology failed to materialize from him, I turned abruptly and, skirting the scorched area, started for the creek.

"I'll take you home," his voice came behind me.

"No need," I said, not looking back. "It's much quicker this way."

Nothing could have kept me from church that evening. I took extra pains with my hair and wore a sophisticated wide-brimmed white hat and a beaded white dress I thought Mark hadn't seen before. It was really very dressy with its high-laced collar, tight bodice, and long sleeves, but I looked older in it, and so I wore it anyway.

I rode in the wagon next to Mama. I had avoided speaking with Peter all afternoon. Tomorrow I'd find him in the fields and do that housecleaning Mark had spoken of. The whole thing *had* gone too far. But I'd tell him gently, I reassured myself, and in such a way that Peter would always be my good friend, and I, his.

The chapel was nearly full when we came into it. I took Katy with me, and the two of us sat on the end of one of the rows next to old Sister Lacey. The rest of the family and Peter went forward to a stretch of bench still empty. I felt Peter's eyes on me as he passed, and pretended interest in Sister Lacey's beaded handbag. Only when Peter had had ample time to seat himself did I dare look up. I was upset, and yet I felt a confusing feeling of tenderness for him. Remembering the night before, I was afraid I knew what had precipitated his buying of the Blaven place.

Last night after the family had returned and Mark had gone, I told them about my narrow escape with Chester, and Peter, hearing the full story for the first time, stopped his scowling in the corner and came to sit beside me. He took my hand and asked with a sudden boyish awareness if I had truly been taking *him* food when Chester attacked me.

It was obvious now that Peter had seen the whole incident in the wrong light, and he'd wanted—in his way—to do something special for me. He'd given up the property adjacent to the Miller place and purchased land right next door to home, thinking that's what I would prefer.

Mark wasn't sitting with the Ashleys as he usually did, but further back with the Brinton family. He turned once and nodded to me. I nodded back and swung my eyes back to the speaker, hoping my color hadn't changed.

I didn't hear much of the service. I was in my own private world, interrupted only when Sister Lacey turned her head to ask in an embarrassingly loud voice, "What page did Brother Frawley say?" or "Such a nice talk, don't you agree, dear?"

When the meeting was over, Wally and Laurie worked their way to me and asked why I'd resigned from the choir.

"I suppose I've had enough excitement for a while."

Laurie laughed, linking her arm through Wally's. "I think I know what you mean. You did get a little more than your fair share."

"What'd you do to yourself?" Wally frowned at the scratches along my face. "Run into a barbed-wire fence?"

"A couple dozen apple trees. It's a long story you wouldn't want to hear."

"Oh, no?" Laurie smiled, wetting her lips. "Everything that happens to you is exciting."

I began reluctantly and then caught the flash of a purple stone on her left hand. "Laurie! What's that?"

"An amethyst. My birthstone."

"It's beautiful." I looked from her to Wally. "Does it mean—?"

"Yes! In October. Isn't it wonderful?"

"I'll say. And you're going to the temple?"

"Of course." She beamed at Wally. "We've already talked with the bishop."

Others within hearing swarmed to congratulate them too, so I said good night and moved down the crowded aisle with Katy.

Outside in the dusk, we were walking to the wagon when I saw Mark coming toward us across the grass. I hurried Katy onto the wagon.

"Good evening, Anne."

"Mark."

"I want to drive you home." He spoke softly at my side, his hand catching my elbow. "I still have Charlie's buggy."

"I don't know, Mark. I—"

"I'm not going to apologize, Anne," he said. "It was just a kiss after all. But despite the temptation to do otherwise, tonight the ride will be pleasant for you. I promise I'll behave every minute." His smile was beguiling, and I loved the feel of his arm around my shoulders. "Now come along."

"There you are!" Delores called from the walk. She tipped her head to one side and shook a playful finger at Mark. "Grandmother says you're to come home with me tonight for suet pudding—no excuses!" She tossed her loose hair and gave me a smile, confident of her hold on Mark.

"I think you have a little housecleaning of your own to do." Before pulling away I managed a smile at both of them, then moved back to the wagon.

I waited with Katy for the family to come, wishing all the time that I'd gone with Mark. But the way Delores behaved—as if she owned him! Where did he stand with her anyway?

"Katy, why don't you run and find the folks? Church has been out twenty minutes at least."

She shook her head. "They're visiting, Annie. Mama will scold me and tell me to be patient."

She was right. A lot of the joy of coming to church was the chatting afterwards, and had I shelved a little pride, I would be chatting too—with Mark. It struck me then that pride, as far as Mark was concerned, meant nothing to me.

"Katy," I said jumping from the wagon, "if I don't come back, tell Mama I've gone home with Mr. Staaton."

"But, Annie," her eyes widened under the bonnet, "he hasn't asked you."

"Sure he has. I wouldn't invite myself, would I?"

I ran back along the graveled path to the church. He was where I'd left him—talking with Delores. She stood, half-turned from him, her face pale in the twilight. I froze where I was. They were talking seriously. I couldn't very well go up and interrupt them as Delores had done. I'd have to go back to the wagon.

But Mark had seen. He hollered for me to wait, and saying a final word to Delores, hurried toward me, a slow smile spreading across his face. "Have you changed your mind?" I nodded, my heart pounding uncontrollably. "I'm glad. Now I won't have to change it for you."

He took my fingers in his, and we walked to Charlie's buggy, hand in hand.

Mark took Turner's Lane—a roundabout way home. The horse's hooves plodded an easy rhythm as darkness crept along the little streets and through the fields. The wind tossed the trees, scenting the August air, and one by one, little stars pierced the heavens, first above the mountains and then over the valleys, until the night was dazzled with them.

We talked about anything and everything—Mark's part-time job at the store and his fondness for Charlie and the Brinton family, my performance of the solo, Raymond, and Mark's family in Salt Lake City.

His father worked for the bank exchange, and his only brother, five years younger than he, was attending the university. They'd missed out, he said, not having girls in the family. I agreed, and Mark laughed and I did too. Then he told some amusing stories about his school days in New Hampshire and we laughed over them. It was delightful!

We pulled into the yard too soon.

"Thank you, Mark. I haven't had so much fun in weeks and weeks!"

He lifted me from the buggy, his hands firm on my waist. "Neither have I—not in years!" And, as he set me on the ground, he had a most peculiar look on his face. I thought he was about to kiss me, but he said instead, "I'll never forget the day I caught you running the fence. You're a very enchanting woman, Anne Carrow." Not knowing what to say to that, I smiled. "And I think," he continued, "that I'm going to have to break my promise."

He took me then into his arms...

"You know your father doesn't approve of me, Anne."

"Papa? Of course he does."

Mark's arm tightened on my shoulder as we walked to the porch. "Sit down a minute. We've got a problem, I think."

"But Papa does like you. He's never said anything—"

Mark shook his head. "Tonight he asked in passing when I'd be moving on. When I said not for a while, he asked me not to confuse you. He said if I had no permanent intentions, to leave you alone."

"Oh, Papa," I groaned, mortified at his interference.

"No—he loves you. He has every right to see to your happiness, Anne. But he implied that with my background I might not be able to marry in the temple."

I jumped to my feet. "You shouldn't have let him say such things. You're good, and—"

"Just know this. Despite what your family may have heard, the temple is important to me too. I have a firm testimony of the gospel. I may have been educated in the East, but my desires are as worthy as Peter's or anyone's. I've seen what the world has to offer, and it has only made me more sure of this. I want to have an eternal family, Anne, and when I marry, that is where I'll take the girl I love. Do you understand?" He smiled and cupped my chin in his hand and kissed me again.

TWENTY-ONE

The settlement with Peter came sooner than I expected or wanted it to. He met me at the door and said in a lowered voice, "Staaton doesn't hear too well."

He hears better than you, I thought, but still feeling Mark's warmth, I held my tongue and stepped past Peter into the living room. All the family was there enjoying the evening together. But as I entered, they seemed to melt away, leaving Peter and me alone. I suspected Papa had given everyone orders.

"Well," Peter said, closing the door from the hallway, "I suppose Mark told you about the land?"

"Of course, he did. What did you expect him to do?"

He shrugged. "Keep a confidence."

"*A confidence*?" I flared in Mark's defense. "I know better than that. You *let* him believe I already knew about the land—that we were engaged!"

"So?" Peter's eyes narrowed, and he crossed to me. "That should come as no great surprise. It's what we've planned on."

"No!" I pulled away. "Will you stop it? I've told you over and over again to leave things alone—give me some breathing room, Peter—*some time*—"

"Some *time*? I've given you two full years. How much time do you want?"

"Oh, Peter," I wailed, seeing how badly it was going. I'd wanted it to be so different. "You and I, we've had such *good* times—"

"I expect a little more than good times from the girl I love."

"Don't say that."

"What? That I love you? I do, Anne, and you love me. We're alike—suited—"

"No, Peter—"

"And we're going to be married. I've talked to your pa and the bishop."

"Peter, you don't *listen*. I can't marry you. I'm sorry if you've waited all these years, but I didn't ask you to."

"Staaton's just confused you. I want him out of this!"

"But he hasn't confused me." I sank into Papa's chair and said very quietly, "He's made everything crystal clear."

Peter laughed, his face ugly. "Oh, I know you think you're in love with him."

"I am." I thought of Mark's arms around me and the look in his eyes—yes, *I loved him*. It was all I could do to keep from telling him so.

"Then you don't love me?"

"I—I have a *high* regard for you." I reached for his hand. "You've been like an older brother to me."

"Like a brother? *Thanks.*" His words were bitten through with bitterness. "Just tell me you haven't liked my hanging around all this time—all the attention—the kiss by the barn that night, or—or the continual trps to those—those blasted practices!"

"I haven't meant to take advantage of you. You've been such a good friend to—"

"Oh, a *good friend* now!"

"Peter, please, I don't want to ruin things between us. If you'd just listen to me."

"*You listen to me.*" He pulled me from the chair, his hands pressing unmercifully into my sore arms. "I want you for my wife—*my wife, Anne!* If I can't have that—," he

212

shook me, "I don't want you at all!" He let me go and started for the door.

"Peter—"

"Spare me, Anne!" He strode from the room, slamming the door behind him.

It was over. I suppose I should have been happy to have it done with, but I had a very real fear that what I had just done would come back to haunt me someday.

By Wednesday morning he was gone.

I went down to a subdued table that morning. Two places were vacant. Raymond had stayed in bed complaining of a headache.

"I'm sorry Peter's gone, Papa," I mumbled after the blessing.

"No need to be sorry to me." He dished himself a helping of hash-browns.

"But you've lost your hired hand right before harvest."

"You've lost more than that, I'd say. Emily, pass the butter. I can always get Link Evans to fill in."

"May I be excused, please?"

"You haven't eaten."

"I'm not hungry anymore, Papa." He lifted his eyes to mine. "I don't love Peter," I said, tears starting. "Would you all have me marry him, just to keep him in the family?"

"Anne!" Mama sputtered.

"Well, isn't that what he's saying?"

"Of course not! We loved Peter and we'll miss him. But neither your father nor I would *think* of letting you marry anyone you didn't want to marry. Now stop your fussing and eat your breakfast."

Later I took a tray up to Raymond. I knew in him I had a sympathizer. Peter and he had never been particularly fond of each other. And Raymond was crazy about Mark. I think he somehow knew that I was too.

He wouldn't touch the food. He rolled over in bed, his face flushed and hot.

"But it's creamed eggs, Raymond, your favorite."

"No thanks, Annie. I feel too sick."

By the afternoon of the next day, Raymond was holding his stomach and saying he was "going to die," he was sure. Papa went for Dr. Sloan.

"Oh, I suppose it's a summer complaint of some sort." The doctor smiled kindly at Mama. "Keep him down a few days and away from the rest of the family. I suspect it's contagious. Raymond tells me he spent a lot of time with Chester last week and he's sick too—same thing."

I left Raymond's bedside and joined Mama and the doctor just outside the room. "Excuse me, Doctor, but when did you see Chester?"

"Well, let's see," he thumped his mustache, "I guess it was Sunday. Yes, the day after the benefit. Beth found him in our barn. It was obvious he was sick, and so she made him come into the house and I looked him over. I thought he ought to keep down a couple of days, but he wouldn't stay. He seems changed somehow—I couldn't understand a word he said."

"Will he be all right—wandering around sick?"

"Oh, I think so. He's no sicker than Raymond, and he's used to being on his own."

But that night Dr. Sloan was back, his face sober. He spoke with Raymond privately a few minutes and then asked to see Mama and Papa in the front room alone. I took the younger children upstairs and put them to bed, and when I heard the doctor leaving with Papa I went down. Mama was standing at the door looking out into the night, her face pinched and white.

"Why did Papa leave with the doctor?"

"Is Raymond's door shut?"

"Yes. Is something wrong, Mama?"

"Anne." She closed the door and leaned against it. "The little fork of the creek that feeds the frog pond—they think it might be contaminated. Raymond told the doctor he and Chester both drank from it. Raymond's sick, and

Chester—Parry Thomas found him several hours ago. He was sitting up against a fence post—dead.''

"*Dead?*"

Mama's eyes filled with tears. "He had typhoid, Anne. He hemorrhaged to death. The doctor says evidently Chester had been ill for over a week. That night he chased you—he must have been sick even then.''

"And he just went off to die? Nobody helped him?''

"The doctor blames himself. But you know Chester—no one could've kept him down.''

"But surely, Mama—''

"Don't you know what I'm saying, Anne?'' She pulled away from the door, her body trembling. "Raymond has it too!''

"Typhoid?''

"Yes, typhoid.'' She spoke the word with horror. "Aunt Charlotte died of it—Chester died of it.''

"Mother, Aunt Charlotte was an old woman and Chester—well, you said yourself he wouldn't let anyone help him. Raymond's young and strong. He won't get it. We won't let him.''

"Anne, he *has* it. The beginning stages.''

I gave her a hug. "He'll get better. We'll take good care of him.''

She walked past me into the kitchen, sank into one of the chairs, her back to me, and buried her head in her arms.

"Mama, don't cry.''

"I'm expecting again.''

"But that's wonderful, isn't it?''

"Of course it is.'' She looked at me wanly. "It's just that the doctor tells me I can't take care of Raymond. He wants us to move him out into Peter's old room and have Beth come out and stay there with him.'' Her voice caught. "How—how can I do that? Raymond needs *me*.''

"Well, you can't take care of the family and Raymond at the same time anyway. I'll stay with Raymond.''

"It's a dirty job, Anne. And it would be hard for proud

little Raymond to have his sister wash him and dress him and—''

''What else can we do? Would Raymond rather have Sister Sloan live there with him? Mama, she's—well, she isn't easy for the doctor to live with!'' I expected a scolding for being disrespectful, but Mama just looked at me. ''I'm sure I can handle it. Please! I want to.''

Papa and I removed everything from Peter's room except a small table, the two cots, and the stove. And that same evening, after Papa and the doctor had given Raymond a blessing, he and I moved into the little room. It was mid-August. We would stay there nearly a month.

Raymond openly enjoyed all the attention he was getting. ''It's kind of like having leprosy,'' he said. The lamp cast a dim glow over the rough walls and low ceiling—across the small boy beneath the blankets. ''Once you get it, you lose your friends—family—everything. They put you in a cave to die alone, and when you do, they seal it up and let your bones rot where they lie.'' We hadn't told him about Chester.

''Your case is just a little different, Raymond.'' I blew out the lamp and slipped into bed. ''They've given you company—*me*—a human sacrifice.''

We lay awake in the quiet darkness until Papa called from outside.

''Everything all right, you two?''

''Yes, Papa.''

''Your mother and I are going to bed then. Our window's open if you need us. Say your prayers.''

''We have, Papa. Good night.''

''Good night.''

I listened to his footsteps retreating in the silence, and I lay a long while, trying not to think of Aunt Charlotte, or Chester dead against the fence, or the little birdlike man, Egan Stone, who'd lost his wife to typhoid two years ago last November.

TWENTY-TWO

The next day Raymond's humor began to crack. He'd become nauseated and fretful—one minute demanding more blankets, and the next, cussing about the stuffy room, and couldn't I leave the door open or something.

The doctor brought out a large can of lime and two big bottles of disinfectant. He placed them in a row against the barn just outside the door and handed me a brief list of instructions.

"You know what the disinfectant is for."

"Mama said I was to scrub with it."

"Yes—everything, daily. Starting with Raymond and yourself. You must be very careful about yourself. Wash your hands each time after working with Raymond, and keep them away from your mouth."

"I will, Doctor."

"Most important is emptying his bedpan. Your father has dug a hole several hundred feet from here. Come, I'll show you where it is." He took my arm and we began to walk in the direction of the cottonwoods. "Immediately after Raymond has finished a bowel movement, cover his stools with that lime and empty the pan into the hole. Throw several shovelfuls of dirt on top of it, and repeat the same procedure each time. Do you understand?"

"Yes. I hope I won't forget anything."

"It's on the list. Everything's on the list. The other things you'll see there are to help make Raymond comfortable. There isn't much more we can do than that. You might like to read to him and help him get his mind off himself. Anything to keep his spirits up, and yours. Any questions?"

"What should we feed him? He keeps asking for—"

"You won't have to worry about that. Your mother is thoroughly acquainted with what he should have, and she'll send it out to you each meal. Just remember—no solids. Oh, and Anne—Raymond's temperature will most likely go up and stay up for a while. It's important for us to keep it as low as we can. Cold packs are easiest, but don't be afraid to remove his blankets and sponge bathe him. Use tepid water —that's not hot or cold—and maybe add a little soda. Just sponge him and let him dry. Got that? Now anything else?" He raised a bushy eyebrow.

"Doctor, I know I'll have a thousand questions."

"Tack that list above your bed and when a question comes to you, write it down. I'll drop by as often as I can. We'll go over them each time I come out."

I nodded, feeling the awesome weight of it all falling upon my shoulders. I had to do everything so very right.

The days formed into a routine. Each dawn Papa would tap on the window to wake me—though I often felt as if I hadn't closed my eyes. I'd rise and, after dressing, light the fire to begin once again down the list the doctor had given me: feed Raymond, bathe Raymond, feed self, boil utensils, change linens, boil linens, scrub room, bathe self, feed Raymond . . .

Raymond was now in the throes of the fever. At times he was violently ill, tossing in the cot and talking half out of his head. At other times he'd lay hours in silence, his eyes staring at the ceiling and his face chalk white against the pillow and wet with perspiration. I think those days were the worst, for when I'd leave to empty the bedpan or to take the short walks the doctor had advised, he scarcely seemed to notice me leave.

In the first ten days of Raymond's illness, Dr. Sloan restricted the rest of the family to the farm. Otherwise life went on almost normally for them all.

Katy, Margaret, and Tyler found our camping in the barn novel and exciting. In the beginning they were a big problem. They'd traipse after me each time I'd walk to the hole, or stand on the can of lime and tap on the window continously, or peer through the gauzy mosquito barre Papa had strewn across the open door to keep out the flies, and ask any of a number of pesky questions, one after another:

"Annie, why must you scrub all the time? Can't you ever play anymore?"

"Annie, what's the funny pan for? Make Raymond wake up and talk to us."

"Annie, can't we come in? If we promise not to breathe, can we? We'll be good—please!"

And on and on, until desperate, I'd call for Mama to come and take them away.

After numerous spankings the children learned that the barn was off limits, and so they decided to create their own fun. They'd been especially good one morning and hadn't bothered me once. I glanced out several times to see them mysteriously building a blanket hut between two trees on the lawn near the house. By early afternoon Tyler was lying flat on his back under the shelter, with a dishtowel wrapped around his head. It appeared that he'd contracted typhoid too—against his will.

"Lie *still*, Tyler. You're sick. Katy, make him lie still."

The first few days the little game kept them busy, but it wasn't long before interest waned. The next time I noticed them playing the sick game, they had dug a hole just off the back lawn, and Katy and Margaret would alternately emerge with a cake pan full of leaves and dump it into the hole. They thought that great fun.

And then, returning from a walk one morning, I found Margaret and Katy on the lime can again.

"Hey, you two, back to the house. Off limits, remember?"

"But there's nothing to do, Annie. No one will play with us."

"You've got a sick patient to care for, don't you?"

Margaret shook her head. "Tyler won't play sick anymore, and Mama says we mustn't make him."

"Yes," Katy agreed, "we mustn't make him. I guess we'll just have to tell people he died."

"Or got better," I suggested.

But Katy was insistent. "No, no, he died, didn't he, Margaret?"

"Uh huh." Margaret's face was somber.

"I think that's a terrible game. You shouldn't pretend death. It will upset Mama."

Two pair of eyes looked at me unshaken. And later that day, I came upon them arranging sunflowers in a fruit jar. They were playing funeral, they said. I wanted to shake them good.

On the first of September, the family came out and sang "Happy Birthday" to me.

"When you two move back into the house, we'll have a real party, candles and all," Papa said. "You could have some of your friends out too. Would you like that, Anne, having some of your friends out?"

"Sounds wonderful, Papa."

"And we have a dress for you, dear." Mama gave me a hug. "I styled it after the pink one that was ruined when Chester—you liked that dress, didn't you?"

"Oh, Mama, I loved it!" I thought of the night when I'd selfishly compared it to Delores's boughten dress. I was ashamed to think I'd told Peter I hated it. "What color is it?"

"We'll keep that as a surprise." Papa put up a hand. "We just told you so you wouldn't think we'd forgotten your day."

"I wouldn't think that, Papa."

"Well, you might. You've been working pretty hard, and with not much thanks."

"We do thank you." Mama's eyes misted, and I could see what an effort it was for them to think of birthdays at a time like this.

"And we're proud." Papa pressed me against him. "You've done real fine. The doctor says you'd make an A-1 nurse. What do you think of that? Something to think about, I'd say."

I hugged him. "Maybe I will."

He took Mama's arm. "Well, Emily, we're in the way. Let our girl get back to work."

And that was my eighteenth birthday, and I didn't have time to give it a second thought. Raymond's fever was frighteningly high.

One evening after Raymond had long since been asleep, I crept out of my cot and started a fire in the stove. The evenings were now uncomfortably cool. I threw the extra blanket over Raymond, and after the little stove began to glow, I crawled again beneath my blankets and watched the flames shimmer pleasantly behind the grate. Outside, the wind rattled leaves against the barn, and occasionally dust would shower down from the beams over my head.

Cozy beneath the blankets, I watched the fire, remembering another fire I'd watched with Mark. How I missed him! In the last several weeks my waking minutes hadn't been my own, and I hadn't really been able to think of him in all that time—not since Katy had told me about a dark-haired man on horseback who'd stopped at the quarantine sign posted at the end of the lane. The man read the notice, she said, and then after staring toward the house awhile, turned and rode off in the direction he'd come. She said it had been too far away to be sure of who it was, but I knew it had been Mark. Did it worry him, the sign? Did he miss me at all?

221

With the warming of the room, my eyes grew heavy, but before giving in to sleep, I made a mental note to ask Mama if Mark ever inquired about me at church.

It was dawn. I awoke, suddenly aware of someone standing in the dark above me.

"Anne! What day is it today?"

"Raymond! What are you doing out of bed? Get back under those covers."

"What day is it? I have to know."

"I've kind of lost track—the ninth or tenth of September I think."

I sat up and lit the lamp. Raymond stood gaunt-looking in the middle of the floor.

"I've missed the outing. You let me miss the outing."

I slipped out of bed and led him back to his cot. "You've been sick. Next year—"

"Next year?" He plopped back onto the blankets. "I've waited all summer, Anne, and after all my work—the candy sales, the meetings. If I would have known, I would have left this stupid bed and gone sick. I would have."

"Don't be ridiculous." I covered him and pushed his hair back from a surprisingly cool and dry forehead. "I don't think you know how sick you've been. We've been battling *typhoid*, Raymond. You've been out of your head half the time."

"Well, I'm thinking straight now."

"You aren't if you think you should have gone on the outing. How're you feeling?"

"For one thing I'm hungry, and for something more than watery soup." His eyes seemed too large in the dim light. "And the next vanilla custard I get is going on the floor. You tell Mama. I want something I can sink my teeth into."

"I'm glad you're feeling so energetic, but doctor's orders are—"

222

"How am I supposed to get my strength back eating baby food? I can't even make a tight fist—look at this. Tyler could beat me up easy."

"I'll ask the doctor about it. All right?"

"You do that, Anne." He lay back on the pillow and I pulled the covers over his thin shoulders. Within minutes he was asleep again.

When Papa came out to wake me he found me dressed and the fire going.

"What, up already?" He stood in the doorway, a strange look on his face. "You're a good girl, Anne, and I promise you'll be blessed for all this."

"Papa, I've got wonderful news! Raymond's feeling better. He woke me this morning all upset about missing the outing, and he's demanding food. He's just like his old self, Papa."

"Well," the weariness lifted from his face and he straightened himself, "that is good news! He's on the mend then, isn't he! I'll go tell Emily." He rubbed his hands together. "That's just what she needs to hear."

Later that same day I walked with Mama to the creek. We sat on the grass along the bank and watched the slow water move lazily around the sunbaked rocks and dried logs.

Up on the hills, the oak brush had begun to turn, and I knew we had only until the first frost before the entire valley would once more take on her finery—the violent golds and crimsons of autumn.

"Mama, do you see Mr. Staaton often?" I looped my arms over my bent knees and studied the water at my feet.

"You don't have to pretend to be offhand," Mama said. "I know you like him."

"Well, of course I do. He's very nice."

"And striking and gallant and personable and—," she tossed a hand in the air, "and exciting and everything!" She laughed. "And he has good sense too."

"Then you know that I—I—might love him." Mama grew sober and there was an awful silence that I hurried to fill. "Mama, it's not just that he's—well, fascinating—he's kind and considerate. I know he loves the Church, and he's crazy about all of you."

She put her head to one side. "You don't have to sell me, dear. He's all of that, I'm sure. I trust your judgment. If you feel that way about him, and he feels the same, that's wonderful, and I'm so happy for you."

"Oh, Mama." I leaned over and kissed her cheek. "Thank you. I want you all to like him so much."

"I do now."

"And Papa?"

"Your father sees more than you give him credit for. He knows why Peter went packing. Just give him some time to get to know Mark."

I plopped a few pebbles into the water. "He'll have plenty of time. Mark has really only hinted. But I have a feeling that when things get back to normal and we begin seeing each other again, he'll propose. Does he ever ask about me at church?"

"Well, now that you mention it, I haven't seen him lately. Of course, I've been preoccupied. I might not have noticed."

"You don't think he's down with typhoid, do you? Dr. Sloan says he's had four other cases."

"I'm sure it's not that. I know the families affected. But I'll ask your father tonight. He's no doubt seen him in priesthood meetings."

We watched the creek a few minutes longer before getting to our feet.

After supper Mama and Papa came out to pick up the trays. They stood a moment in the doorway together, both looking very tired, Mama's head against Papa's arm.

"You didn't eat your custard, Raymond. And there's half a glass of eggnog left. You've got to keep up your strength."

"I'm sick of it, I keep telling you. I want some real food. When will you all realize I'm better!"

"It's a critical time right now, son. Your system's been through a lot. Have a little patience."

Raymond threw up his arms and leaned back against his pillow. "Patience? Papa, I'm *starved* all the time. I *dream* of food."

"I know." He stepped into the room and brushed an affectionate hand over Raymond's head. "It won't be much longer," he said quietly, his eyes on me.

"Is something wrong, Papa? You and Mama seem—I don't know, troubled."

"Nothing's wrong, Annie. Your mother and I just have some news we'd rather not have to tell you, that's all."

"What is it?" I put down the book I'd been about to read to Raymond. My heart had already begun to pound. It was about Mark, I could feel it. "Papa, tell me!"

"Well, Annie, Mark Staaton's—well, he's been fired and—"

"Fired? Oh, Papa." I sank relieved onto my cot. "You scared me. I thought he might be ill or something."

"No, I'm sure he's fine."

The tone of his voice brought me upright. "But what, Papa. There's something else, isn't there!"

"Anne, Rachael fired Mark weeks ago. When a man loses his job—," he gave me a pained look, "he has no more reason to hang arou—"

"Bill, hush," Mama said from the door.

"What are you two trying to tell me?"

Mama went to stand at Papa's side. "That he's gone, dear. He left the very week Raymond came down sick."

"Gone? Where?"

"No one seems to know. But he's left the valley—we're sure of that."

"Gone . . ." Her face blurred. I saw Mark's eyes in the moonlight, felt his lips pressing over mine. "But he *can't* be gone. He—" *He loved me*, I finished silently. He did, didn't he?

"Anne," Mama's voice came to me across the hot little room, "he tried to tell you, I'm sure. Remember Katy's man on horseback? Obviously he *wanted* to say good-bye and explain things to you. But we—all of us—were quarantined. What was he to do? You can understand his predicament, can't you?"

"Yes, Mama," I said, though I couldn't understand at all. "I'm sure that's how it was."

"Please don't feel bad."

"I don't." I looked up at them dry-eyed. "I'm fine—really."

"Then I want to see you smile, possum. Let me see my little girl smile."

"Oh, Papa, not now, please."

"Bill—," Mama began.

"Nope." He shook his head. "I'm not leaving till I see some sunshine. Annie, come on. Let me see it. Think of the soldier." Whenever I was unhappy as a child Papa would tell me to think of the soldier—the soldier who got his head shot off and didn't complain once. "Are you thinking of the soldier, honey? There!" He smiled at me. "You see, Emily, she feels better. That makes a lot of difference to this room, don't you think?"

The folks left and Raymond said he'd be glad to forget the story for tonight. After prayers, I put out the light and crept into my cot. Sleep seemed very far away.

"Annie," Raymond said into the blackness, "he wouldn't have left for good. I know Mr. Staaton. He's an all-right guy, and he liked you. I could see it easy."

"Thanks, Raymond. Now go to sleep."

"No, Anne, you listen. I'm just a kid maybe, but you listen. Mr. Staaton'll be back. I promise he will. Annie, do you hear?"

I strained my eyes at the dark figure on the cot.

"Annie? He will—I know it."

"I love you, Raymond."

"I love you, Annie. Good night."

The night passed, and when Papa's tap came at the window, I pulled myself from the narrow bed. My pillow was cold but completely dry.

TWENTY-THREE

"I've got a swell idea, Annie," Raymond said one morning from his bed.

"What's that?"

"You and I are going to make our own little hike as soon as we get out of this."

"And where," I set his vanilla custard and chicken broth in front of him, "are we going on this hike?"

"To that aspen grove above the High Creek ridge. You remember the place, don't you? Grassy and green and rimmed all around with skinny white aspens. It's got a little pebble creek running through it."

"There are a million such places, Raymond. Eat your breakfast."

"You remember it, Annie. We picnicked there—the whole family. We were kids then."

"Raymond." I handed him his spoon. "You're a kid now. Your breakfast's getting cold."

"Breakfast, dinner, supper. It's all the same. I want bacon, eggs, pancakes, and syrup. I want gravy and potatoes, roast, hot rolls, and butter." He pushed the tray away.

"Eat now. I'll talk to the doctor later." I set his food before him again.

"What is this? You're talking like some old lady humoring me. I'm *serious* about that hike and about the food."

"Eat, Raymond. *Just eat.*" The tray went clattering to the floor.

"Raymond!"

"You talk to the doctor *today*, and see to it that he understands this. I'm not eating another sickening spoonful of that mushy guck." He shook a bony wrist at me and then lay back on the bed and turned to the wall. He was crying.

"Raymond, I'm sorry. If you tell me about the hike again I'll listen. I think it's a wonderful idea. I do—really. We'll do it as soon as we can, but you've got to get completely well first, right?"

He nodded. "But I'm *hungry*, Annie, all the time. It's just awful."

"I'm sure it is." I touched his shoulder. "Tell you what, I promise I'll give you some real food as soon—just as soon as it's safe. All right?"

He sighed and rubbed the tears from his eyes. "All right."

After Raymond had gone to sleep, I carried the tray of spilled food back to the house and set it on the porch, leaving with it a note for Papa to get Dr. Sloan. Then I returned to the barn, but I didn't go in. For some reason I'd started to cry and I couldn't seem to stop.

"Are you all right?" the doctor asked when he came.

"Raymond's miserable with hunger. We've got to give him food."

The doctor led me to the shade of one of the cottonwoods behind the barn. "The lad's getting to you. You mustn't let him."

"But he *pleads* for solid—"

"I know, but I've explained it all before. The intestinal walls are weak. Food would perforate them. That would be fatal."

"But are we to starve him? He seems so much better. His temperature's been normal for a week."

The doctor took one of my hands in his. "Anne, if he eats what we give him he'll hardly starve."

"He's sick to death of eggnogs, custards, soups—"

"Yes, but he must eat them just the same. Understand?"

I nodded wearily.

"You're not taking very good care of yourself, Anne." He rubbed a hand over mine. "Let me give you some salve for those callouses."

I slipped my hand from his and hid it in the folds of my skirt. "Thank you, doctor. They're awful, I know."

"Are you sleeping all right? You've circles under your eyes and your color isn't good."

"I sleep all right."

"Well, you should be getting better rest now that Raymond's mending."

"I'm fine. It's Raymond who needs your concern." I began back toward Raymond's room, feeling the doctor's all-seeing eyes on the back of my head.

It was the nineteenth of September. Mark had been gone from Ashley a month.

After Dr. Sloan had gone, I left Raymond sleeping and walked to the edge of the Blaven property line. Because Peter had gone, the land was never officially sold to him and went instead to Wally Brinton. He and Laurie had told me about buying the land themselves. I'd come upon them several days ago in this very place, walking out the acreage. They were full of plans for the land and the little house they'd build in the spring with the ward's help. They were sorry, they said, that things hadn't worked out for Peter and me.

I stood with my feet pressing in the blackened growth and my eyes riveted on the spot of ground where Mark had kissed me. Peter would never have left me at a time like this.

When I returned to the barn Raymond was gone.

"Raymond? Mama! Come quick!" I flew to the house and pounded on the back door.

"What on earth is it, Anne? Has something—"

"Raymond's gone—he's *vanished!*"

"Oh, Anne." Mother's face melted into a smile. "You scared the daylights out of me."

"But he's gone, Mama."

"Well, not far, I'm sure." She let the screen door close behind her. "I'll help you find him—poor boy. I guess he's about had it, stuck out there all this time."

I walked at Mama's side resenting her sympathy for him. *I'd* about had it! We crossed back to the barn just as Raymond came around the corner.

"Where have you been?" I exploded at his cocky smile. "You scared us sick!"

"You're not the only one who needs fresh air. That barn reeks of disinfectant."

"You're not supposed to be up. Now get back in—"

"Anne—," Mama pressed her fingers gently but firmly into my arm, "there's no need to be upset. Raymond's fine, you see? The little walk probably did him good."

"Thanks, Mom. It did—I can tell you that!" Raymond said jauntily. He gave me a sly smile of victory and strode, looking ridiculous in the short nightshirt, into the barn.

"Mama, you shouldn't encourage him. He's hard enough to manage."

She shook her head. "Go easier with him. He's been so sick. I love to see him behave normally."

I sighed, thinking of the feverish little Raymond of a week ago. "You're right. I don't know what got into me."

"You're tired." She brushed a strand of hair back from my eyes. "But soon you'll be back in your soft bed again. Won't that be wonderful—life back to normal?"

"Yes," I agreed, though I dreaded the return to normalcy. That would mean facing up to Mark's absence. I would never be able to do that.

That very afternoon Raymond began to complain of a stomachache again. His temperature had gone back up.

231

"Get the doc, quick," he bellowed from the bed.

"You shouldn't have gotten up. See what you've done?"

"I don't need a scolding. I need the doctor."

"Raymond, stop rolling around and tell me where it hurts."

But he continued to toss in the cot, his legs drawn up beneath his chin. I couldn't understand the sudden change in him.

"Raymond, is it like before—the pain?" But I knew before he managed to answer me that it was worse—far worse. His color had begun to change. His lips were blue. The cool efficiency that had grown inside me shattered. Something was terribly wrong.

I ran to the house after Mama. She was in the fields, Katy said, with Papa.

"Get them both, *quick!*"

"What's the matter?" Katy asked maddeningly, pulling one of her braids across her mouth.

"Just *get them*, Katy!" I hollered at her, running back to the barn.

"Raymond, you've got to help me. Where does it hurt? High or low? Raymond," I shook him, "please!"

"Low, low," he moaned. I felt his stomach. It was rock-hard.

"Raymond, this isn't normal. Something's gone wrong. You haven't eaten anything you shouldn't, have you? *Have you?*" But of course—that morning when he'd left the barn, his sly smile . . . "Raymond, *what did you eat?*"

"It wasn't that, Annie. That made me feel real good."

"*Raymond!*" I screamed, pulling him toward me. "*What was it?*"

"Apples," he whispered between pale lips.

"But how could you?" I sobbed, holding his convulsing frame against me. "We've been so careful. How could you throw it all away?"

His brown eyes closed with pain. "I'm sorry, Annie."

By the time Mama and Papa returned from the fields, Raymond had slipped from consciousness. Two hours later, while Dr. Sloan worked over him, he died.

I don't really remember much about Raymond's service, but I do remember Mama sitting rigid between Papa and me—her eyes forever on the open coffin and Raymond's lifeless profile. I remember, too, the closing hymn. The words were somehow as comforting as anything that had been said:

"Lead, kindly Light, amid th'encircling gloom;
Lead thou me on!
The night is dark, and I am far from home;
Lead thou me on!
Keep thou my feet; I do not ask to see
The distant scene—one step enough for me."

As the words to the final verse were sung many voices broke, weeping for the small boy who'd so loved his life. And I prayed desperately that my little brother was happy.

"And with the morn those angel faces smile,
Which I have loved long since, and lost a while!"

We buried Raymond in the windy cemetery on the hill next to baby Richard John and Grandmother Carrow. There were a lot of flowers.

TWENTY-FOUR

The beautiful valley around me mocked the sudden emptiness of life. For weeks I'd risen at dawn to work the day away. There had always been something vital to do, a needed service to perform that had brought fulfillment and peace. But now I found myself with only chores to fill the endless hours. I never allowed my eyes to stray to the southeast hills that held Raymond's body, and I vowed that as soon as the family—Mama especially—was over the strain of Raymond's death, I would leave Ashley. I'd teach somewhere as Phyliss was doing, or perhaps take up some kind of nurse's training as Dr. Sloan had so frequently suggested. Anything, so long as it was useful and time consuming.

For the present Mama worried me. I once came upon her sitting in the dark, her hands thrown over her swelling stomach.

"Two sons," she whispered, rocking in the chair by the bed. "Bill's two sons . . ."

"Mama, are you all right?" I stood at the door of her room.

"Anne? Yes, I was just resting."

"But you were talking, Mama."

"Was I?"

I went into the room. "You shouldn't sit in the dark. Shall I get a lamp?"

234

"If you'd like, dear," she said, her eyes fixed ahead of her. I returned with the lamp and sat on the bed at her side.

"Raymond was a good little boy," she said softly.

"He was, Mama, the best."

"Such a little individual, wasn't he? So full of life and so sure of himself."

"Mama." I took her cool hand into my own. "Richard John and Raymond were special children, so special they didn't have to live long to prove it. We'll have them again, Mama, before you know it, and what a wonderful reunion the resurrection will be. Think of it!"

At length she turned to me. "Yes, Anne," she pressed my hand against hers, "I know, I know. We are so blessed to have the Church, and the promise of eternal family life. I just—I just need you to remind me, I guess. And oh—how I miss Raymond."

I put my arms around my little mother then, and we cried, the two of us, as if our hearts would break.

The harvest was a difficult one that year because the weather turned cold early. On October 26 we had our first good snowfall, and by mid-November the pass to Ogden had begun to fill with snow. Travel would become increasingly difficult as winter deepened. If I wanted to leave—and I did—it would have to be soon.

One Sunday evening I spoke with Dr. Sloan on the steps of the churchhouse about the training he'd mentioned. He seemed delighted with my interest.

"Tell you what," he wrinkled his craggy brow over his eyes, "next weekend Prescott's coming up. He works at the Ogden Medical and Surgical Hospital, you know."

"Yes, I know. I bet you're very proud of him."

"Oh, we are. He's done very well. He's officially a doctor now."

I thought of the tall, shaggy-haired Prescott who'd always been so taken with Phyliss.

"Well, he'll be driving back to the hospital the following Monday morning. That would be a week from tomorrow. Maybe you'd like to go back with him. He could show you the place—introduce you to Miss Eardley, the head nurse. You could see if that sort of life might interest you. If it doesn't, well, you're only out a day."

"It'd be wonderful, Doctor—if I won't be in Prescott's way."

The doctor smiled. "I think the boy would like the company of a young lady. He hasn't had much time for that, you know. Shall we make it firm, Anne?"

And so the date was set. And at last I had something to look forward to in the days ahead. But I felt a little guilty in even considering the training. In the past weeks Mama had adjusted somewhat, but I hated to think of what a quieter house would do to her. In the days before Peter's leaving and Raymond's death, she'd had eight around the table. With me gone, she'd only have five—that would make Raymond's absence all the more apparent. I spoke to Papa about it.

"Well, that's a fine how-de-do." He threw his head back and laughed as I hadn't seen him do in ages. "Your mother's been worried sick about *you*. It's obvious you're not happy, and we want you to be, Annie. Tell your Ma, Annie. She'll be delighted."

She *was* happy about my going to Ogden—especially with Prescott.

"He's such a fine young man, don't you think, Bill?"

Papa nodded agreement. "He's a stable fellow—reliable."

"I'm going to see the *hospital*, you two—not to snag a man, and especially not Prescott."

"What a thing to say!" Mama scowled at me. "Whatever is wrong with Prescott?"

"Nothing. He's a good fellow."

"Well, then why *especially not* Prescott?"

"I'm going on business. Besides, Prescott's always had his eye on Phyliss. I'd like to see them get together. He's so big and gruff. He'd dominate Phyl and if she gave it a chance, she'd like that.''

''Well, I want you to wear your new dress just the same. It never hurts to turn a man's head.''

''I do want to look nice, Mama, and the new dress will be perfect.'' My birthday dress turned out to be a vivid rust color, different from anything I'd ever had before. It was very sophisticated, I thought. The lines were stylish, and it fit perfectly. I'd pin my hair up and wear a hat—something I rarely did. I suddenly felt a little like my old self again. ''You know that perky little black hat—''

Papa groaned. ''A total waste of money. You've never worn it.''

''I've just never had the proper place to wear it, Papa. I think if we add a little rust velvet ribbon, it'll look good with my dress.''

''Yes!'' Mama laughed. ''And I know just how we'll do it. Let's get it out now.''

And so my little trip to the city became a major project for us to put our minds to. Even Papa joined in the planning, and the following day, he came home from Charlie's with a black velvet purse to match my hat, and a dark fur muff to wear with my winter coat.

It was snowing when Prescott came by Monday morning. I'd stood at the front room window watching the puffs of winter lace fall and cling to the hardened ground, waiting for nearly an hour, and when at last I saw the buggy coming up the lane, I hollered for Mama to come. She helped me pin on my hat by the hall mirror and slip into my long coat.

''I hope you don't look too worldly.'' She frowned at my reflection.

''Shouldn't I wear the hat?''

''No, it's lovely, dear. I'm afraid it isn't the hat.'' Her eyes filled instantly, and she turned away. ''. . .Or the dress this time.''

"Mama, what's wrong? I won't go if you're unhappy about it."

"Oh, Anne. It's nothing. I want you to go." She blinked back the tears. "You're just so grown." She kissed my cheek. "You have fun today, and if you'd like to become a nurse, I want you to accept, understand?" I nodded, suddenly regretting that I'd ever spoken to the doctor about it. I didn't want to leave Ashley—not ever.

"Fetching," was Prescott's first remark as I met him at the door.

"Hello, Prescott." I smiled, taken aback again by the immense size of him. He'd always been respected in Ashley, I think partly because of his size and partly from the fierce expression that could cross his wide brow without a moment's notice. I was always relieved to find the soft gray eyes of his father in the rugged face. "I'm all ready. I hope this doesn't inconvenience you."

"Not at all. It's my pleasure, I assure you."

He immediately put me at ease, and as we rode, he talked some of Phyliss, and I was glad to see his interest still there. I suggested he drive up and see her.

"I don't know," he drawled, giving me a sidelong glance. "She never had much time for me before. I always had the notion she was interested in that hired hand of yours. What was his name? Tate—yes, Pete Tate."

"Peter? Phyliss?" I laughed.

"You don't think so?"

"Well, I just never considered that before." But it made sense, I had to admit to myself. It was a possible explanation for the distance that grew between Phyliss and me so suddenly and her abrupt decision to leave the valley and go into teaching. We rode in silence after that.

The still, snow-stuffed canyon was beautiful. The evergreens were almost black against the white. The horse's hooves seemed muffled, and except for the quiet plodding

238

and an occasional animal's cry, the pass was void of sound —a quiescent wilderness.

I couldn't shake the notion that Phyliss might have been interested in Peter. The more I thought about it, the more it made sense. Poor Phyliss. Her jaunty attitude may have just been a mask for a hurt I couldn't—or wouldn't—recognize. And I'd thought Phyliss hadn't understood *me*.

It was after twelve when we arrived in Ogden. Here it still seemed autumn. Many trees held their leaves though they were dry and brittle and rattled in the wind, and the ground was only patched with snow. The sun shone warmly overhead. Prescott suggested we eat before going on to the hospital, and he turned the horse down toward the city. As we drew along the tree-lined streets, we passed dignified houses of every design. Perhaps it would be fun to live in Ogden, just awhile anyway.

We reached the business center of the city, and Prescott pulled the buggy up in front of Dylan's Cafe and Confectionary. "Best food in town." He smiled at me. "Everybody comes here. No matter what else you order, I insist you start with rabbit stew. They serve it with hot bread and apple jelly."

The food was good. We ate leisurely in the crowded room, but I worried that I might be keeping Prescott from his work. He leaned back in his chair, talked as much as he ate, and didn't seem in the least pressed for time.

"So—you think I ought to ride up and see your friend!"

I laughed. "Sure. You obviously like Phyliss. Why not *do* something about it?"

He ran a hand through his hair. "Maybe I will. She can only send me away, I guess."

"Prescott, don't tell me you're shy." I touched his hand across the table. "Phyl's hard to read, but I can tell you this —she's hardest on the fellows she likes best. She's afraid she won't be able to handle it." And as I spoke the words I knew they were completely true.

"Well, Miss Carrow," he gave my hand a squeeze, "we'll see if you're right about your friend. Finished?" He pushed his chair back from the table. "Let's go take a look at the hospital—that may be your future home."

He helped me on with my coat, and we made our way through the maze of tables toward the door. I had a sudden feeling of being watched, and turned to glance back at our empty table. But I saw only a young man sitting beyond it with his eyes on me. He nodded and smiled at my attention. I turned and hurried out the door on Prescott's arm.

As we came into the bustle of the street, I remembered my muff. "Prescott, did I take my muff into the cafe? I seem to have left it."

"Yes, I remember seeing it on the table. You stay put and I'll go back and get it." But when he returned, he was shaking his head. "Maybe I was wrong. You probably left it in the buggy."

It wasn't there either. I tried to reassure Prescott that it wasn't important, but I felt unaccountably depressed at losing it. The muff had been a gift from Papa, and he'd been so proud that I'd worn it today. I was certain I'd left it on the cafe table. Perhaps that young man who'd watched me leave had—no, I shouldn't think such things. But from that moment on, my new enthusiasm for the city had dampened.

We spent the rest of the afternoon at the hospital. I hadn't been there an hour before I realized that for the time being at least, nursing wasn't for me. Raymond seemed to lie in every bed. The eyes of the patients were all his eyes, and everywhere was the inescapable odor of disinfectant.

At five, Prescott drove me to the mouth of Ogden Canyon as planned, and we met Papa waiting with the buggy. After I thanked him for the lovely day, I climbed up beside Papa, suddenly feeling tired and relieved to be going home.

"Nice day, possum?"

"Yes, Papa. But I don't think I want to be a nurse. Not for a while anyway."

He left it at that, and I settled back in the buggy to sleep most of the way home.

In Ashley, Papa roused me. Wally and Laurie were coming in the opposite direction. They'd been married now two weeks.

"We're having a party Friday. Can you come, Anne?" Laurie shouted from the wagon.

And so the day hadn't been a total loss after all. I had another date to circle on my calendar.

TWENTY-FIVE

"Annie! Look, a letter. To Miss Anna Carrow." Katy burst into my bedroom Friday afternoon, waving a pale blue envelope. "Shall I open it? Shall I?"

"Let me see it first." I dropped the needlepoint I'd finally become adept at and went to sit beside her on the bed.

"Well, then take it, Anne." She thrust the envelope in my lap. "What's wrong? Why don't you look at it?".

"I am, Katy." I forced my eyes down to the thin square of paper, but the writing wasn't Mark's heavy scrawl. It was from Phyliss. The return address read Mendon.

"All right, honey, you can open it. Read it, too."

"Hey, thanks, Anne." She grabbed the letter, tore it open, and began laboriously reading. As Katy stumbled over Phyliss's flamboyant hand, I got up from the bed to stand by the window and watched the blowing snow fling itself against the barn, blasting the weathered door of the room where Raymond had died—Peter's old room. Had it ever been summer?

"Well, isn't that great, Annie? Annie?"

"What?"

"I said isn't that great about Phyliss and Prescott Sloan?"

"Hmm—read that part again, will you?"

It was a long letter, three full pages—both sides—and

said essentially this: Phyliss was in love. Prescott Sloan had called on her and "incredibly enough, Anne, I about fell through the floor at the sight of him. He's really very attractive, don't you think? I like him very much, and, brace yourself, Anne, I'm certain I'll be engaged before Christmas."

Katy finished the letter and stuffed it back into the envelope.

"Are you sorry you didn't get Prescott Sloan, Anne?" she asked, studying my face.

"Of course not! I'm very happy for Phyliss."

She shook her head slowly from side to side. "Uh uh. I bet if I left right now you'd cry."

"Silly." I dropped into my chair and took up the needlepoint again. But it was true—I was close to tears. What was the matter with me?

Friday evening, for lack of anything better to do, I piled my hair up on my head for the party as I'd done for the trip to Ogden, and I wore the new rust dress and little hat.

"I want to drive myself in tonight," I said to Papa as I came down the stairs.

He shook his head. "Looking like that you're liable to bring the Indians right out of hiding. I insist. Get your coat."

The party was at Sister Lacey's home. Until spring Wally and Laurie would make their home there. Sister Lacey always moved in with her daughter for the cold months.

Papa dropped me off in front of the large old house, where a dozen or so rigs and horses had already been tied.

"I'll be back for you at ten. Have fun," he called as the buggy disappeared into the pale night.

The moon lighted the path ahead of me. I hurried toward the house, and as I did so, a dark figure stepped off the porch and waited for me to approach.

"Hello?" I called. But the man made no move to reply. "Going to the party, too?" I asked as I neared him warily. And then I saw who it was and stopped short, my heart slamming in my throat.

"Anne." Mark spoke softly from where he stood.

I had the strongest impulse to run—run anywhere. But my feet remained where they were, and I said in a forced voice, "Mark! I thought you'd left our fair valley."

He closed the distance between us. "I rode out to tell you I was leaving, Anne, but—"

"We were quarantined. Yes, I know."

"You do?"

"Katy saw you."

"Well, good. I didn't want you to think I'd just go without a word. I thought of writing a note, but I didn't think I could explain things too well on paper. I'm sorry, though, that—"

"No need to be sorry, Mark. Papa says when a man loses his job he has no more reason to hang around."

"Anne—"

"It's cold out here. I think I'll go in." I stepped past him and moved toward the house.

"Anne, I'm very sorry about Raymond. I—I just heard. I had no idea he was so sick. He was a fine fellow."

I stopped again. Why did you leave me? He had *typhoid fever*. "Thank you, Mark. Now if you'll excuse me, I'm late."

But he put a restraining hand on my arm. "You said you were cold. Maybe this will help." He turned me around to face him, and slipped my hands into the fur muff I'd lost in Ogden.

"Mark," I gasped, "where did you find it?"

He laughed at the sudden loss of my formality. "Still the same Anne after all. I'm relieved. You seemed so changed."

I backed away. "I asked where you found my muff."

"In a cafe. I eat there every day."

"You do?" I looked into his eyes and remembered the impression I'd had in the cafe that someone had been watching me. So Mark had been there too. "You live in Ogden now?"

He nodded. "I'm hopeful of getting a job there, Anne. I—I had no idea it'd take so long to get it. I'd hoped to have the thing sewn up before coming back, but Monday when I saw you in the cafe—who's your new friend?"

"Prescott Sloan." I straightened up. "*Doctor* Prescott Sloan."

"The old doctor's son? You were having such a good time with him—in that ridiculous hat."

I touched my hat and looked at him icily. "I'm sorry you don't approve. Yes, we did have a good time—all day. Prescott and I—well, we've become very close." I felt the lie burning in my cheeks, and said more curtly than I'd intended, "Now, Mark, it really is cold—"

"You're right." His face had grown grim, and he released my arm with a jerk. "You work pretty fast. Have fun at your party." With that he turned on his heels and strode down the path.

I watched after him, feeling like stone. I looked toward the warmth of the house. The laughter of people having fun drifted from the bright windows. Somehow everything had gone wrong. I could have said anything—but *a lie?* Hadn't I learned?

I couldn't go in. I stood on the porch, my hand about to knock, but I couldn't go in. "Mark?" I called to the darkness. "Mark?" I ran back down the path. "Have you gone?"

"No." His voice boomed from out of a buggy near me. "Decided against the party, have you?"

"Why didn't you write? All that time, why didn't you write just once?"

He fumbled inside his vest and pulled out a tattered envelope. "You see I did write."

"Oh." I closed my eyes against stinging tears. "It didn't do either of us much good in your pocket." My voice broke, and I turned back to the house.

"Annie, wait." He dropped out of the buggy at my side. "I told you once you had some housecleaning to do, remember?"

"As if it were any of your business."

"Well, *you* returned the suggestion, my sweet," he said, taking my shoulders. "And it cost me, Anne; it cost me *my job*. I was no longer free to court seriously. As your father will tell you, a man must have work to court seriously—and I was serious about you, Anne."

"Are you telling me you left for the noble purpose of securing a job so that you could continue to court me?"

"I am."

"I don't believe you, Mark. You would have written at least."

"Anne, Anne." He drew me to him, his warm lips brushing my forehead. "The letter is a proposal. I couldn't mail it until I had some word on my position with the Weber Academy. Besides, you knew how I felt about you, and I thought you'd have a little faith in me—that you'd wait. But Monday when I saw you with that man—well, I saw then we'd have to have a little talk—job or no job."

I tried to push out of his arms, but he pulled me closer.

"Darling, listen to me—"

"No!" I shook my head and forced myself to think of all the grief of the past months.

"Listen—"

"You said I seemed changed." I wriggled free of his hold. "Well, that's because I have. I'm no longer that little girl who waited for your every glance and word. I've grown up, Mark."

"I've never thought of you as foolishly young!" He kicked the gate. He was so suddenly angry that I raised my head to look at him. The moon partially lighting his shoulders and profile showed his face creased in a scowl. "You've been through it, and through it alone. I know that.

246

But you seem to think I rode out of here without a backward glance. It was all I could do to keep from running back jobless, which is *just what I did* when I saw you with that—that bear of a man, Sloan. I haven't been gone even three months and you're chasing with him—holding hands across the table."

"Oh, I haven't been chasing with anyone, Mark Staaton. I've been sitting home night after night wondering what made you up and leave. Prescott's just a friend, a good friend."

"Yes, like Peter. You make good friends easily."

"No! Not like Peter!" I stamped my foot and glowered at him. "Prescott's in love with Phyliss—with Phyliss! They're nearly engaged. Do you hear me? *The whole darned valley's nearly engaged.*"

There was a sudden commotion from the house. The door burst open and several young men came noisily across the porch and down the steps. Behind them, the light caught the gleam of auburn curls, and Delores swung out onto the porch.

I pressed into the shadows next to Mark. Delores stood laughing down at the group on the walk and wagged a playful finger at the tallest of them, Jerry, her latest beau.

"Mark—"

"I see her."

"Let's go somewhere quickly before—"

His fingers closed around my wrist. "What does it matter if she sees us?"

I moved farther into the shadows, and as I did so, he pulled me into the circle of his arms. "So it isn't true? You're not really close to this fellow—at least not in the way you wanted me to think?"

"Mark, I think they all may be coming."

"Why don't you just relax and accept the way we feel about each other." His lips were on my forehead again.

"And how do we feel?"

"I won't let you get away with that, Anne. *You love me*, and I'll make you say it! But first," he caught me against him, "first I must tell you that you are dearer than all the world to me, and were you truly engaged to Prescott Sloan, I'd break it up!" His biting tone had returned, and he forced my face up to his. "*You're mine,* Anna Jeanette! You've been mine from the moment you walked through the doors of the chapel in that blue dress, your eyes just daring me to compliment you. I tried not to want you, not to love you. There was nothing settled in my life. It was of all times the wrong time to fall in love, but at the dance—seeing you in everyone's arms but mine—I knew the truth. I couldn't leave Ashley without you."

"Oh, Mark!" I threw my arms about his neck. "Do you mean it? Honestly?"

"You're a stubborn woman, Anne—hard to convince. I love you—*love you.* Marry me—for now and for always!"

"Yes, *yes,*" I sobbed, laughing and crying—my ecstasy almost too much to bear. I hugged him hard, pressing my face into his chest. "And I *do* love you, Mark. I've loved you forever and ever, it seems, and I think you've been *positively spiteful* keeping away so long!"

He kissed my hair, and when I raised my eyes to him, he kissed them too. "I'll spend the rest of my life making it up to you, darling. The rest of eternity too."

And so it was as Raymond had promised, shaking a thin finger across the darkened room. "Anne, you listen to me. I'm just a kid maybe, but you listen. Mr. Staaton will be back. I promise he will! Annie? Annie, do you hear?"

Above us the stiff branches of the winter cottonwoods creaked in the wind—creaked and rattled.